DETROIT PUBLIC LIBRARY

3 5674 006073

W9-CAD-919

DETROIT PUBLIC LIBRARY

BROWSING LIBRARY
5201 Woodward
Detroit, MI 48202

DATE DUE

Sneaks

by the same author A WOMAN'S HONOR–THE DEATH TRAP

THE MARK OF LUCIFER–ROTTEN APPLES

Sneaks

Edith Piñero Green

165

82 8861

E.P. DUTTON • NEW YORK

C.1
M

Copyright © 1979 by Edith Piñero Green

All rights reserved. Printed in the U.S.A.

No part of this publication may be reproduced or transmitted in
any form or by any means, electronic or mechanical, including
photocopy, recording or any information storage and retrieval
system now known or to be invented, without permission in writing
from the publisher, except by a reviewer who wishes to quote
brief passages in connection with a review written for inclusion
in a magazine, newspaper or broadcast.

For information contact: E.P. Dutton, 2 Park Avenue, New York, N.Y. 10016

Library of Congress Cataloging in Publication Data
Green, Edith Piñero.   Sneaks.
I. Title.
PZ4.G78885Sn   [PS3557.R367]   813'.5'4   79-1300
ISBN: 0-525-20632-9

Published simultaneously in Canada by
Clarke, Irwin & Company Limited, Toronto and Vancouver

Designed by Barbara Huntley

10 9 8 7 6 5 4 3 2 1

First Edition

BL

MAR 2 4 '80

to Jason and Jeremy

Sneaks

Whitney's Funeral Home is a symmetrical white frame building tucked among a row of arty storefronts on the outskirts of
Greenwich Village. The cornerstone bears a date of 1801 and
the building's design is attributed to Asher Benjamin, although the actual builder is said to have been Moses Harwood,
a local carpenter of the period. The edifice was originally the
First Congregational Church of Wagon Green, and the steeple
and steeple bell remain, as does the air of austere reverence.

Dearborn V. Pinch eyed the building with the same dis-
taste he brought to the contemplation of wicker toilet seats and
television sets housed in Duncan Phyfe cabinets. A funeral
parlor should look like a funeral parlor, not like a church.
Dearborn, over six feet tall, presented a distinguished figure in
his fur-collared greatcoat and homburg, and, with his scowling
face and determined cane-swinging stride, he looked more like
an elder statesman on his way to a United Nations conference
than like a gentleman returning home at 10 A.M. from an
evening's revel.

Ah, the fair Emmylou. Eager, practiced, and cheerful.
Juicy as an orange. Sweet as a peach. Soft, pliable, and sweet-
scented with lemon verbena and Sen Sen. Also musical. He
conjured up a vision of her mellow flaccid posterior undulating
to his vocal accompaniment. And his own recklessness. "Another glass of champagne? Another few moments of ecstasy?"

What benevolent fate had sent him into Schrafft's, induced
him to choose the small table against the back wall, cast before
him the buxom, accommodating Emmylou, pencil and pad in
hand, ripe bouncing spheres oscillating at eye level? "What
can I do for you, sir? And how do you like your eggs?" Sunny
side up, my dear. "And what would you say to an English
muffin? Or would you rather have a bacon roll?" A bacon roll

by all means. Thick, not too crisp, smoky-flavored, and preferably streaked with fat. Ah...

Dearborn smiled reminiscently. Delivered as ordered. That and more. He hummed in finger-snapping counterpoint to "Nearer, My God, to Thee."

"Is this the Wiggins funeral?" an anxious voice asked.

Dearborn glanced down at the small black-clad woman who had popped up under his elbow. "I shouldn't be surprised," he ventured.

"Would it be on the ground floor?"

"I suggest you follow the sounds of lamentation, madam."

Pity about Emmylou. No sooner found than lost. A sick brother in Boise, a second mortgage on the tiny three-room converted garage on Macdougal Street, a loan outstanding. She'd spoken of Boise with loathing, but she had no choice. And if she didn't get the five thousand dollars she needed by March first, then it might be Boise on a permanent basis. Dearborn shook his head, thinking of her warm pulsating flesh languishing in Boise. And she was leaving that very afternoon.

The organ gave out a rude flatulent wheeze and fell silent. The rise and fall of a voice sermonizing took its place. Dearborn couldn't make out the words. He didn't need to. They were always the same. A beloved spouse, a dear friend, a heavenly reward, reverence, respect, love, a ray of light, a generous heart, a caring nature. He'd been to so many funerals. Each individual finally reduced to a sentimental memory. Not for Dearborn V. Pinch. He would have himself cremated and boxed. Dozens of matchbox-sized containers. Distributed with appropriate messages. The New York Telephone Company... "Your time will come too, you crooks." Otto Rothschild... "Find a legal loophole in this, you shyster."

Otto. Otto would find some reason to keep Dearborn from contributing the five thousand dollars to Emmylou. And even if Dearborn prevailed, Otto would shoot his mouth off to Benjamin, supply all the intimate details to Dearborn's banker, try to persuade Dr. Moltke to have a heart-to-heart talk with him. It was unendurable, the lengths they would go to in order to interfere with Dearborn's life.

Dearborn's attention was momentarily distracted by a pair of abandoned shoes lying under a bush on the other side of the fence. The phrase "tossed aside like an old shoe" skipped through his mind. Poor Emmylou. Banished to Boise. Her Schrafft's uniform relinquished. Her little white cap tossed aside. To say nothing of her apron, that attractively skimpy garment utilized so charmingly for domestic interludes. "I'll just slip it on while I pour coffee. Wouldn't want to scald myself." Heaven forbid, sweet lady. Heaven forbid.

Dearborn leaned forward and fixed a little more intently on the pair of shoes. It looked as if the owner had scuttled his socks as well, and wasn't that a scrap of trouser leg? Buzzing noises erupted inside Dearborn's head. He suffered the opposing sensations of a dry mouth and damp eyes as he clung to the fence as if he had been frozen to it. A less disciplined person might have panicked. Dearborn drew in his breath and waited for the shock to pass. The shoes weren't jetsam. Or if they were, they were only the most incidental part of the wreckage.

When Dearborn's heart stopped pounding, he went partway up the steps and climbed, not without a certain awkwardness, over the stone balustrade onto the patch of yard between the fence and the building, then stooped to part the bushes. He found himself staring at a body, the very still body of a tall young man wearing a poplin storm coat buttoned to the neck and a tweed cap jammed onto a head of blond curls. His arms were crossed over his chest as if he were asleep, and his open eyes were dark marbles staring out of a ghastly china-doll face. He looked like one of those celluloid Kewpie dolls that had been all the rage back in the thirties. Dearborn noticed that he had a large brownish bruise under his chin on the left side of his face. It was the only wound that Dearborn could see and yet he knew instinctively that it had been a violent death. He rose, pulled himself back over the balustrade onto the steps, and made his way hastily into the cool dim vestibule of the funeral home.

A somber gentleman, like a carnationed St. Peter, stood guard in front of the ground-floor chapel. "Wiggins or Van Nuys, sir?" he whispered.

"There is a corpse on the premises," Dearborn declared in a stage whisper.

The man nodded, his expression blandly receptive.

"Do you hear me?" Dearborn demanded.

"Yes, sir. You said that there is a corpse on the premises. There are four, to be exact. And whose remains have you come to view?"

"None of 'em," Dearborn snapped. "I am trying to tell you that there is a loose cadaver out front. A stray body, a dear who has departed in the front yard."

The funeral director stepped back for a better view of Dearborn and then hurried to the front door. Dearborn waited. A moment later the funeral director returned. "I'm going to call the police. We must do something about this before the Wiggins service is over."

He scurried off through a door in the back of the vestibule while Dearborn remained behind to contemplate the efficiency attendant upon one's dying, as it were, at the very threshold of one's last earthly stopover.

"You still insist that it was a mugging?" Dearborn demanded.

Niccoli's eyes were on a stack of pink forms on the desk in front of him. "Suppose you leave that to me. Just sign the statement and you can go home."

"Your promotion hasn't smoothed the rough edges, I see."

"Lieutenant Galton's supposed to be handling this, not me."

"I wanted to talk to you. I know you."

"It's not my job anymore."

Behind Niccoli's shoulder, on the other side of a soundproof glass partition, Officer Stefanich bent over his typewriter, forehead wrinkled, fingers plunking at the keys.

Dearborn went on coolly, "We are not discussing a traffic violation. It is not that simple."

"It is that simple," Captain Niccoli contradicted firmly.

_____4

"The victim is shot and dumped in front of Whitney's. His wallet is missing. His cuff links are ripped off. From the looks of his right ring finger it's plain a ring was pried off."

"There was no blood on the outside of his coat. What does that suggest to you?"

"That the mugger buttoned up the victim's coat to cover the wound. Passersby don't stop to check on drunks."

"He had a bruise on his chin," Dearborn pointed out. "He must have struggled with his attacker. Did they check his fingernails?"

"That bruise wasn't something he got from fighting off a mugger. That's certain. It wasn't that recent. Looked like it could of come from a strap buckle rubbing on his chin. Like on a motorcycle helmet. Something he wore a lot."

"You intend to go on insisting that some idiot mugged that man, robbed him, and then, instead of running, buttoned his coat, dragged him to a ridiculously inaccessible spot, lifted him over a stone banister, and hid him behind a bush?"

"There's a lot of nutty people in the world," Captain Niccoli replied evenly, with a brief but burning glance at Dearborn.

The telephone on Niccoli's desk rang. He leaned over to pick it up. "Yeah? Okay. What? He was dead how long? Over twenty-four hours?"

Dearborn raised an eyebrow.

Niccoli jotted something down on the edge of his blotter. "Thanks." He hung up and read aloud to Dearborn, "Louis Martin, Olmstead Arms, West Eleventh Street."

Dearborn showed no signs of chagrin. "And how, may I ask, did your men find that out?"

"One of them pulled the guy's wallet out of the corner mailbox by Whitney's. It had an identification card in it."

"Peculiar," muttered Dearborn.

"What's peculiar?" Captain Niccoli returned shortly. "Typical M.O. for a mugger."

"I'm referring to the fact that the body was not discovered for twenty-four hours."

"The body was hidden behind the bush," Niccoli declared exasperatedly.

"I noticed him," Dearborn insisted.

"You would." Niccoli shifted his attention back to his forms, filling in a line, flicking a piece of lint from the paper, flipping the paper over to fill something in on the back.

Dearborn walked to the glass partition and rapped on it. Stefanich looked up and smiled cordially. Dearborn pointed to the statement still in Stefanich's typewriter. Stefanich held up one hand, tapped out a final letter with his other, pulled the statement from the machine, and stood up.

"It's about time," Dearborn greeted him as he came through the door.

"What'd you expect?" Stefanich said cheerfully. "It's almost two pages long."

"I could have typed *War and Peace* in less time," Dearborn informed him. "And I type with only two fingers."

Niccoli rose from his desk, made a neat edge-to-edge bundle of his pink forms, and weighed them down with a cracked ceramic coffee mug. The truth was that he was not so indifferent to Dearborn as he pretended. Dearborn was not a stranger downtown. Niccoli had been heading up the detective squad on the Vernon Tree murder case when Dearborn came to his attention, first as a suspect and later as an unwelcome collaborator. It still rankled that the case had ballooned into the Rotten Apple murders and that Dearborn had received a major portion of the credit for solving the case. Niccoli took the statement out of Stefanich's hand. "Sign it, please, Mr. Pinch."

"That's right," Stefanich chimed in. "Just sign on the old dotto."

Dearborn reached into his pocket for his glasses, settled them over his ears, took the statement from Niccoli, and commenced reading. " 'Corpus delicti' are two words, not one," he pointed out. "Blah blah, eyes open, blah blah. I did not say 'appeared to be dead.' I said 'dead as a doorpost.' All right, never mind. Spoke to funeral director. Stayed with body until police arrived. Yes, yes, it's essentially correct except that you have misspelled 'inconvenience.' "

Niccoli handed Dearborn a pen. "Okay, Mr. Pinch. We don't want to keep you here any longer than we have to. If you'll just . . ."

"It is all right so far as it goes," Dearborn went on calmly, "but it is incomplete."

"How so?" Stefanich asked. "What'd I leave out?"

"What now?" Niccoli barked.

"I want it officially noted that I do not consider the murder to be a casual one. Where's your pencil, Officer . . . what is it? Stefanich?"

"You remembered," Stefanich exclaimed with a flattered grin. He took a pencil off Niccoli's desk and picked out a discarded envelope from the wastebasket. "Yeah?" he said expectantly.

"Hold it," Niccoli interrupted. "We want facts, not opinions."

"I wish to have it on record that you and I do not see eye to eye, Captain."

"Put it in a letter and mail it to me." Niccoli tossed a slip of paper to Stefanich. "Call this number. They've got the victim's wallet. This number was in it. Be careful what you say."

"Wait a moment," Dearborn declared, detaining Stefanich with a strong hand. "What is that number?"

"It's—"

Niccoli yanked the slip of paper out of Stafanich's hand. "That's it. Either you get out of here or you go into the tank with the other loonies, Pinch."

"Unreasonable as ever, I see."

"Out," Niccoli said firmly.

Dearborn sighed. There was nothing to be gained by arguing. He slipped into his coat, fastened the buttons with deliberate calm, and slung the curved handle of his cobra-head cane over his arm. He ignored Niccoli's glare as he picked up his suede gloves and worked his fingers first into one and then into the other. "Good day, Captain," he said at last. "If you need me you know where to find me."

2

"The cops said he left the place without signing his statement. Niccoli said he was making waves, interfering with routine. Niccoli told me if I don't keep him away he's going to arrest him for disturbing the peace."

"Can he do that?"

"You bet your sweet ass he can," Otto Rothschild declared.

"Let me get this straight. He's not directly involved, is he?" Benjamin Pinch asked. "He was just passing by. Am I right?"

"Yesterday morning. The guy was mugged and killed and dumped in the bushes. Your father discovered the body."

"So what's wrong, then? Niccoli didn't say he wanted to talk to me, did he?"

"It's the first thing he said," Otto replied. "I told him you're away on vacation. I told him you left last week and you won't be back until the first of March."

"Thanks, Otto. I won't answer the phone for a couple of days. Talk to you soon."

"Wait a minute. I'm not done. You've got to go see your old man."

"Why?"

"He called me a few minutes ago to hit me for five thousand dollars."

"What?"

"You heard me."

"What for?"

"What do you think for? For another one of his 'investments in my well-being and peace of mind' projects."

Benjamin groaned. "Not another Avon lady."

"Your guess is as good as mine," Otto returned morosely.

"What did you say to him?"

"I told him to find some other hobby. Sometimes I wish he'd get another lawyer. Anyway, I got the full treatment from

'After all it is I who retain you' to 'Your father, were he alive today, Otto, would bow his head in shame.' "

"Balls."

"So you've got to get over there and talk to him."

"Shit."

"Ben?"

"Okay, Otto. I'll go."

"Soon, Ben."

"Yeah, yeah. Right away."

The walls of Dearborn's apartment on upper Fifth Avenue were thick, the humidifying system efficient. In the library polished rosewood and teak, thick-tufted leather, and heavy silver predominated. The warm reds and oranges of a Chagall on one wall were complemented by the cool blues and greens of a Gauguin opposite.

Dearborn, wearing his favorite red silk lounging robe and black patent leather slippers, was sitting at his desk when his housekeeper tapped on the open door. "What? What is it? What now?"

"Mr. Pinch?" She was wearing an aqua uniform and a string of simulated pearls the size of olives. "Your son called again about ten minutes ago."

"So what?"

Mrs. Woolley was Dearborn's aesthetic opposite, small, hennaed, plump, and generally pleasant-tempered, but this evening her nerves were frazzled. "I don't know what to tell him."

"This is the third time this evening you have invaded my privacy to deliver that repetitive and depressing message."

"He's coming over."

"Do not open the door."

"For your own son?"

"For anyone's son, Mrs. Woolley."

"He's been phoning all day. It's probably something important."

"Nonsense."

"Also somebody named Edward Roycroft."

"What?"

"Called."

"When?"

Mrs. Woolley narrowed her eyes and stared at the telephone on Dearborn's desk. "I don't know why you keep the telephone unplugged. You could find everthing out for yourself if you'd just—"

"It's my generous spirit. Why should I deprive you of the pleasure of prying into my personal affairs, Mrs. Woolley?"

"He called about five minutes ago. He said he'll call back."

"Who's that?"

"This Edward Roycroft."

There was a ripple of chimes in the front hall. Mrs. Woolley turned.

"Don't answer it," Dearborn instructed.

"But . . ."

"No buts. Just go somewhere and do something useful. Make me a cup of tea. Bake a pie. Do whatever it is you do at this hour."

"I generally go to bed," Mrs. Woolley said huffily.

"Then do so."

The chimes reverberated from wall to wall.

Mrs. Woolley shook her head and marched off.

"Dad?" The voice was muffled behind the rolling chimes and thick front door. "Dad!"

Dearborn applied himself to the letter he was composing. "And so, Emmylou, although I must still . . ."

The shouting picked up in volume. Dearborn began to hum. There was an abrupt silence. Then it began again. "I'm warning you, Dad. I'm not going away."

" . . .work out a few of the details . . ."

"Oh, for pity's sake!" Mrs. Woolley marched past the open library door. "What will the neighbors think?"

Dearborn slapped the desk with the palm of his hand. "Damn the neighbors, Mrs. Woolley!" He shook his head angrily. "He doesn't know when he's not wanted. No more sense than a . . . than a . . ."

"Than a basketball bum?" Benjamin suggested amiably as

he loped into the room and mimed a jump shot at an imaginary basket.

"You suggested it, not I. One would think that some of your education might have rubbed off on your confreres. Instead they have succeeded in corrupting you beyond redemption."

"Not beyond redemption, Dad. I'd hate to think that. Now that I've retired from the NBA there's some hope, isn't there? After all, I'm only thirty-two."

"I was president of Pinch Enterprises when I was twenty-seven. What do you want, Benjamin? Why are you bothering me?"

Benjamin's resemblance to his father was striking. He was about the same height, with dark eyes, thick black hair, a slender frame and stooped shoulders. He diverged only in manner of dress, tonight wearing faded jeans and a coarsely woven linen shirt open at the neck. His hair was neatly combed but it curled under his ears, and he was sockless, his sneakers shabby to the point of dilapidation. Dearborn eyed him with disgust. He rose and circled his desk, planting himself directly in front of Benjamin. "You have an antipathy toward barbers, I take it?"

"Otto told me what happened yesterday, Dad."

"What is that?" Dearborn returned innocently.

"Your run-in with Niccoli. The dead body. The murder."

"You have come to hear the sordid details?"

"No. I'm just mentioning it. Otto was scared you were going to get involved, but I told him you wouldn't."

"It was not an altogether cut-and-dried situation."

"So I hear. It's still better to leave it to the police. That's their job."

"I have washed my hands of it, Benjamin."

"Glad to hear it, Dad."

"Although I shall never understand what the body was doing on the other side of the fence or how it could have lain there unnoticed for twenty-four hours."

"The other side of the fence?"

"The killer," Dearborn elucidated, "took time to hoist the body over a fence and push it under some bushes. I cannot understand it. And the man had been dead some twenty-four hours when I found him. To me that seems peculiar. But there's no talking to Niccoli. Spiny as they come. I thank God I'm not cut from the same cloth."

"Nothing spiny about you, Dad."

"I'll say not. One of these days I'm going to investigate city policy in regard to the qualifications for joining the police department."

"Thinking of joining the force?"

"I don't like smart alecks, Benjamin. Now, if you're satisfied that all is well, you might as well leave."

"There's something else." Benjamin's eyes shifted to the door. "Uh, you think Mrs. Woolley could scare up some ice cream or a couple of cookies?"

"I do not."

Benjamin sighed resignedly and threw himself down into an easy chair, draping one long leg over the cushioned arm.

"Don't you own any hose?" Dearborn asked, eyeing Benjamin's bare ankle.

"What's the five thousand for, Dad?"

"Is that unexpected question intended to throw me off guard? The answer is that what I do with my money is my business."

"The rub is that your business is usually funny business. The last time, it was the Avon lady. The time before that, you were all for dipping into your capital to subsidize the diet-pill lady. What was her name? Ruby something or other? You remember what those diet pills turned out to be? Otto had one hell of a job keeping your name out of it."

"I misjudged the woman."

"I'll say you did. You almost misjudged yourself into a jail cell. You've got a taste for crazy ladies, Dad."

"Benjamin," Dearborn returned with dignity, "it was not I who found himself facing an irate husband on the sidewalk in front of Regine's."

"Don't let's bring that up again."

"Or whose visage was reproduced on the front page of the

New York *Daily News* below the headline 'Basketball Star Named Corespondent.' "

Benjamin swung his legs over the chair arm and propped his feet up on the coffee table. "The point is that five thousand dollars isn't pin money and Otto wants some kind of accounting before he agrees to let you dip into your account."

"It is my money, Benjamin, and it is I who have the final say."

"Since you pay Otto for advice, you should try taking his advice once in a while."

"When his advice is sound I take it. When it is high-handed and arbitrary I ignore it."

Somewhere in the back of the apartment a telephone rang. Benjamin reached over to the extension on the coffee table, followed the dangling cord to its source, inserted the loosened prong into the wall jack, and picked up the receiver. "Hello? His son here. Just a second." Benjamin put his hand over the mouthpiece. "Somebody named Edward Roycroft."

Dearborn took the telephone out of Benjamin's hand. "Yes? What do you want? What? Oh, you're the person my housekeeper mentioned. Any relation to Burgess Roycroft? You don't say. Well, what's this all about?" Dearborn's face registered astonishment and then quickly composed itself. "Just a moment." He waved his free hand at Benjamin and whispered, "You might as well go. I'm tied up now."

Benjamin shook his head.

Dearborn said into the receiver, "I cannot talk to you over the telephone. Would you like to come and see me? Yes? All right, then. When? Yes, all right. Come ahead. Good-bye, Mr. Roycroft."

Dearborn hung up and said firmly, "And good-bye to you too, Benjamin."

"Dad, you still haven't told me—"

"Never mind. My friend Edward Roycroft is stopping by. This discussion will have to be postponed."

"Your friend? You never spoke to that guy before in your life. Who is he, Dad? Does this have anything to do with that five thousand bucks?"

"A buck is a male deer, rabbit, sheep, goat, or antelope."

"What am I supposed to tell Otto?"

"Tell him that I do not appreciate his sneaky underhanded tactics in sending you here. Tell him that if he has something to say to me he can say it in person. Tell him that if his father were alive today he would bow his head in shame."

3

"You say you're Buggy Roycroft's nephew?" Dearborn asked. "How is Buggy? Still racing at Indianapolis, is he? I remember when he raced against Pete Depaolo in 1924, or was it 1925? The date's fuzzy but it was a Duesenberg beat him. I'm sure of that. Buggy was driving a Peugeot, or was it a Fiat? Well, no matter. He didn't win the race. Pete Depaolo did. Or was it Frank Lockhart? Peculiar sport that. About on a par with Russian roulette for amusement, but I suppose there's no accounting for tastes."

"Dead," Edward Roycroft said.

"Come again?"

"Dead. Uncle Burgess died in 1945. To tell you the truth, I never knew him."

"No scruples," Dearborn rallied. "None whatever. A bon vivant and a bit of a scoundrel. Made off with Juanita Froebel right after Buzz Beckwith made off with her porcelains. I'll never forget it."

"Come again?"

"That's a long story. Never mind. Now, look here, if Buggy died in '45 you can't be coming here to see me about him, can you?"

"No, I can't. As a matter of fact I just used his name as an introduction. Your name was in the papers a while back in connection with those Rotten Apple murders and that's when my mother told me you and Uncle Burgess had been at Harvard together. I took a chance you might have known him."

Dearborn examined Edward Roycroft closely. He certainly didn't look much like Buggy's nephew. He appeared to be in his early thirties and he was tall, as tall as Buggy had been, but his carriage was stooped, his manner self-effacing, and he walked stiffly, with a slight limp. His dark hair was worn short and his face was pinched behind rimless spectacles. Buggy had been sandy-haired, with an open countenance and an arrogantly self-assured manner.

He had also been a natty dresser. Edward Roycroft wore an uninspired knee-sprung brown suit under a respectable but badly cut tweed coat, and he looked as if he might bolt at the least hint of unfriendliness. It wasn't "like uncle, like nephew" at all. Sad how the generations had a way of deteriorating. Dearborn sighed, as much for himself as for poor old Buggy.

"It's about the body you found yesterday," Roycroft blurted out.

Dearborn was surprised. "You're from Homicide? Don't tell me one of the Roycrofts stooped to becoming a flatfoot?"

"No. As a matter of fact I'm ... was a friend of Louis Martin, the man whose body you found, Mr. Pinch. He and I were friends. We met in high school. The High School of Music and Art. I'm a musician. Lou was into theater arts."

"You're a musician, you say?"

"I've been with the Metropolitan Symphony since 1968. Thanks to Lou."

"Thanks to Lou?"

"He saved my life once. I was attacked by a street gang up on 169th Street. They grabbed my violin, roughed me up, and one of them was getting ready to hit me over the head with a piece of lead pipe when Lou came along. He started throwing punches and shouting to attract attention, which got rid of them, but not before Lou was hit with the lead pipe. Broke his hip bone. He was in the hospital for six weeks."

"Harrowing experience," Dearborn allowed.

"Lou said he was glad it happened," Roycroft added wryly. "He was 4-F after that. He said it kept him from getting killed in Vietnam, but I never got over feeling guilty about it."

"I sympathize."

"You can see why I feel like I do about what happened to Lou. We saw one another once in a while over the years, until Lou left New York. Then we lost track. He came back to New York about four months ago and called me. He was staying with me when it happened. I can't tell you how rotten I feel."

"Why have you come to see me, Mr. Roycroft?"

"When I found out you had been at the police station, that you were the one who found Lou—"

"They told you that, did they?" Dearborn sensed that he wasn't being called upon to commiserate.

"I decided I'd come and talk to you about it. You see, Mr. Pinch, I have these doubts. About whether or not it was a mugging. More than doubts. Lou was in good shape. It wouldn't have been easy to mug him. Even with a gun. I mean, someone might have walked up and shot him point-blank but if he had any forewarning he would have put up a fight." Roycroft took a deep breath and plunged ahead. "To tell you the truth, I don't think Lou was killed by a mugger. I think it was someone with a grudge against him. And I think I know who."

They were standing in the library doorway. Dearborn gestured toward the couch and Roycroft sat down. Dearborn took a seat opposite. He hadn't expected anything so stimulating. They had spoken of Buggy on the phone and Dearborn had naturally assumed that it was Buggy who would be the topic of conversation. This was infinitely more intriguing. "Tell me, Mr. Roycroft, why are you bringing me this story?"

"When the police called me down to identify Lou, an officer there named Stefanich mentioned your name and I recognized it. He happened to say that you didn't think it was a mugging murder and since I don't think so either..."

"Yes, yes, go on. Give me the specifics."

"About four months ago I got a call from Lou. He said he'd just arrived in New York from Florida and that he was strapped for money. He asked me if he could stay with me for a few weeks until he found a job. I have an apartment in the Olmstead Arms in the Village."

"No wife?" Dearborn interrupted to ask.

"No wife. And I'm not home much. I work nights. I do a lot of practicing and rehearsing."

"So you were agreeable to having him."

"I was glad to help."

"Four months is stretching it a bit, though, isn't it?"

"I owed it to him."

Dearborn prodded him along. "Let's get to the heart of it. What makes you think your friend was murdered?"

Roycroft went on, "Lou had been living in Florida. He was involved with a woman. Her name is Molly Beggs. She's married. When it started getting serious Lou wanted out. He was afraid of trouble."

"From the woman?"

"From her husband."

"Ah hah."

"The husband wasn't anybody Lou wanted to tangle with. Monday, when Lou came in, he said he'd seen this blue Lincoln parked in different parts of town all day. He thought he was being followed. He asked me to go downstairs and check it. He was right. There was a blue Lincoln just pulling away from the curb as I came out of the building."

"You got the license plate number, of course."

Roycroft shook his head. "Lou had told me he'd taken it. But I don't know now what he did with it."

"It wasn't among his personal effects?"

"You mean when they found him? No."

"You've looked for it at home?"

"Everywhere."

"I see. Go on."

"Lou didn't go out Monday evening. Next morning, that was Tuesday, I went down to check for him again. Nobody was there, so I gave Lou the all clear and he left. It was about nine in the morning. He didn't come back. I didn't know what had happened until the police called yesterday."

"Why didn't you call the police when your friend failed to return home on Tuesday evening?"

"Lou knew a lot of people. I thought he'd decided to stay with one of them until the thing blew over."

"And for some reason you haven't yet told the police all you know about this affair?"

Roycroft looked miserable and shook his head. "I'm afraid to tell them."

"Afraid? Why should you be afraid?"

"Because of who Molly Beggs's husband is."

Dearborn asked impatiently, "And who is he?"

"Leo Beggs."

"The Florida land speculator?" Dearborn returned with relish. "The Cracker Tycoon? The Everglades Gladiator?"

Roycroft nodded. "Molly was his chauffeur's daughter. Beggs married her a few years back. They live in this hotel Beggs put up near Silver Beach."

"Ah yes. La Playa. The ultimate resort. Isn't that what they call it? Never been there myself. Not fond of ultimates."

Roycroft rubbed his hands on the knees of his trousers. "I haven't been to sleep in two days. If Beggs gets away with this it'll be my fault. I know that. But I can't help thinking that if he had the nerve to kill Lou, then he isn't going to think twice about killing me."

Dearborn said dutifully but without much enthusiasm, "You should report it to the police."

"I'm not crazy, Mr. Pinch. The police said Lou was shot with a .38-caliber bullet. Beggs is a crack shot. That's what Lou told me. He could have done it. If I could prove that Beggs has a .38-caliber gun or if I could prove that Beggs was in New York when Lou was killed or maybe that he rented a car, or if Molly Beggs could be persuaded to talk—"

"I should be very surprised," Dearborn cut in dryly, "to discover that Mrs. Beggs would be willing to risk losing ten million dollars for the sake of a dead man."

"I thought of that," Roycroft said eagerly, "but I was counting on the surprise element. She doesn't know Lou's dead yet. How could she? Beggs wouldn't tell her. Nobody but me knows about it. When she finds out, the shock might make her blurt out something."

"Blurt out what?" Dearborn asked.

"That she and Lou were having an affair. That her husband found out about it. Then if we can prove Beggs was in New York Monday and Tuesday..."

"We?"

Roycroft looked at Dearborn expectantly. "If someone could get to her..."

"Someone?"

"I can't go down there, Mr. Pinch. I'm no good at this sort of thing. I'd botch it up."

Ah, there it was. The crux of the matter. Dearborn regarded Roycroft with pleasure. A man of discrimination, if not much fiber. If only Dearborn didn't have other irons on the fire.

"Would you consider helping me, Mr. Pinch?"

"I am sympathetic to your plight," Dearborn allowed agreeably, "but..."

"I thought you could take a tape recorder."

"A tape recorder?" Dearborn said, intrigued.

"Maybe a bugging device."

"A bugging device?" Dearborn echoed delightfully.

"If you pretended to be a guest at the hotel..."

"Infiltrated, you mean?"

"I know it's a lot to ask. Believe me, it took a lot of nerve for me to come and ask."

"Not more than you possess, I notice."

"I was even," Roycroft added with an embarrassed laugh, "going to offer you money."

"Money?" Dearborn began to reevaluate the possibilities. "Did you say money?"

"It shows you how desperate I am."

"What sum had you in mind?"

"I'd be ashamed to tell you."

"Spit it out, Edward. Mind if I call you Edward? After all, you are Buggy's nephew."

"Why would you want money? I mean the kind of money I could pay."

"Charity?" Dearborn prompted helpfully. "I could contribute it to my favorite charity?"

"I suppose."

"Come, come. No shyness now. What had you in mind? Are you talking in the hundreds or the thousands?"

"I was thinking of five thousand. I know it's not much. I'm sure it's chicken feed to you."

"You're right, of course. It isn't an enormous sum. . . ."

"I'd offer more if I had it."

"But then, what do I need?"

"Nothing. I know that."

"Still, there are charities."

"A lot of them."

"Can I deprive them . . .?"

"You're thinking about it, then, Mr. Pinch?"

"I have considered it, Edward."

"And?"

"Done," Dearborn informed him benevolently.

"You accept? My God, that's wonderful!"

"There is a charity to which I contribute. A little-known charity but one to which I am partial. Now, this is what I propose. This particular charity is underfunded. Been in difficulties lately. Needs money by the first of March, as a matter of fact. I propose, since time is of the essence, that you agree to make your check payable to the . . . er . . . secretary of the organization, a lady in Boise. I'll write down the particulars. And when I notify you that I have successfully completed the assignment, you may forward the check to her with a note appended explaining that it was sent at my behest. That should be sometime within the next week or so. Does that meet with your approval?"

"Anything you say, Mr. Pinch."

"Very good." Dearborn suddenly cocked his head and held up his hand for silence. Then he boomed, "Mrs. Woolley! Show yourself!"

A red-faced Mrs. Woolley poked her head around the door. "I was just coming in to ask if you still want tea."

"Who asked you for tea?"

"You did. You told me before—"

"Nonsense. You have been skulking around trying to hear what I'm saying. Benjamin has been instructing you in the fine art of spying, has he not? Answer me, Mrs. Woolley!"

"He has not," she replied with aplomb.

"Hoof it back down the hall and out of earshot."

Mrs. Woolley, with a mighty expiration of breath, withdrew. Dearborn turned his attention back to Roycroft. "Now, where were we?"

"I was just about to thank you, sir."

"And I was about to give you the address of the lady in Boise." Dearborn wrote it on a slip of paper and gave it to Roycroft.

"It's marvelous. I can't believe you said yes." He held out his hand.

Dearborn took it. "Your appeal to my altruistic nature did it."

Dearborn escorted Roycroft to the door. He was humming when he returned and sat down again at the desk. He crumpled the letter he had been writing earlier and took out a fresh sheet of paper. "Dear Emmylou, the Hindu vernacular includes a word called 'karma'. . . ."

4

"This is where he slept," Edward Roycroft said, throwing open the door and preceding Dearborn into the room.

The room contained a double bed covered in channel-quilted blue cotton and was decorated with a dozen or so throw pillows, an art-deco blond night table, and a modern sling chair in white canvas. Under the double windows at the far side of the room were bookshelves, a floor arrangement of potted plants, and another sling chair.

"Where are his belongings?" Dearborn asked.

"He didn't have much. What he had is in a suitcase in the living room. I turned out his pockets. There wasn't anything worth saving. The police still have his wallet. I suppose his watch and ring are lying in some sewer, wherever Beggs threw them."

"He left no papers?"

"Nothing."

"And you didn't find the slip of paper with the license plate number of that blue Lincoln?"

"I'm afraid not."

Dearborn crossed to the night table. The two small drawers in it contained nothing of significance. He started to turn away when he spotted something on the floor behind the table and stooped to pick it up. It was a clear plastic pill container.

"What are they?" Edward asked.

"Ephedrine. From the Hardwicke Pharmacy on Coral Street in Silver Beach. Was Martin ill?"

"He had low blood pressure."

Dearborn put the container in his pocket. Then he got down on his knees and reached under the bed. All he felt was puffs of dust. "Did you check the rest of the apartment?" he asked, struggling to his feet. "It would simplify our task if you could locate something to connect Louis Martin to Molly Beggs, a letter, a trinket of some sort."

"I turned the place upside down," Edward replied. "I guess they were smart enough not to exchange letters."

Dearborn dusted off his hands. "Let us go into the parlor." He followed Edward down the hall and into the living room. It looked, Dearborn thought, like the room of an artist, theatrical and Sybaritic. The walls were enameled red with matching vertical blinds at the windows. Centered on the black floor was an oriental rug in shades of red and yellow. Soft black leather couches faced one another over a six-foot-square chrome and glass cocktail table. Dearborn crossed to the baby grand piano that occupied one corner of the room, its black form stark against the red-enameled walls.

There were photographs everywhere, the one on the piano a large framed likeness of the conductor of the Metropolitan Symphony Orchestra, Luigi Uberdini. The inscription in the lower corner read "To Eddie, from the Maestro."

A violin and bow lay next to the photograph. The violin case lay on the floor. "Practising, were you?" Dearborn asked, picking up the violin.

Edward shook his head. "I haven't touched it since Monday."

Dearborn plucked at the violin strings and ran his fingers along the fine rosined horsehairs of the bow while Edward watched him glumly.

"You didn't play last night's concert?"

"I called in sick."

"It doesn't do to fall apart at the seams," Dearborn lectured. "You aren't falling apart at the seams, are you, Edward?"

"No, sir."

"Because if you are, I have a friend, a doctor named Moltke..."

"I'm okay, Mr. Pinch."

"In that case, let us proceed. I should like to see Martin's suitcase."

"It's over here." Edward crossed the room to a console table on which rested a small suitcase. He snapped it open.

Dearborn joined him and together they examined the contents. There were two pairs of slacks, a sports jacket, a white dress shirt, a sports shirt, a couple of ties, and two changes of underwear and socks.

"The funeral's tomorrow," Edward said. "I gave Lou's suit to the funeral director to bury him in."

After a tactful pause Dearborn asked, "Did you check the pockets first?"

Edward nodded. "Empty."

Dearborn lifted out a fancy leather toilet kit. "This might have been a gift," he reflected, "but I suppose there's no way to find out if it came from Molly Beggs." He picked out a razor, then scrabbled around among the other items. "I find it hard to believe that these few things constitute the sum total of Martin's possessions."

Edward sat down heavily on the couch. "Well, that's it. That's all he brought with him."

Dearborn put back the toilet kit and addressed Edward with severity. "That may be all that he brought with him, but it does not necessarily follow that it is all he owned."

"He was down on his luck, Mr. Pinch. From what he told me he was having a hard time making ends meet. He'd been working for this radio station in Miami."

"Radio station?"

"Yeah. He had some idea about becoming a sportscaster. When he lost that job he went up to Silver Beach. The radio station there hired him on a year's trial basis. He was making peanuts. He couldn't even afford an apartment. He was living in a rooming house."

"Is it not possible that he left something behind?"

"I guess anything's possible. He didn't say he didn't leave something behind."

"Do you know his address in Silver Beach?"

"He never told me. Only that it's a rooming house."

Dearborn patted his pocket. "In that case this little container will come in handy. The next step will be to check with the police to verify the caliber of the bullet and to collect whatever other tidbits of information they may have to offer."

"Are you going to call them?"

"I am going to call *on* them. I shall go downtown and have a little talk with Captain Niccoli."

"You won't say too much."

"No more than necessary."

"Or bring my name into it."

"You may rely on that."

"I don't know what kind of gun," Stefanich said, peering up over his typewriter, "and if I did I wouldn't tell you. If the captain was to come in I'd get chewed out for even letting you up here."

"I should like to see the file on Louis Martin."

"Are you kidding? I can't show you that."

"I insist upon my right to add a paragraph stating that I am not in agreement with Captain Niccoli's assessment of the case."

"Not that again."

"By the way," Dearborn said offhandedly, "was Martin shot from a distance or at close range?"

"I forget. You know how many muggings we get in here in a week?"

"I have some recollection that the captain mentioned a .38-caliber bullet."

"Your guess is as good as mine."

"He wasn't carrying any odd scraps of paper, was he? Anything with numbers written on it, say?"

"Now look, Mr. Pinch, it's lucky for you that you come up here while the captain's over to the borough commander's office. He wouldn't be too happy to see you. I think you better split before he gets back."

They were sitting at Stefanich's desk at the end of the room nearest Niccoli's office. Between them and the exit was a jumble of desks and file cabinets, a water cooler, a coffee machine, a switchboard, and a teletype, all of which were in use. "You can see what's goin' on around here," Stefanich pleaded. "There's no time for horsin' around."

"You will not change your mind?"

"What am I doin' discussin' this with you? I'm goin' to get myself in Dutch here."

"May I remind you," Dearborn announced in stentorian tones, "that I am a tax-paying citizen of New York, one of that common breed to whom you owe allegiance."

"Say again?" Stefanich asked in a bewildered voice.

Dearborn, in his soft-brimmed tattersall cap, belted cashmere coat, and fur-lined suede gloves, belied the word common although his indignation was genuine. He said, "I do not intend to leave here without satisfaction."

"I'm not tryin' to give you the bum's rush, Mr. Pinch, but the captain could walk in anytime now."

_____ 25

"Where is it?" Dearborn demanded, and although Stefanich didn't reply, the flicker of his eyes told all.

"In Niccoli's file cabinet, eh?"

"The captain isn't kiddin' about clappin' you away," Stefanich warned. "It took him a long time to get over that other business, and he told me the other day if you start interferin' again he's goin' to arrest you, son or no son."

Dearborn bristled. "What did he mean, son or no son? What has Benjamin got to do with this?"

"He's the only thing standin' between you and the slammer. Lucky for you the captain's a basketball fan."

"My son no longer plays basketball."

"The Super Runt's the Super Runt whether he's playin' or not. Listen, if he decided to go back tomorrow he could write his own ticket. Any team, any city in the country."

"I'm not here to discuss my son's athletic prowess."

The phone on Stefanich's desk rang. He picked it up. "Hi, Captain," he said, opening his eyes wide at Dearborn and pointing to the receiver with a free finger. "Yeah, I know where it is. I filed it last night, remember? You want me to bring it over myself or send it? Okay, in about ten minutes." He hung up. "You gotta go now, Mr. Pinch."

"Do you intend to give me access to that folder?" Dearborn asked.

"You're givin' me a headache."

"You, Stefanich, are giving *me* a headache."

"I'm tryin' to let you down easy. I'm goin' to end up havin' to tell the captain you was here if you put me on the spot."

Dearborn turned and stalked toward Captain Niccoli's office. Stefanich jumped up and followed him. "Maybe you got a suicidal impulse," he declared, making an unsuccessful attempt to place himself between Dearborn and Niccoli's desk, "but I don't."

Dearborn brushed him aside and sat down in Captain Niccoli's swivel chair.

"It's not going to do you no good," Stefanich exclaimed. "You're stickin' your head in the lion's mouth. And what about my head?" he added in an inspired mixed metaphor. "My head'll roll along with yours."

Dearborn looked up at him with a thoughtful expression. To Stefanich's surprise he suddenly nodded and said, "You may be right. Though not for the right reasons. Perhaps my coming here was a mistake."

"Now you're talkin'."

Dearborn started to rise, then, halfway out of the chair, sat down again and put his hand up to his forehead.

"What's the matter? You sick?"

"No, no," Dearborn muttered.

"Somethin's the matter."

"My blood pressure. That's all. I have low blood pressure. Nothing to worry about. Forgot to take my pill this morning." He reached into his vest pocket and pulled out the pill container he'd picked up from the floor in Edward Roycroft's apartment and waved it at Stefanich.

"I told you," Stefanich groaned. "I knew it. I thought somethin' was the matter with you. You want some water?"

"It would be appreciated."

"Hot damn!" Stefanich rushed out of the office and started across the floor toward the water cooler.

Dearborn waited until his back was turned, then rose from his seat, slipped the pill container back in his pocket, and crossed to the file cabinet. "M." It took only a moment to locate the drawer, pull it out, and retrieve the folder labeled "Martin, Louis." Dearborn snatched the folder, left Niccoli's office, and was halfway down the stairs before Stefanich had filled the paper cup with water.

5

"What was the other thing you wanted to talk to me about?" the borough commander asked. He and Captain Niccoli were seated on opposite sides of the desk. Niccoli's briefcase lay on the desk between them along with two empty Styrofoam coffee cups and an ashtray full of butts.

"It's about a homicide, a murder in the Village Tuesday."

"What about it?"

"A man named Louis Martin was shot and dumped in front of a funeral parlor down there. It looked like a mugging murder at first, but now I don't know."

"What do you mean?"

"A couple of things about it struck me as fishy—the way he was dressed, the placement of the body, the amount of time elapsed between the killing and the discovery of the body. Nothing concrete. Just enough to make me suspicious. When we checked up on him we found out he'd been in trouble in Florida."

"What kind of trouble?"

"He was booked on attempted burglary a few months back."

"So? Don't small-time hoods ever get mugged?"

"It was the circumstances. He was caught in a lady's bedroom, supposedly stealing the family jewels. The husband surprised him. The husband had a gun. He held him and called the police."

"Well, what's so strange about that?"

"Martin cooled his heels in jail for a day or two and then the husband bailed him out."

"The husband?"

"Yeah. There was a lot of talk that this guy wasn't burglarizing the apartment at all and that the wife wasn't shouting thief either when the husband walked in. The guy had a job. He was working for a radio station in Silver Beach, so he wasn't your run-of-the-mill burglar. Anyway, he jumped bail and came to New York. Now he's got himself killed. What I'm wondering about is how come the husband stood him for bail and could there be any connection between his coming to New York and getting himself killed?"

"Silver Beach, Florida?"

"Yup."

"Did Galton call the Silver Beach police?"

"How do you think I got all the information?"

"I mean," the commander said irritably, "did he ask them to check up on this husband?"

"No."

"Why not?"

"Touchy."

"How come?"

"The husband is Leo Beggs, the guy who turned a lot of sand into a lot of dollars."

"The Florida Cracker Tycoon?"

"That's the guy."

The commander grunted and stared at Niccoli expressionlessly.

"He pays a lot of tax dollars into the state. What's more, he owns La Playa, which resort also brings in more tourist dollars than Miami and Palm Beach put together."

"You don't think they'll cooperate?"

"They'll cooperate, but they won't initiate, if you get what I mean."

"So what do you propose we do about it?"

Niccoli shrugged. "We could forget the whole thing, but there's this oath I took a few years back."

"Nobody's suggesting you forget about it. What have you done at this end?"

"Nothing so far."

"What do you intend to do?"

"This guy Martin was sponging off some old friend of his up here. The friend identified the body. We can go see him. Maybe he'll be able to shed some light."

"He didn't say anything when you talked to him?"

"No. He didn't volunteer and we didn't ask. It wasn't until later we found out about Martin's record."

"You think this friend might know something?"

"He's kind of a mouse," Niccoli replied. "Plays the violin for a living. Not too sharp. You never know, though."

"No possibility that the mouse is a wolf in mouse clothing?" the commander asked. "Does he have a motive?"

"Anything's possible, but I wouldn't bet on it."

"What else do you want to do, Tony?"

"You can't guess?"

"You want to gather some hard evidence."

"That's right."

"And turn it over to the Silver Beach boys so they'll be forced to act."

"That's right."

"You want to send somebody down there."

Niccoli looked surprised, as if he had expected the commander to know the answer without asking.

"But not officially. So it's got to be someone who'll keep it under wraps."

"Now you're talking," Niccoli declared.

"Not one of your men."

"Uh uh."

"Sometimes I think you should have refused that promotion, Tony."

"Sometimes I think so myself."

"The final okay has to come from upstairs."

"A good word from you will help."

"I'd like to see the report."

"Galton only spoke to Silver Beach on the phone. He doesn't have anything from them in writing. I can get copies of their folder on Martin when I'm down there, whatever match-ups we need, mug shots, prints, that stuff. . . ."

"What's the matter? Their equipment break down? Why can't they wire us that stuff?"

"What equipment? Silver Beach isn't New York. I think they're still hand-cranking the phones down there. What's the difference? We've got enough right here to go on. I can get it here in a couple of minutes."

The commander pressed a button on his desk and said into the intercom, "Plug this into Captain Niccoli's office. Ask for . . ." He raised his eyebrows.

"Stefanich."

"Officer Stefanich." The commander handed the phone to Niccoli.

"Listen, Ben, none of that bim, bam, thank you, ma'am, business. I like a little foreplay, know what I mean?"

"I don't keep a copy of *Psychopathia Sexualis* on the bed table for nothing." Benjamin snapped up the lid of the cube-shaped cocktail table and pushed a couple of buttons. "The liquor's in that rolling cart over by the window. You pour. I'll get the ice."

He glanced into the bedroom on his way to the kitchen. Shit. He'd forgotten to make the bed that morning. He dodged inside and began plumping the pillows. To think how hard he'd tried to wiggle out of that telethon. Six hours sitting on his ass making small talk to a bunch of celebrity hounds. He must have said "How nice of you" five hundred times. His tongue had begun to cleave to his teeth on the five hundredth "Thank you." Then came the five hundred and first call and Natalie, that sultry voice that was maple syrup pouring out of the receiver. "Listen, Ben baby, I've been a fan of yours for years. What are you doing after the show?"

She'd turned out to look as good as she sounded. That was the second miracle. Benjamin smoothed the sheets, pulled up the quilt, and jammed yesterday's socks and shirt into a drawer. He splashed a little Brut on the back of his neck and pivoted back out into the hall just as the strains of Ravel's *Bolero* thrummed out of the loudspeakers. He didn't hear the door chimes over the beat of the music. It wasn't until Natalie glided into the kitchen to say that he had a visitor that he felt the first shiver of foreboding. "Who is it?"

"An old man."

"The super, maybe?" Benjamin speculated, clinging to hope while his spirits plummeted.

"Not unless the super wears a cashmere coat and fur-lined gloves."

"Shit."

"Benjamin!" The voice was imperious, irritable, and unmistakable.

"Who is it?" Natalie whispered.

"Don't ask. Look, why don't you get out the ice cubes while I get rid of him."

"Whatever you say, Ben baby."

Benjamin loped down the hall. Dearborn was prowling the living room, poking at the furniture with his cane.

"What's up, Dad? What are you doing here?"

"Where is the Victrola?" Dearborn demanded, lunging at the drapes.

"It's after midnight, Dad."

"Don't tell *me* it's after midnight. You're the one causing the commotion." Dearborn pulled open a cabinet door and poked at Benjamin's television set. "Your neighbors are either remarkably tolerant or stone-deaf."

Benjamin crossed to the stereo and punched the "off" button. "Are you in some sort of trouble, Dad?"

"I am not in trouble. I am not in any sort of trouble."

"Then what are you doing here?"

"I happened to be passing—"

"At midnight?"

"And it occurred to me that I might not have mentioned—"

"When have you ever 'mentioned'? You haven't made an incidental remark to me in the last twenty years."

" . . . that I might not have mentioned," Dearborn went on unconcernedly, "the fact that I have decided to take a little vacation."

"Uh oh."

"Don't 'uh oh' me, Benjamin. There's no reason why my announcement should inspire suspicion or distrust. I have simply decided to cast off for warmer waters."

"Which warmer waters?"

"Acapulco."

"Who are you going with?"

"I am going alone," Dearborn replied.

"Come off it. I know you better than that. It's your new girl friend, isn't it?"

"If you insist."

"She isn't married, is she?"

"She is neither married nor a fortune hunter. There will be no scandal."

"So what do you want with me, Dad?"

"Nothing at all."

"That's a relief."

"Or almost nothing," Dearborn amended.

"Uh oh."

"Again 'uh oh'? It is simply that I need some information. Nothing much. Has to do with an old friend of mine."

"Who's that?"

"Leo Beggs."

"*The* Leo Beggs? The Florida Cracker Tycoon?"

"The very one."

"I didn't know you knew him. Not exactly your kind of guy, is he?"

"Don't be a snob, Benjamin. You know how I feel about snobs."

"Sure."

"Leo was in town last week. He rented a car, a blue Lincoln. He's not sure whether it was Hertz or Avis or one of the smaller agencies. His secretary arranged it. They delivered the car to his hotel. Anyway, the point is that Leo thinks he may have dropped a very valuable ring back of a cushion when he was adjusting the car seat."

"And you want me to track it down."

"Exactly."

"Some assignment."

"Benjamin, you are always offering to help me. Now I've found a way for you to do it."

"Hurrah."

"I shall phone you to see what you've found out," Dearborn said, heading for the door.

"When are you leaving, Dad?"

"Now."

"No, I mean for Mexico."

"Mexico? Oh yes. Tomorrow."

"How are you going to phone me, then?"

"They have phones in Mexico, don't they?"

"Dad, you're not going to get into a jam, are you? I mean, you've got a way of getting tangled up with kooky broads."

"Don't be vulgar."

"I mean, hell, if you don't care about me, at least have a little consideration for Otto. You've had him in court twice already this year. Give the guy a break."

"Don't nag, Benjamin."

"Bullshit."

"Vulgarity. It's a quality you inherit from your mother." Dearborn walked to the door and turned with his hand on the knob. "Benjamin," he said casually, "you may get a call from Captain Niccoli. I would appreciate it if you did not tell him that I've left town."

"Why? Wait a minute. What are you saying?"

Dearborn disappeared through the door and Benjamin sprinted after him. "What are you talking about? Why should I get a call from Niccoli? I thought that whole thing about the stiff in the Village was settled."

Dearborn, who was already standing at the elevator, ignored Benjamin's question and concentrated on jabbing the point of his cane against the elevator button.

"Do you hear me, Dad?"

"The entire twelfth floor hears you," Dearborn observed calmly.

"Bullshit."

The elevator doors opened and Dearborn stepped inside. He turned to face Benjamin, slinging his cane over his arm so that his hands were free to tie his coat belt. As the doors closed he said firmly, but with a sad shake of the head, "It wasn't my fault. I will not shoulder the blame. I did the best I could for you, Benjamin. Blame it on your mother."

6

"I verified the fact that it was a .38-caliber bullet," Dearborn informed Edward Roycroft triumphantly, crooking the telephone between chin and shoulder to spread marmalade on one of Mrs. Woolley's homemade buttermilk biscuits.

"You didn't say anything to the police about me, did you?"

"Certainly not. I merely asked to see the folder on the case to satisfy my own curiosity. I think you might be interested to know, however, that the folder contains a note that your friend skipped bail in Florida."

"Skipped bail? What are you talking about?"

"You didn't know about his arrest?"

"What arrest?"

"Apparently Leo Beggs had him arrested for breaking and entering, then bailed him out."

"Lou was no thief. Beggs must have found him with Molly and trumped up the charges."

"My thought exactly."

"Beggs must have wanted Lou out so he could kill him."

"It's possible, my boy."

"Do you think the police thought of that?"

"Not a mother's son of 'em is bright enough to put two and two together."

"What else did you find out, Mr. Pinch?"

"I found out that the bullet was fired from a Colt revolver, that Martin was hit only once at medium range, the bullet penetra—ah well, never mind. No need to go into lurid detail.

Let's pass to another topic. I have completed my travel arrangements. I have a bedroom on a train leaving Pennsylvania Station today at four forty-five. I'll have to switch trains at Tampa, but I should arrive in Silver Beach tomorrow afternoon."

"You're going by train?"

"That is my usual mode of travel. I see no reason to alter it. One day more or less will hardly make a difference. I shall not, by the way, be registered at La Playa under my own name. I have, for the duration, assumed the name of Burgess Roycroft."

"Uncle Burgess?"

"Correct. There are many people who associate my name with the Rotten Apple affair. I don't wish to call undue attention to myself. Burgess Roycroft's name carries with it a degree of distinction. Roycroft soft beverages. It's a name to be reckoned with."

"But suppose someone there remembers that Uncle Burgess is dead?"

"He's been dead for over thirty years. People are vague about that sort of thing. Even I thought Buggy was still alive, and I have one of your more trustworthy memories." Dearborn was sitting at the breakfast table in his bedroom. He sipped his coffee. His luggage, a matched set of buttery brown calfskin suitcases with thick straps and buckles, festooned with what amounted to a world Baedeker of travel stickers, was lined up at the foot of his bed. His closet, behind mirrored doors, was open, so that he could examine the contents while he breakfasted.

"Mr. Pinch," Edward went on, "I'd like to thank you again for all you're doing for me."

Dearborn made a mental note to leave his sky-blue dinner jacket but to take the one in white linen. He wondered whether his dress pumps were in respectable condition. It had been raining the last time he wore them. "Save the deep-felts for another time," he replied, his mouth full of buttermilk biscuit. "Did you play last night?"

"Yes, sir."

Dearborn asked suspiciously, "What was on the program?"

Edward hesitated. "Beethoven?" he suggested tentatively after a moment's pause.

"Berlioz!" Dearborn boomed into the receiver. "The *Fantastic* Symphony! Just what I thought. Edward, you've got to pull yourself together, get back into the swing of things. Don't pamper yourself. Everything's going to turn out all right."

"If you say so."

"Pick up your fiddle and play. *Sul ponticello*, Edward. *Sulla tastiera.*"

"I'll try, Mr. Pinch."

Dearborn's secretary, William Rhodes, a gray-haired meek individual with a perpetual frown and at the moment an expression of harried anxiety, accompanied Dearborn to Penn Station. He checked through six of Dearborn's seven pieces of luggage and stashed the overnight case in one corner of the bedroom. "I think that's everything, Mr. Pinch. Here are the baggage checks. Here are the magazines you asked for: *Time, Fortune, U.S. News & World Report, Barron's, Esquire, The New Yorker*, and *Ellery Queen's Mystery Magazine.*"

"Where are the chocolates, William?"

William dug around in his pocket and produced a half-dozen Hershey bars.

"Nuts!" exclaimed Dearborn.

William quailed.

"I told you nuts. Did I not say nuts?"

William gazed bleakly at the flat brown wrappers in his hand. "They didn't have any more with nuts," he explained. "I went to three different stands."

Dearborn took the candy bars and tossed them onto the seat. "If I'd asked for peanut brittle you'd have brought that without nuts."

Outside on the platform the conductor was shouting for the last time, "All Aboard!" causing William, his dismal face brightening, to suggest that it was time he left.

"Can't wait to run off, eh, William? Taking the rest of the day off?"

"Not at all, Mr. Pinch."

"Get going, then. And no hanky-panky while I'm gone. Benjamin is not the only one with spies. Forward the bills to Mr. Rothschild and don't open anything that looks personal."

"Yes, sir."

"And keep your paws off Mrs. Woolley."

"Sir?"

"You know what I'm talking about. Don't play the innocent with me."

Dearborn's admonishments to tend to business and not commit outrages upon the person of Mrs. Woolley pursued William down the narrow passage and sent him dashing out of the car in a scramble that was barely short of a gallop.

"Idiot," Dearborn muttered in his wake. "If I didn't feel sorry for him I'd have fired him long ago."

The train pulled out five minutes later, and five minutes after that Dearborn had tracked down the car porter, remonstrated with him for not having answered the buzzer with more alacrity, tipped him ten dollars with a promise of more at the other end of the journey, been supplied with extra towels, pillows, and soap, had his change of clothes hung in the small curtained niche that passed for a closet, and was on his way to the club car.

Train travel, he reflected, was not so luxurious as it once had been. Certainly not so luxurious as it had been when he was a child traveling in his father's private parlor car. That extravagance, with the name Rollo Ashville Pinch inscribed on its side, had been all mahogany and polished brass with brocade swags, upholstered seats that turned into beds at night, and Tiffany lamps with beaded pulls that shimmied and jingled with the sway of the train. And even later, when it had become unfashionable to flaunt one's wealth, it had still been possible to travel first class on the big streamliners, observing the civilities and enjoying the creature comforts. Nowadays, however, Dearborn was forced to admit, all that had changed. The trains were shabby, the service inadequate, the porters barely accommodating, the food unpalatable. Nevertheless, he still found it more civilized to effect his transitions in this leisurely fashion. Who enjoyed being whisked from one climate to another with scarcely time to shed one's overcoat?

The club car was almost empty. A woman and two children occupied the curved banquette near the door. They were drinking Cokes and playing cards. At the far end of the car, with his back to the room, was a lanky young man drinking beer directly from a beer can. Halfway down the car, curled in a chair with one leg under her, sat a heavily made-up young woman with a mass of fuzzy brown hair that was so full it dwarfed her face and made her head look out of proportion to the rest of her. She was dressed in loose cotton slacks, a green cotton blouse, a man's red plaid vest, and hiking boots. Dearborn disapproved of the bizarre attire, the painted face, the relaxed posture. In his day young women didn't dress like gypsies or show such disregard for convention. Or if they did, they did so with style. He sauntered up the aisle and placed himself in front of her. "Young woman."

"Hi."

Dearborn pointed to the foot protruding from under her backside. She looked down at her foot and then back up at him.

"Varicose veins."

"From sitting on my leg?"

Dearborn lowered himself into the chair next to her. "Impaired circulation."

"Why not? Everything else is wrong with me."

"Phlebitis," Dearborn added. "Arthritis."

"Bursitis?" she asked, getting into the spirit of it. "Tendonitis?"

"Treat it lightly if you wish," Dearborn reproved. "But ten years from now you'll suffer the consequences."

She slid her leg out from under her. "My name's Cooky Gillette. Short for Cordelia."

"Dearborn V. Pinch." Dearborn waved to the club car attendant, who had just delivered another beer to the young man at the far end of the car.

"Want to buy me a drink?" Cooky Gillette asked.

"Do you often ask men to buy you liquor?"

"Only when I'm short on cash."

Dearborn was shocked but felt that it would be caddish under the circumstances to refuse. "What would you like?"

"What are you having?"

"Campari and soda."

"Okay. I'll try it."

"You *are* old enough to drink, are you not?"

"I'll be twenty-two my next birthday, which is next Friday, Valentine's Day."

The girl, Dearborn thought, was so thickly shadowed, mascaraed, and rouged that her actual face was all but camouflaged. It was hard to tell just how old she was. Dearborn ordered the drinks and cast about for some excuse to sit elsewhere.

"Before you came over," Cooky confided, "I was trying to figure out some way to get that guy's attention." She waved her hand toward the beer drinker. "But I don't have much luck with anybody under forty. At least, in New York I don't."

"You are a New Yorker?" Dearborn inquired mechanically.

"The Bronx. That is, I live in the Bronx. I work in Manhattan. That is, I work in Manhattan when I'm working."

"You are currently unemployed?"

"Fired," she said matter-of-factly.

"Regrettable," Dearborn commented.

"Yeah but understandable. I can't take shorthand. I'm a lousy typist. And bookkeeping? Forget it."

The waiter delivered their drinks and Dearborn postponed the conversation while he paid for them.

"You always travel by train?" she asked Dearborn.

"Usually. You prefer train travel to plain travel, Miss Gillette?"

"I'm scared of planes. It runs in the family."

"Fear," Dearborn remonstrated, "is not an inherited trait."

"It is in my family. My mother had it."

"Had?"

"My mother's dead. But she was afraid of planes too. So's

my uncle. I'm going to visit my uncle, by the way. How about you? Where are you going?"

"I'm taking a little vacation at one of the Florida spas."

"Which one?" She sipped her Campari and made a wry face. "It tastes like cough medicine."

"Would you prefer a soft drink?"

"I'll stick to this. What's the name of the resort you're going to?"

"La Playa," Dearborn informed her.

She opened her eyes wide and grinned. "Are you kidding? That's where I'm going."

Dearborn was bewildered. "Didn't you just tell me that you are going to your uncle's?"

"My uncle owns the place."

"He isn't . . ."

"Leo Beggs. The rich side of the family. Hey, what did you say your name is?"

"Dear—" Dearborn paused, swallowed, and then supplied, "Burgess Roycroft" in a loud voice, repeating it twice in an effort to superimpose the name over the one he had already given her. "Burgess Roycroft."

"I thought you said Pitch. Delbert or Deerfield or something?"

Dearborn cleared his throat. "That is correct," he returned finally. "That is to say, it is not correct, but it is the name I let slip. That is, not let slip. Fabricated. Yes, that's the word. Fabricated. I made it up. One can't be too careful with strangers, can one?"

"My name is really Cordelia Gillette," she pointed out. "I gave you my real name."

"Next time you should be more cautious," Dearborn remonstrated.

"Maybe we'd better start again." Cooky held out her hand. "How do you do. I'm Cooky Gillette."

Dearborn took her hand and said slowly and distinctly, "Roycroft. Burgess Roycroft."

"I'm on my way to my uncle's place. I always go for my birthday because La Playa throws a big bash every year to celebrate Valentine's Day. What are you doing next Friday?"

"Pardon me?"

"Want to take me to the party?"

"I may not be at La Playa that long," Dearborn said primly.

A porter strolled into the car to announce the first call to dinner.

"We can talk about the party later," Cooky said. "I'd be willing to settle for dinner right now."

Dearborn was disconcerted. He wasn't sure whether he should cultivate the acquaintance or sever it as quickly as possible.

"Oh, come on," Cooky insisted, seeing him hesitate. "Let yourself go, Burgess. Don't be an old stick-in-the-mud."

The club car had been filling up and, as they rose, Dearborn saw that most of the seats were taken. He guided Cooky past the outthrust legs toward the dining car, holding her arm as she marched up the aisle. As he prodded her from behind he made a mental note to be more circumspect in future. He would not allow anyone again to catch him so blatantly off-guard.

But that promise was short-lived. As he passed the last table in the car he glanced down to see what sort of young man would travel first class yet imbibe his beer directly out of a beer can. The sort, he discovered, was the sort who chose Princeton over Harvard, played basketball instead of golf, and disgraced the name of Pinch with predictable regularity. It was Benjamin, sprawled in his chair and looking even more self-satisfied than usual.

7

Dearborn and Cooky were met by the La Playa limousine. The chauffeur relieved Dearborn of his coat, took his and Cooky's baggage checks, and handled the transfer of luggage while they settled themselves in the car.

It was a balmy day and Dearborn reveled in the warmth, the clear air, the semitropical scenery. What could be better, he thought, than a salubrious atmosphere and an adventure in the offing. True, there was an abrasive note or two, one being Cordelia Cooky Gillette, who continued to cling to him like a lamprey to a shark, regaling him with boring and interminable anecdotes about her childhood in the Bronx while remaining stubbornly uncommunicative when he tried to pump her about La Playa in general and her uncle in particular. All he had succeeded in finding out was what he already knew, that Leo Beggs was rich, that he had a young wife and a son Cooky described as a "weirdo," and that Cooky was not just Leo Beggs's favorite niece but his only niece.

Then there was Benjamin, who had buttonholed Dearborn on the station platform a few minutes before and insisted on accompanying him to La Playa.

Dearborn recalled the conversation on the station platform with renewed irritability.

"Otto called me at eight-thirty yesterday morning, Dad. From your place. Where the hell were you?"

"In my bedroom. Packing."

"While Otto was in the library?"

"Mrs. Woolley told him I was out."

"He was spitting nails."

"Otto is too easily excited."

"Excited, Dad? I suppose you have no recollection of what it was you did to excite him?"

"I do not."

"You went down to Captain Niccoli's office and stole his goddamned file!"

"Benjamin," Dearborn had cut in to ask, "did you find out which car rental agency Leo Beggs used when he was in New York?"

"How could I? I was on the horn all day yesterday trying to book a flight to Florida. I could have made arrangements to go to the moon easier. It was the train or nothing. Lucky somebody canceled a roomette or I'd have had to sit up all night in the coach."

"Have you no sense of responsibility? I asked you to do me a favor."

"Otto's doing it. We can call him from the hotel."

"Not 'we,' Benjamin. 'I.' "

"Dad, Otto gave Niccoli the same song and dance you gave me about going to Mexico. But Niccoli's too smart to swallow that story."

"Why shouldn't he? Otto lies very well. It's nothing to concern yourself over."

"Yeah? Then why am I concerned?"

"I venture to say it's because you have an unnatural attachment to me. Don't you think it's time you severed the cord?"

"What did that Edward Roycroft want, Dad? And don't give me the 'old friend' routine. It had something to do with the guy whose body you found, didn't it?"

"Mrs. Woolley had a little difficulty hearing that part, did she?"

"Look, Dad, if you have any sense you'll mail back that file folder and lie low for a couple of months."

"I sent back the file folder by messenger before I boarded the train."

"You did? Are you sure you did?"

"With an additional paragraph that should have been included in the original report and over which the captain and I had our basic disagreement. I think you may rest assured that by now Niccoli has called off the bloodhounds and forgotten the incident."

"That's a relief."

"Benjamin, it would be a relief to me if you would stop following me wherever I go."

And finally Benjamin had agreed to stop following him. It might only be a temporary reprieve, but Dearborn didn't feel he would need more than a few days.

The chauffeur got into the driver's seat, started the engine, nosed the car out of the parking lot, and turned south. It was a smooth ride along a silky strip of highway. The vegetation on either side was dense but occasionally opened out to sand and scrub pine, affording Dearborn a glimpse of the gleaming blue-green waters of the Gulf.

After a fifteen-minute drive they veered onto a narrow road leading to the private causeway separating La Playa from the mainland. The car slowed down at the near end, where a large sign announced that they were about to enter private property belonging to the hotel and that only hotel guests were welcome. The chauffeur saluted the guard at the entrance booth and steered the car onto the ribbon of concrete. Dearborn, leaning forward to squint through the windshield, saw a stone archway with the name "La Playa" inscribed on it, beyond that a line of cabbage palms, and beyond those an area of lush greenery. "Where's the hotel? Place looks like a jungle. Can't believe it's habitable."

"This part *is* jungle," Cooky said. "The island's about a half mile wide and four or five miles long. The hotel's at the southern tip."

They swung off the causeway onto the island and turned left onto a road that ran along the edge of the bay. Now only a narrow strip of beach separated them from the Gulf, and Dearborn could actually see schools of small fish darting and turning in the shallow water near shore. The mainland beyond was an endless green strip, with here and there clusters of low white buildings on luxurious lawns.

"Uncle Leo owns all that," Cooky informed Dearborn proudly, pointing to the mainland. "They're called the Silver Beach Cottages. Every apartment has its own sauna and there's a golf course and two swimming pools."

On the right side of the bay road was a curtain of green

that, in places, encroached on the road with creeping vines and overhanging branches. After a mile or two the road curved to follow the edge of a deep cove on their left. To their right, a section had been cleared to make way for tennis courts. Directly opposite the tennis courts was a broad beach dotted with chaises lounges and small octagonal tents. A few people were sitting on the sand and a few more were wading in the bay water. Up ahead at the far end of the cove was the marina where a fleet of small craft was anchored; sailboats, motorboats, and bicycle pontoons, with here and there a yacht. Dearborn noticed some small open blue and white buses parked at the edge of the marina with "La Playa" printed on their sides.

"No private cars are allowed on the island," Cooky said. "The guest parking lot is on the other side of the causeway. We passed it coming over."

"What's behind that wall?" Dearborn asked, pointing to a high brick wall to their right.

"The gardens back of the hotel. There aren't any sidewalks, so if a person wants to walk to the marina or the tennis courts or the bay beach they generally walk through the gardens." She pointed to an arched wooden gate in the wall. "You can go in and out of the gate over there."

Dearborn still couldn't see the main body of the hotel. It wasn't until they had driven another quarter of a mile and cut sharply inland to pass under a natural archway of oaks that he spotted the red tile roof. It lay behind the brick wall, and as they approached from the northeast he was able to tell that the building, only the second story of which was visible, was shaped like a capital E with all three wings the same length.

The chauffeur drove the limousine around the building to the front entrance: a portico constructed from the same weathered brick as the wall behind, shallow steps leading to the lawn, French windows, and magnificent brass-studded wooden doors that were open and pushed back against the walls of the building. The actual doorway was protected by delicate filigreed gates giving the whole structure the appearance of an elegant Spanish hacienda.

"There's Uncle Leo," Cooky exclaimed excitedly, as the car drew up to the steps. She rapped sharply on the window to attract his attention.

Dearborn peered at Leo Beggs through the car window. He was a burly, bearded man wearing a beige safari suit and hiking boots. Dearborn noted, with some discomfort, that he also wore a cartridge belt and that the belt contained a neat row of bullets. He was an outdoorsman. That was obvious. His complexion was leathery and his squint so extreme that Dearborn couldn't make out the color of his eyes. His hair was thick, coarse, and white and his neck was stringy and loose-fleshed. Dearborn put his age at about sixty, though it was possible that the Florida sun might have added a few years to his looks.

"Where you been?" Beggs bawled as he pulled open the door. "Damn it, Cooky, you was supposed to be here last night. You take that goddamn train again?"

"I'm afraid of planes," Cooky claimed in an equally strident voice. "You know I'm afraid of planes, Uncle Leo."

"You shouldn't be afraid of planes."

"You're afraid of planes, Uncle Leo."

"I'm older than you are. Now, lookit, I been waitin' to go shootin' with you. I got all the 'quipment in the wagon."

"So give me a chance to get out of the car. I'm hardly here and you're already pulling at me."

Beggs took Cooky's arm and hoisted her out of the car. Then, before Dearborn could object, he reached in and performed the same service for him. Once upright, Dearborn towered over Beggs by at least three inches, but he felt somehow that it was the other man who was the more formidable.

Cooky introduced them. "This is Mr. Roycroft, Uncle Leo. We met in the club car of the train yesterday. We hit it off right away."

Beggs's grip was crushing, his expression suspicious. "What's the little girl to you?" he demanded without preliminary.

"He's a friend, Uncle Leo," Cooky said firmly. "Now, don't start in with that 'innocent kid' business."

"Cooky's an innocent kid," Beggs boomed at Dearborn.

"I have no reason to doubt it," Dearborn assured him.

Cooky pounced on her uncle, threw her arms around him, and gave him a noisy kiss. "I'm the only twenty-one-year-old old maid in captivity."

"Don't be funny," Beggs said reprovingly. "Don't be looking to lose it to the first old geezer that comes along." Beggs treated himself to another baleful look at Dearborn over Cooky's head.

Dearborn was ruffled by Beggs's animosity, and even more so by his own helplessness to return insult for insult. He couldn't afford to give offense, but it rankled nonetheless. It certainly rankled.

A couple of suntanned young men bounded down the front steps to tend to the luggage and Dearborn moved to a discreet distance to supervise the unloading.

"Where is everybody?" Cooky asked. "I thought this was supposed to be the middle of the season. We didn't see but a dozen people down at the bay and there's nobody at all on the tennis court."

"Siesta."

"You're full-booked, then?"

"Yup. Except somebody checked out of the Cloister wing this morning. Complained his suite was noisy. I told him my apartment's in Cloister. The noise don't bother me none. 'I got the apartment right next to yours,' I told him. 'The noise don't bother me none. If you don't like it,' I says, 'get out and go on over to Palm Beach.' "

"Where'd you put Burgess?"

"Who's Burgess?"

Cooky pointed to Dearborn, whose attempt to assume an air of affable unconcern resulted in a forced smile that Beggs took for a leer.

"Cooky's an innocent kid," Beggs declared. "We got some nice old ladies stayin' here. I'll introduce you to them."

"Oh, Uncle Leo," Cooky remonstrated, "behave yourself."

"Come on, Cooky." Beggs grabbed her by the arm and began propelling her up the steps.

"Burgess," Cooky called back over her shoulder, "I'll see you later, okay?"

Dearborn responded with a stiff bow, then clipped his cane over his arm and marched up the steps behind them. A fine start, he thought. Plagued by Benjamin, adopted by a garish young female barely past puberty, set upon by the one individual Dearborn wanted least to antagonize. What next?

8

The lobby displayed an extravagance of Moorish arches and stucco columns, silk-cushioned benches and heavily carved refectory tables, presided over by two wood nymphs pouring water out of conch shells into an alabaster fountain. Dearborn could see, through the archways at the back of the lobby, cultivation gone berserk in a garden of oversized hibiscus and cacti, and the front desk to his right completed the exaggerated decor with a semicircular slab of mosaic tile beneath an elaborate crystal chandelier.

Dearborn announced himself to the unctious-looking young man behind the desk.

"Yes sir, we have your rooms. Tahitian wing. Suite 76." He opened the register, flipped it around to face Dearborn, and proffered the pen.

Dearborn signed the register with his pseudonym but gave his New York address, then said peremptorily, "The Tahitian wing won't do."

"Won't do, Mr. Roycroft?"

"Won't do."

"It's on the ground floor with sliding glass doors that open directly onto the beach."

"Save it for Buster Crabbe."

"The bathroom has two sinks."

"I have only one face."

"It has a marvelous view of the Gulf."

"Is it noisy?"

"I can assure you that it is not. It is extremely quiet."

"I like noise," Dearborn promptly informed him. "The noisier the better."

The clerk's face began to settle into an expression of martyred patience common to desk clerks. "You *like* noise?"

"I get all the quiet I need at home. On vacation I like it lively."

"I don't know where else I can put you, sir. We're quite solidly booked. This is the height of the season."

"I understand that someone didn't go for the cacophony in the Cloister wing."

"The what, sir?"

"The noise. The noise. Someone checked out of the Cloister wing this morning."

"They did?" The clerk checked his records and then said with relief, "We did have a checkout before I came on duty this morning. Second floor, Cloister. Number 63."

"I'll take it."

"I'm not sure . . ." the clerk said dubiously.

"Isn't it noisy?"

"Yes, sir, it is."

"That's what I want."

"But we don't have elevators, Mr. Roycroft. There are only two stories. Generally we put the . . . um . . . more mature guests on the ground floor. They generally appre . . ." His voice faltered as Dearborn held his eyes with a chilling stare. "But if you insist . . ."

"Where's my husband, Stan?" a voice behind Dearborn said.

The clerk's eyes swept past Dearborn, who saw a deep flush suffuse his face. Dearborn turned. A stunning woman in a white tennis dress, carrying a tennis racket, had walked up to the desk.

"I'm not sure, Mrs. Beggs. I thought I saw him go by a minute ago."

Molly Beggs more than fulfilled Dearborn's expectations. She was a beautiful woman, not the wholesome pink and white type he'd pictured with a name like Molly but an exotic beauty with high cheekbones, deep-set dark eyes, a wide mouth, and remarkable hair, silky and black like the hair of an Oriental, reaching almost to her waist.

"Excuse me, madam," Dearborn broke in, "my name is Roycroft. Burgess Roycroft."

"Oh?" She cocked her head inquiringly.

"I had the pleasure of sharing the limousine from the station with your niece. We arrived about ten minutes ago."

"Cooky's here?"

"Your husband greeted us at the front steps. I believe he said he was thinking of going hunting."

"That's all he ever thinks of," Molly Beggs said irritably. "Guns, hunting, and more guns."

The desk clerk was fussily going about his business, locating Dearborn's key and signaling the bellboy. "I'll have someone take you to your suite, Mr. Roycroft." He announced officiously to the bellboy, "Suite 63, Cloister."

"You're in 63?" Mrs. Beggs noted. "That's next door to us."

"Really?" Dearborn returned innocently. "You don't say."

"It's noisy."

"I am not at all bothered by noise, Mrs. Beggs."

"I wish to God I wasn't." She shrugged, waved her hand, and walked away from the desk, calling back over her shoulder, "If you *should* see Mr. Beggs, Stan, tell him I'll be with Stuart Ripple down at the courts."

Suite 63 was noisy, as predicted. The living room opened out onto a terrace and the terrace was only forty yards or so from the swimming pool. What seemed to Dearborn like an army of children were busying themselves in and around the pool and communicating with one another in whoops and bellows. And although the bedroom was a little quieter, it had a balcony that was in earshot, if not in sight, of the pool. Nevertheless, Dearborn was where he wanted to be. Next to Beggs.

He set himself to the task of unpacking. He prided himself on being able to adapt to any situation and he would have considered fatuous any attempt to describe the adaptation process in reverse. The fact remained that his forte was people and that he was at a loss in contending with inanimate objects. At home Mrs. Woolley saw to Dearborn's wardrobe and normally William traveled with him. Left to his own devices, Dearborn couldn't get the hang of things. The shoe trees didn't seem to fit the shoes, the trousers persisted in falling off the pants hanger, and the tie rack defeated every effort to make it behave. Dearborn finally piled his ties on the dressing table, left his shoes with the flexible metal rods hanging out the backs, and lined up his trousers on one of the twin beds. Even so, it took him almost an hour to organize himself, and by then it was too late to do anything else but shower and take a brief nap before going downstairs.

The Starfish Lounge was located on the ground floor of the Bay wing facing the water. The entire east wall was glass, protected on the outside by a low box hedge and on the inside by a six-foot-deep border of flowering hibiscus. A waterfall behind the bar ran the length of that wall, and three rows of tables were arranged in tiers to afford each table a double view of waterfall and the Gulf beyond.

Dearborn, in beige linen slacks, pastel blue silk sports jacket, and brown and beige silk shirt, arrived at seven-twenty to find the room crowded and the cocktail hour in full swing. He had thought that meeting Cooky Gillette might work to his advantage, and it might, but rectifying the unfortunate impression he'd given Beggs was the first order of business. It would be a strain on his powers of diplomacy but he must make the effort.

He looked around for Beggs and spotted him standing at the bar next to a tall thin handsome man of about sixty, dressed in a guayabera, the Cuban version of the sports shirt; white slacks; and tinted sunglasses. Beggs and the elegant gentleman weren't talking to one another but they seemed to be together, and Dearborn thought it might be a propitious moment to initiate a friendly exchange.

Dearborn sidled between the tables and approached the bar. "Good evening, Beggs. Mind if I join you and your friend?"

"Hello, Roycroft," Beggs greeted him gruffly.

The important-looking personage held up a magisterial hand, said something in Spanish, then picked up a bowl of peanuts from the bar and held it out to Dearborn.

"Thank you," Dearborn said politely, plucking a peanut from the bowl and popping it into his mouth.

"Cooky said you asked her to supper," Beggs said conversationally.

"Cordelia asked me to supper," Dearborn corrected. "She told me that you are occupied this evening and that she couldn't dine with you."

"Bullshit. She just felt like eatin' in the dinin' room. She's got a crush on the maître d'."

Dearborn raised a noncommittal eyebrow.

"I'm tellin' you that so you don't go gettin' ideas about her. She's just an innocent kid."

Dearborn felt his hackles rise. "So you said earlier, Mr. Beggs."

"Just so you remember it."

"My conscience is clear."

"It better be."

Dearborn held his tongue and addressed himself to the Spanish gentleman. "My name is Roycroft, sir. Burgess Roycroft." He held out his hand.

The Spanish gentleman took his hand and said, "Raúl Baki."

"There are always people suckin' up to me or my family, Roycroft," Beggs informed Dearborn.

"I am not in the least surprised. I, too, have my problem with hangers-on."

"That's why I worry about Cooky."

Dearborn laughed hollowly. "I hope you do not put me in that category, Beggs."

"I'm explainin' why I worry about her."

Dearborn clucked sympathetically.

"She don't know her ass from her elbow," Beggs went on.

"She's still very young."

"That's why she's a pushover for any punk who happens by."

"I am not a man of limitless good humor," Dearborn said stiffly.

"I'm not necessarily talkin' about you."

Dearborn was getting hot under the collar. He felt constrained to change topics. He said to the Spanish gentleman, "I'm Burgess Roycroft of Roycroft Beverages, Hula Cola, Chugola, Spritz Fizz."

"Roycrap?" the Spanish gentleman inquired.

"Not 'crap'; 'croft.' Burgess Roycroft."

"I'm a self-made man," Beggs went on. "It wasn't all smooth sailin', I can tell you that. A lot of misery went along with the climb. But I never asked nothin' from nobody."

"I have the utmost respect for your enterprise and accomplishments," Dearborn assured him.

"And if there's anything I won't put up with, it's spongers. I'd as soon shoot 'em as look at 'em. I'm a crack shot, Roycroft. You know that?"

Dearborn was suddenly more receptive. "So I have heard," he said encouragingly.

"I got quite a gun collection upstairs. Shotguns, rifles, pistols, you name it, I got it."

It was on the tip of Dearborn's tongue to do just that, but he decided that it might lack subtlety to mention the Colt .38 at just that moment. "You don't say?" he commented interestedly.

"Believe me," Beggs declared, "I'm ready for anything. I learned to shoot as a kid. Used to shoot 'gators down in the Glades. Taught Norbie to shoot too. That's my son, Norbie. He don't like huntin' like me. But he can shoot. I seen to that. Not Cooky, though. I offered to teach her but she don't want to. She'll come along to keep me company but she balks at shootin' anything. Takes after her father that way."

"The Gillette side of the family, eh."

Beggs nodded. "The garbage collector side of the family. He don't like me and I don't like him. The only good thing I can say about him is he's not a sponger."

"I should say that's a strong point in his favor," Dearborn remarked.

"You shoot?" Beggs asked challengingly.

"I do not."

"Nothing like it. Getting out into the great outdoors, trackin' down your own supper, knowin' you can take care of yourself. Best feelin' in the world."

Dearborn said to the Spanish gentleman, "Are you an outdoorsman too, Mr. Baki?"

"You're wastin' your time talkin' to Raúl," Beggs informed Dearborn. "He don't speak English. The only one can talk to him is my wife Molly and the help."

Dearborn regarded the Spanish gentleman curiously. "His name is Raúl Baki? Seems to me I've heard that name somewhere."

"He used to be head of Ronbaki Distilleries in Havana. He's been livin' in the United States for the last twenty years."

"And he doesn't speak English?"

"He's a little . . ." Beggs nodded to fill in the blank. "You know. He was livin' here on La Playa when it was still a deserted island. He owned it, lucky for him. Castro took everything he had in Cuba. Affected his mind. He got out of there and came here. Was livin' here like a hermit. Then I come along and bought the island off him. Part of the terms was he could live in the hotel free once it was built. With that and the money I paid him he's been makin' out okay. Except for his thinkin'. He's an oddball. I'm runnin' the only hotel in Florida with its own resident kook. He thinks Castro's got men out lookin' for him. To assassinate him. He's always lookin' over his shoulder."

"Why? Why does he think they're after him?"

"He's got this here plan to retake Cuba."

"Single-handedly?"

"I told you, he's a little . . ." Again Beggs nodded.

Mr. Baki, realizing that he was the focus of their attention, reached into his pocket to pull forth some papers. He peeled one sheet off the top and handed it to Dearborn. It was a flyer with a headline that read "BAKI, CUBAN PATRIOT."

"Thank you," Dearborn said loudly. "Very nice. Thank you."

"My fran," Mr. Baki declared, "we moss sahv Cuba."

"That's my cue to leave," Beggs announced drily. "Remember what I said about Cooky. Cooky's off limits." He slapped Dearborn on the shoulder and began threading his way toward the door.

Dearborn watched him go with mixed feelings. The man was abrasive but peculiarly likable. It was not going to make Dearborn's task any easier.

 9

Cooky collared Dearborn in the shopping annex in front of the dining room. She was wearing knickers, knee socks, and a red and black plaid cotton shirt, an outfit that seemed relatively conservative compared to the costume of her companion, a dark-haired, suntanned willowy individual of questionable gender dressed in a skin-tight green sequined jumpsuit with matching snood. As if the costume weren't attention-getting enough, there was a bass fiddle in a brown case on rollers strapped to his back.

"Burgess, where have you been?" Cooky exclaimed. "I called your suite and you weren't there. I've been looking for you."

"I was in the bar with your uncle and a gentleman named Raúl Baki."

"Raúl the ghoul," Cooky's companion intoned.

"Burgess, this is my cousin Norbert."

"The Musk," Norbert amended.

"That's his stage name," Cooky explained. "Mildew and the Musk. They're the relief band at the Monsoon."

"The Monsoon?" Dearborn inquired.

"There are two nightclubs here, the Tropicala Roof Garden and the Monsoon."

"You're the dude Cooky was telling me about?" Norbert asked.

"Burgess is the president of Roycroft Beverages, aren't you, Burgess."

"He looks more like the head of Geritol," Norbert returned with a snicker. "My father know you're dating Cooky?"

"He knows it," Cooky said shortly. "Come on, Burgess, let's go in."

"Are you certain," Dearborn asked, "that you wouldn't prefer to eat with your uncle and aunt?"

"Uncle Leo's got a meeting."

"That's not what he told me, Cordelia."

"So I lied," she returned agreeably. "Besides, I was with Uncle Leo all afternoon."

"What about your aunt? You weren't with her all afternoon."

Norbert looked at Cooky slyly. "Maybe he's right. Molly must be pining for your company, Cooky. Why, she said to me just the other day—and you know how close Molly and I are—she said to me, 'Norbie, you have no idea how much I'm looking forward to seeing dear, sweet Cordelia, that darling girl. I just wish she could find herself a dear sweet little husband to take care of her so she doesn't have to depend so much on dear sweet little Leo.'"

Norbert's recital caused Cooky to respond with, "You know what she told me? She told me she hopes her dear sweet stepson will go off on his dear sweet own soon and stop being such a pest."

Norbert didn't find Cooky's remark so amusing as his own. "I have to go," he announced abruptly, and started down the hall with his bass fiddle rolling along behind him.

"See you later," Cooky called after him, then added to Dearborn, "Isn't he weird? You know, he doesn't talk to Molly. He hasn't said one word to her for about a year."

"I would suppose his father would step in."

"They don't get along so well either. In fact, nobody really gets along with anybody. Come on Burgess. I'm starved."

Dearborn looked at his watch. It was after eight. He'd eaten lunch at eleven-thirty and consumed the last squashed Hershey bar in the tub a few hours before. The only thing that had stood between him and starvation in the last hour had been a handful of peanuts. "After you, Cordelia."

The dining room was high-ceilinged and softly lighted, with white tablecloths and fresh flowers on each table. Dearborn was gazing around the room appreciatively when Cooky stopped inside the entrance and grasped his arm. "Look who's there."

"Where?"

"There."

Dearborn looked where she was pointing. He might have guessed. Benjamin was sitting at one of the tables. "Who is it?" Dearborn asked, affecting not to remember.

"It's that guy from the train."

"What's he got on there?" Dearborn murmured. "That looks like my . . ." He squinted and thrust his head forward in an effort to identify the midnight-blue dinner jacket.

"Want to say hello?" Cooky asked.

"I do not."

Cooky's voice suddenly rose as she said affectedly, "Oh, hello, Fernando."

A slender, tall, dark-haired young man with large dark eyes, a sweet smile, and a handful of menus said, "Miss Gillette, when did you arrive?"

Cooky clutched at Dearborn's arm. "Today. How's everything, Fernando?"

"Very fine, thank you. And with you?"

"Cool."

"Have you been dancing since I saw you last?" he ventured.

Cooky blushed. "I told you I don't really like to dance very much."

Fernando's smile faded. "Would you like a table near the window?" He led them to a table about halfway down the room facing out onto a narrow, winding pebbled path lit with old-fashioned street lamps and bordered with hedges of full-blooming pink and red and white azalea. He held Cooky's chair, asked them if they wished to order from the bar, and when they declined handed them menus and withdrew.

"You've dated that young man?" Dearborn asked.

"Of course not. What gave you that idea?"

"He asked you if you'd been dancing?"

"Oh, that. Uncle Leo paid him to teach me to dance last time I was down. He's a terrific dancer. Not that he could teach me much. I'm too much of a klutz."

"Nice-looking young fellow."

"He is? I never noticed."

"Spaniard? I thought I detected the faint trace of an accent."

"Cuban. Florida's full of Cubans. They came after Castro took over. Most of the help here at the hotel is Cuban."

"So I understand."

"Fernando only came about five years ago. He had some kind of trouble there. They wouldn't let him leave so he escaped in a motorboat. Don't you think that's romantic? He was studying to be a jai alai player in Cuba, but he left before he started playing professionally."

"You seem to know a great deal about him."

"That's because Uncle Leo likes him a lot. He's always pushing me at him."

"You object to that, do you?"

"I'm not interested in Fernando," she said demurely, "and he's not interested in me. He's nice to me because of Leo and Molly."

"Fond of your aunt?" Dearborn noted interestedly.

"That's a nice way of putting it."

"Is there another way?"

"Yeah. My aunt's fond of Fernando. Not that she lets my uncle know that. He's very possessive."

"So I've noticed."

"How could you notice that?"

"I noticed it in regard to you, Cordelia. As a matter of fact, that is something we should talk about. Your uncle is under the impression that my intentions toward you may be, shall we say, less than honorable? It's a source of some embarrassment to me."

"Uncle Leo can be a pain."

Dearborn decided that the situation called for complete candor. "Cordelia, we are separated by tastes, interests, and time."

"How much time?"

"Too much time."

"So?"

"So I suggest that during your vacation you seek out more suitable escorts."

"Friday's my birthday. And that's the night of the Valentine's party. Who'll take me if you don't?"

"Surely there must be someone here your own age."

"Come on, Burgess, don't run out on me just when I thought I had a date for the party."

"I shall inquire around, find some nice young—"

Cooky reached out to put her hand on Dearborn's arm. "Please, Burgess? I don't want you to bribe somebody to take me. Please?"

Dearborn sighed. There was no reasoning with the girl. He pointed to the menu. "Shall we start with the soup, Cordelia?"

"You're a doll, Burgess."

The cuisine was Spanish and it was excellent, beginning with the delicate canja, chicken soup made with lemon and mint, through the white rice with mussels and the green salad with onions, to the dessert of a soft cinnamon-flavored custard. Dearborn was sufficiently pacified by the end of the meal to feel somewhat optimistic about his abilities to fend off Cooky, get the better of Benjamin, and at the same time successfully carry out his mission. After all, it was simply a question of footwork, a bit of shadow-boxing, a duck and feint operation. Difficult for a novice, granted, but no great undertaking for a man of his competence.

"You've really been around, haven't you?" Cooky said, at one point.

Dearborn was distracted just then by the sight of something behind Cooky, on the other side of the picture window.

"I mean, everybody's been to France and England. But Paraguay and the Shetland Islands and Borneo. That's really something."

Dearborn lowered his demitasse, bestowed a tolerant smile on Cooky, and let his eyes slip past her to the spot left of her ear. A couple were standing outside the window half-hidden behind the azaleas, and they were arguing. It was Leo and Molly Beggs. The thick glass that separated them from the diners was effective soundproofing and Dearborn could hear nothing, but Molly's face was furious. She seemed to be doing most of the talking while Leo listened, his belligerence reflected in his stance, legs planted far apart, hands clenched at his sides.

"What are you looking at?" Cooky asked, starting to turn around.

Dearborn reached across the table to swipe at her ear. "There. Gone."

"Ouch. What was it?"

"Fly."

Behind her, Molly raised her hand and struck Leo across the face. He reached out, grabbed her by the shoulders, and shook her. Suddenly she spotted Dearbor through the window and spoke sharply to Leo. Beggs turned, glowered at Dearborn, dropped his hands, and with a quick shove pushed his wife aside and strode off.

"You *are* looking at something." Cooky pushed back her chair and peered through the window. "Oh, it's Molly." Cooky's voice was colorless and she didn't raise her hand in response to Molly's shaky salute. She pulled her chair back around and picked up her coffee cup.

"You're not too approving of your aunt, I notice."

"She's a gold digger. She married Uncle Leo for his money."

"She told you that?"

"Are you crazy?"

"Then how can you be sure?"

"She fools around. She flirts with every man she meets."

"For instance?" Dearborn prompted.

"Fernando, for instance."

"I see."

"And Stuart Ripple, the tennis pro, and a pack of others. Even Raúl Baki."

"Surely not Mr. Baki."

"Why not? He's good-looking and far-out. Molly'll try anything for kicks. Come on, Burgess, I don't feel like talking about my aunt. Let's get out of here."

Dearborn put on his reading glasses to sign the check, then slipped the glasses under his plate before following Cooky out of the dining room. He paused in the lobby to slap his pockets and then excused himself to return to the dining room with the ostensible excuse of having left the glasses on the table. Benjamin was still seated, just pushing aside a plate containing a residue of cake crumbs and reaching for a bowl of fresh fruit.

"What is the meaning of this?" Dearborn demanded, stalking up to the table. "What are you doing here? You promised me you would go home and now here you are again. How did you succeed in getting a room?"

"There was one accommodation left. A suite in the Tahitian wing. Rates are a little steep but the view's terrific. Ground floor. A couple of hundred feet from the water. Quiet. Cool. Couldn't ask for nicer."

Dearborn's mood was not improved by knowing that Benjamin was occupying the suite he himself had turned down. "And what are you doing in my dinner jacket?" he demanded.

"I didn't have one of my own. Listen, Dad, I spoke to Otto

before dinner. There's no record at any of the rental agencies that Leo Beggs rented a car. That includes Hertz, Avis, and a half dozen smaller places."

"I see. I appreciate the information, but it wasn't necessary to check in, in order to tell me that. I suppose there is no way to persuade you to check out again?"

"No way."

"In that case I shall expect you to keep your distance."

"Whatever you say, Dad."

"Roycroft. I am registered here under the name of Burgess Roycroft."

"How come?"

"None of your business."

"I hope the real Burgess Roycroft doesn't get wind of it."

"The real Burgess Roycroft is dead."

"You had nothing to do with that, I hope."

"Don't be funny, Benjamin. I have enough to think about without having to deal with your adolescent sense of humor."

10

Dearborn hadn't gotten away from Cooky until nearly two. She had inveigled him into a visit to the Monsoon, a club that attracted the younger crowd, the ones with stamina, a taste for discordance, and a tolerance for clamor. The Monsoon was on the beach, a building with three stationary walls and one composed of bamboo panels that could, on special occasions, be removed to join with an outdoor pavilion. The inside of the club was dim, almost dark, except for the dance floor, which was lit by flashing neon lights and moving green and black spots. Sequin balls rotated overhead and the elevated bandstand was bathed in a silvery glow that made Norbert the Musk Beggs and his Mildews appear to be specters floating in space.

Dearborn had, during intermissions, been subjected to the company of Billy, Riff, Fleece, Spik, and a double-jointed individual named Skinzo who played the drums and who had enlightened Dearborn on the finer points of "juggling the sticks."

Now, finally quit of them all, Dearborn was embarked on a tour of the Cloister wing. There were, he determined, twenty-four rooms to the second floor and twenty on the first floor. Apparently the main entrance to the Beggses' duplex was on the ground floor because it was there that Dearborn found their nameplate on a door flanked by two shrub-filled urns.

He circled the outside of the Cloister wing and found that the duplex had the unique feature of an additional door leading directly into the rose garden. Lounge chairs and an umbrella table near the door provided the Beggses with what amounted to a private patio, since the only other point of entry to the garden was from the north around the corner of either the Tahitian or the Cloister wing. Overhead was the Beggses' terrace, as well as the terrace outside Dearborn's bedroom door, the division between them being a dense double hedge in back-to-back planters.

Dearborn's suite, number 63, was at the extreme end of the wing and took up its entire width. Investigation showed that behind his living room was Room 61 and behind his bedroom was the Beggses' duplex. As to which room shared the mutual wall and terrace with his own, Dearborn had no idea. Not even the industrious application of ear to toothbrush glass to wall had provided Dearborn with any enlightening sounds beyond a slight murmur that might have been conversation but might also have been the sound of running water.

He went out onto his terrace and examined the hedge dividers. By standing on one of the patio chairs on his side he could just peek over the top, which meant that the barrier was almost eight feet tall. Since each hedge was about eighteen inches thick, there was a vaulting depth over the top of about three feet, all in all not an inconsiderable obstacle.

Dearborn formulated his plans while he was lying in bed. He must find some way to get into the Beggses' apartment so that he could look for the gun. He must also try to determine where Beggs had been the weekend before. He would go into Silver Beach to try to locate Louis Martin's boarding house, and when the moment was ripe he would confront Molly Beggs with the news that Louis Martin had been murdered. He would then make a strenuous effort to elicit from her testimony of a damning nature and finally would himself personally notify Captain Niccoli that he had—what was the expression—broken the case.

He woke late. It was almost nine when he rolled over in the unfamiliar bed and peered at his watch. He was annoyed at not having left instructions at the desk for a seven o'clock call. He liked to exercise and bathe first thing in the morning and he liked his breakfast in his room at eight o'clock sharp. He got dressed and went out the door, bending down to run his fingers under the carpet until he found a loose flap and then slipping his door key under it. The key was attached to a leather disk that was awkward to carry in one's pocket, and Dearborn didn't want to leave it at the desk. Too easy for Benjamin to see whether he was in or out.

"Good morning, Mr. Roycroft," the desk clerk chirped when he approached the desk. "How are you this morning?"

"I have a headache," Dearborn replied, "and constipation. That's what comes of altering one's routine."

"Did we err in some way?" the desk clerk asked. "I wasn't aware that, ah—"

"You didn't err and I'd rather you didn't ah," Dearborn returned shortly. "Just write it down there somewhere that starting tomorrow I wish to be wakened at seven."

The desk clerk, his face pink, pulled over a note pad, and began writing down Dearborn's instructions. Behind him the office door opened and a woman wearing a putty-colored slack suit minced out, fluttering her hands and looking agitated. She was tall and top-heavy, with broad shoulders, large pendulous breasts, no waist to speak of, formidable hips, and long spindly legs. Her face put Dearborn in mind of a caricature he'd once seen of Abraham Lincoln: nondescript hair, a long narrow face, small pale eyes separated by a high-bridged nose, thick lips, and deep facial creases. Her ugliness made all the more absurd her affected mannerisms and prancing walk. "I was promised the afternoon off," she was saying, "and I'm taking the afternoon off."

From behind her a disembodied voice proclaimed, "I'm the manager, Alberta. You're supposed to do what I say."

"Speak to Leo about it."

"I'll speak to Molly," the voice threatened, with a trace of brogue, "and let her speak to Leo."

"Open your eyes, Collis," the woman responded. "Molly hasn't been able to twist Leo around her finger for a long time now." She withdrew her head, slammed the door, and lifted the hinged countertop to let herself out. "Buzz Mr. Beggs, Stan. Tell him I'm on my way up."

"He's in the lounge," the desk clerk informed her. "He came down about ten minutes ago."

The woman veered right and headed for the bar. Dearborn watched her march across the lobby, a middle-aged woman with a shape like a mushroom and the most incredibly homely face he'd ever seen.

"Who is that female?" Dearborn asked.

"Miss Van Curl, the assistant manager."

"Did you say Mr. Beggs is in the lounge?"

"Yes, sir."

"And where is Mrs. Beggs?"

"She's at the beach."

"Are you sure?"

"She told me she'd be there if anyone wants her. Do you want me to page her?"

"That won't be necessary." Dearborn started away from the desk.

"Hi, Burgess." It was Cooky, wearing khaki Bermuda shorts, a long-sleeved work shirt, white ankle socks, and sandals held on her feet by means of several yards of brown cord. "I phoned your room a couple of minutes ago but you'd left. Did you eat yet?"

Dearborn decided swiftly that no breakfast would be preferable to getting tied up with Cooky just then. "I finished breakfast," he answered.

"So did I. Listen, Burgess, I've got a cool idea. Up at the end of the island there's a place called Shell Cove. You can't walk to it but you can get to it by motorboat. It's got the most fabulous shells—"

"I'm busy now, Cordelia."

"We can't go now anyway. You can only get there during high tide because of the coral beds. High tide is at five. We could go sometime between four and six."

"Tomorrow," Dearborn said.

"It might rain tomorrow. Fernando says there's a storm moving this way from off the coast of Cuba."

"Didn't I tell you yesterday that you must try to busy yourself with people your own age? Since Fernando seems to be so nautical-minded, why don't you ask him to go boating with you."

"Not boating. Shelling."

"Whatever."

"Fernando works a full day Monday. Besides, he wouldn't give me the time of day."

"Why not? He's already given you the tide tables and the weather report."

Dearborn turned to see Benjamin hurrying across the lobby with a worried look on his face. He caught sight of Dearborn, slowed down, and attempted to signal him. Dearborn pretended not to notice. Benjamin grimaced and began gesturing toward the gardens. Dearborn gave an almost imperceptible shake of the head. Benjamin strode up to the desk and said loudly, "I'm expecting a call in my room from a friend of mine, a priest, name of Father Dearborn. Put him right through to me, please."

"Yes, sir."

Benjamin looked at Dearborn penetratingly to make sure Dearborn had understood and then walked away.

"So then how about going swimming?" Cooky asked. "Want to go swimming?"

"Absolutely not. I have an appointment with the masseur."

"When? Now?"

"Right now, Cordelia. Right now."

Benjamin was growing increasingly restless. Why hadn't his father called or come over? Hadn't Benjamin made it clear enough? He'd spoken loudly. He'd made it explicit. Why hadn't Dearborn responded?

"Damn," he mumbled, pacing the floor. "Damn it all." He checked the time. Ten-fifteen. He went out onto his patio and gazed up and down the beach. Then he went back into the living room and picked up the phone. "Suite 63, please." He listened for Dearborn to answer, but he didn't. "Where is he?" Benjamin asked aloud. "Where the—"

A knock at the front door cut the oath short.

"It's about time!" Benjamin bounded to the door and opened it. A woman was standing there, a beautiful woman, tall and long-limbed, with sleek dark hair, extraordinary eyes, and white teeth in a deeply suntanned face.

"I'm not who you were expecting," she said.

"Let's put it this way. I'm not disappointed."

Molly Beggs accepted the compliment with a graceful nod. "Can I come in?"

Benjamin threw open the door and ushered her into the living room.

"You're Ben Pinch, the basketball player. I'm Molly Beggs, Leo Beggs's wife."

"Lucky man," Benjamin said appreciatively.

"He owns the place. How do you like your suite?"

"Fine. How do you like your scotch?"

"I like it after five, thanks." She strolled to the couch and sat down. She was wearing a white ankle-length terry robe slit to the waist to reveal shapely legs and a bit of white satin bikini. "I looked twice when I saw your name in the register."

"Why's that?"

"We met once. Don't you remember? About three years ago in New York?"

"We did? How could I forget that. Where was it?"

"At some party or other. I don't really remember too well myself. I was a model back in those dim dark days. And a blonde, believe it or not. Molly McAuley. You made a pass at me."

"I would have been a fool not to. I guess you wouldn't give me a tumble?"

"I couldn't. I was engaged to Leo."

"And now?"

"I still can't. I'm married to Leo."

"There must be something you can offer me."

"There is," Molly Beggs rejoined. "I can offer you dinner tonight at my place."

"What do you have in mind?"

"I'm having a few people in for dinner, including my father, who's a basketball freak. I thought it would be a nice surprise for him if you came. Besides being very pleasant for me, of course."

Benjamin realized that there was a good possibility that neither he nor Dearborn would be at La Playa that evening, but he could cancel if he had to. "Thanks," he said. "I'd like to."

"Terrific. Eight o'clock, then. Cloister wing. Suite 42–62."

11

Dearborn staged a raid on the garden, a foray which was almost thwarted by one of the gardeners who appeared as Dearborn was in the act of pilfering the gladioli. Dearborn slunk out of sight, to resurface after the gardener disappeared into the tool shed.

Dearborn tried out a variety of excuses in the event that

Molly or Leo Beggs came home. *"Came over to see your gun collection."* He hadn't been invited. *"Thought we could discuss your niece."* God forbid. *"Just passing by."* Carrying a dozen gladioli? *"Wanted to apologize for the disturbance last night. What disturbance? You mean you didn't hear anything? That's a relief. Felt sure you had. Brought this little peace offering."* Not bad. Not bad that last.

Dearborn knocked on the door and stepped back to look up at the terrace overhead. Somebody was up there. He could see a hand running a cloth over the railing. A moment later a round head bound with a yellow kerchief popped over the edge.

"Jes?"

"Is Mrs. Beggs at home?"

Two small dark eyes in a round face blinked down at him. "No. Che's gone to the bitch."

"Mr. Beggs?"

"Not jere."

"Oh, I see. Well, I have something for Mrs. Beggs. Will you take it?"

The head withdrew and a minute later the door opened to present Dearborn with a tiny woman with bright dark eyes and chipmunk cheeks, dressed in a loose-fitting garment that reminded Dearborn of a nightgown but that was probably a smock.

"How do you do," Dearborn greeted her. "You say Mrs. Beggs is not at home?"

"I tole chu, che's out."

Dearborn glanced over the maid's shoulder into the room beyond. It was a dining room with a glass and chrome table and gleaming chrome and white leather chairs. At the near end of the room was a circular staircase leading to the second floor. "In that case I'll leave the flowers," he suggested, attempting to slither past her.

"Gif them to me," she instructed, blocking the way. "Wha ees jore name?"

"Roycroft," Dearborn answered. "What is your name?"

"Conchita."

"Conchita, Mrs. Beggs told me she wants these flowers placed in the Limoges vase on the piano in the living room."

"Piano?" Conchita repeated bemusedly. "Wha piano?"

"I meant to say the étagère," Dearborn corrected himself, thrusting the flowers into her hands. "Be sure to put them into the Limoges vase with the fleur-de-lis border."

Conchita looked at the flowers, then back up at Dearborn. "Wha you say?"

"Tut tut. Never mind. I'll do it myself." Dearborn pushed past her and sailed to the foot of the stairs.

"Chu better wait ontil I get Señora Beggs," Conchita cautioned.

"Nonsense. I'll be in and out in a minute." He clattered up the stairs, his head emerging at floor level to take in a polished white tile floor, gray upholstered couches and chairs, an expanse of mirrored wall, and glass doors opening into a broad plant-filled terrace. There was no piano, no étagère, and no Limoges vase, but there was a hallway to his left and a door on the north wall that Dearborn decided to open. It turned out to be the master bedroom. He took it in at a glance, the wardrobe, the doors to the terrace, the platform bed with its art-deco headboard against the far wall. That answered the question of which wall Dearborn shared with the Beggses. But where was the gun collection? It wasn't in the living room or in the bedroom or in the dining room downstairs.

"Wha chu wan in there?" Conchita asked indignantly, poking her head in the door.

"Where *is* the Limoges vase?" Dearborn demanded.

"I doan know. You chudn't go in there."

"Where's the den?" Dearborn inquired.

"Wha?"

"The study. The playroom."

Conchita's suspicions were aroused. She pointed to the flowers in her hand. The stems showed the effects of having been twisted roughly off the parent plant. "Where you got theze? You got theze outside?"

"I beg your pardon?"

"Wha chu wan here?"

"That is none of your affair. It is the affair of Mrs. Beggs and myself."

The reprimand had the opposite effect from the one intended. The diminutive Conchita puffed up like a pouter pigeon and made an abrupt dash at Dearborn. "Affair? Chu get out of here. Chu want to bother Señora Beggs? I tell Señor Beggs. An ole man like you. *Viejo!* No shame! *Sinvergüenza!*" She raised the flowers and advanced.

"You misunderstand," Dearborn returned. "I was not talking about that kind of affair."

"Chu get out!" Conchita struck him on the elbow, scattering gladioli petals over his and her feet as well as over a considerable section of floor.

"I assure you, madam—"

"Chu get out or I tell Señor Beggs! Chu chud not be here!"

"You are misinterpreting the situation utterly."

"Chu push chor way in here!"

"Nothing of the sort," Dearborn responded irately, forgetting that that was precisely what he had done.

Conchita destroyed what was left of the bouquet on Dearborn's kneecaps and shins and continued to flail at him as he fled down the stairs and out the door.

"An doan chu come back," she shouted. "Doan chu come back, heh?"

Dearborn, chastened, returned to his suite to find Benjamin sitting on the sofa tinkering with the tape recorder. Benjamin looked up when Dearborn walked in. "Where the hell have you been, Dad?"

"How did you get in here?" Dearborn demanded, shutting the door behind him and crossing to the bar.

"I came in while the chambermaid was cleaning up. Do you mind telling me where you were?"

"Benjamin, last night you said you weren't going to bother me. First thing this morning you create a scene in the lobby with your cryptic messages and ogling. Now you're vandalizing my tape recorder."

"What are you doing with a tape recorder anyhow?"

"Don't quiz me. I don't like to be quizzed."

"Didn't it occur to you, Dad, that I had a very good reason for wanting to see you?"

"That is the one thought that never occurs to me," Dearborn replied. He chose a bottle of port from among the bottles on the bar and poured himself a drink.

"Before lunch?" Benjamin asked. "You're really going to hell with yourself."

"I had an unnerving experience, a run-in with one of the hotel employees. Help is not what it used to be."

"I'll say it isn't. You're about to have a run-in with another hotel employee, Dad."

"What are you talking about?"

"Anthony Niccoli."

Dearborn put down his glass. "What was that name?"

"Niccoli. He's here. I saw him. I was out jogging on the beach about five-fifteen this morning and I saw this guard patrolling the grounds. He was wearing a La Playa uniform. I wouldn't have looked twice except he spotted me and did a double-take, so I backtracked a few minutes later and caught a good look at him. It was Niccoli."

"Ridiculous."

"I'm telling you. He was just as shocked to see me as I was to see him."

"What would he be doing here?"

"Suppose you tell me?"

Dearborn regarded Benjamin thoughtfully and then murmured to himself, "It's possible. Not probable, given the man's limited capacities, but possible."

"Which brings up the question of what you're doing here," Benjamin interjected.

"I suppose he could be after the same thing I am," Dearborn mused.

"Which is?"

"Your presence, Benjamin," Dearborn snapped, recovering his equanimity, "only complicates an already complicated situation."

"Dad," Benjamin pleaded, "tell me what's going on. I know

it has to do with that murder. So you were right. There was more to it than a mugging. I give you that. Niccoli wouldn't be here otherwise. It has to do with that Roycroft character who came to see you. It doesn't take a genius to figure that much out. You signed the register as Roycroft, so Roycroft has something to do with it."

"Don't play detective, Benjamin."

"You asked me to check up on Leo Beggs. I never swallowed that crapola about losing a ring in the upholstery. You wanted to know whether or not he hired a car. Am I right?"

"You don't actually think I intend to confide in you, do you?"

"Why not?"

"You are a blabbermouth, Benjamin."

"Thanks a lot. I didn't let Niccoli know I saw him, did I? I didn't tell him you're here, did I?"

"Also you have no skill at subterfuge. Your performance this morning proved that. All that prattle about priests. Those idiot smirks."

"I was trying to attract your attention," Benjamin explained.

"And while we're on the subject," Dearborn went on, "I'd like you to know that I do not appreciate your electing Mrs. Woolley into your league of spies. In fact, I am so unappreciative that I have decided to give her her walking papers when I return to New York."

"Dad—"

"Also I am making plans to transfer my business out of Otto's hands. If it weren't for his machinations I would not find myself in the lowly position of investigating a murder for a paltry five thousand dollars when I could be—"

"So that's it! Edward Roycroft hired you to investigate a murder."

Dearborn was abashed at having become so reckless as to make the admission. He covered his embarrassment by stridding across the room and wresting the tape recorder out of

Benjamin's grasp. "Where did you get this? I had it in the bottom drawer of my bureau."

"I was looking for a pair of cuff links—"

"Thank you for calling, Benjamin. Enjoy the remainder of your stay. Sorry I can't chat any longer. Good-bye."

"Not so fast," Benjamin said. He leaned forward. "What happens when Niccoli finds out you're here?"

"Do you intend to tell him?"

"I don't have to tell him. Sooner or later he's going to run into you."

"I am traveling incognito."

"Some incognito. An assumed name isn't incognito, Dad. How long do you think it'll be before Niccoli tips to you?"

It didn't please Dearborn to admit it, even to himself, but Benjamin had a point. Niccoli's presence presented a problem.

"Sooner or later," Benjamin pointed out, "you're going to find yourselves in the same place at the same time. And unless I miss my guess, any run-in you have with him is going to end up with you in the cooler."

Benjamin's argument was irrefutable. "I suppose I could try having him called back to New York, a faked phone call perhaps. . . ."

"Come on, Dad. He's not going to fall for those Marx Brothers tactics. I have a better solution. Niccoli doesn't know why I'm here. Otto already told him I'm somewhere on vacation. No reason why he shouldn't think this is the place I came to. He's got nothing against me, and so long as I go on acting like a guest he's going to go out of his way to avoid me. It's the perfect setup. I've got free run of the place. Anything you want to know I can find out."

"You don't know Leo Beggs."

"Maybe not, but I've already got an invitation from his wife."

"You do?"

"I'm going to dinner at their place tonight."

"Your mysterious appeal to women, Benjamin, never ceases to amaze me." The idea of taking on Benjamin as a confederate was not one that Dearborn found in any way appealing, but it was no bleaker than the alternative possibilities. "Will you give me your word that you will follow any and all of my instructions to the letter?"

"A to Z."

"And restrain yourself from engaging in any fanciful improvisations of your own?"

"No winging it."

"Very well, then. I see I have no choice. I am going to have to trust you, Benjamin, against my better judgment and despite your past performances."

"Nothing ventured, nothing lost, I always say."

"If that aphorism is meant to be reassuring, Benjamin, it fails utterly."

12

Dearborn rode into Silver Beach in one of the La Playa buses. He got off on Cabinet Street in front of the post office and went into the nearest stationery store to purchase a street map. Coral Street was within easy walking distance, but before he set off he made a stop in a clothing shop where, under the assumption that no one would glance twice at a retired clothing salesman, he had himself outfitted according to the tastes of an obliging clerk named Arnold Stubbs.

The results were more than satisfactory. His piercing eyes were hidden behind sunglasses. His unhighlighted black hair was tucked under an adjustable golfing cap, and his tall, lean body was camouflaged within a lime-green polyester leisure suit and flowered Hawaiian shirt.

"Very snappy," Arnold Stubbs pronounced when the

transformation was complete. "The beauty is you can throw everything in the washing machine, even the cap."

"That certainly is an advantage," Dearborn allowed, watching his cotton cord slacks, his Givenchy tie, and his blue and yellow silk Bill Blass shirt disappear into a shopping bag. "You might try putting a little tissue inside that blazer."

The Hardwicke Pharmacy on Coral Street was a dispensary specializing more in hair preparations and mouthwashes than in drugs. The proprietor was amiable and his professional demeanor lackadaisical. Getting Louis Martin's address was simply a matter of asking for a repeat on the prescription for ephedrine. "Doctor's out of town. You've filled it before. Sure you've got the right Martin? What address do you have on that card?"

Half an hour later, Dearborn cautiously approached the boarding house. It was galling to have to slink around like a fugitive. One should be able to tackle problems directly, face up to vicissitudes openly, deal with trouble head on. That he, who abhorred deceit, sham, and dissemblance, should be forced into this masquerade was deplorable. Surely Edward Roycroft hadn't changed his mind and gone to Niccoli? It made no sense. Dearborn had tried to phone Edward in New York before leaving the hotel but there hadn't been any answer at his apartment. Until Dearborn spoke with him he must proceed on the assumption that Niccoli was, indeed, unaware of Dearborn's presence and operating on information acquired from some other source, but Dearborn's lack of information made things disagreeable.

The house was a three-story brown clapboard with a wraparound screened porch, a latticework base, and a cracked cement walk. It was easy to see that it had originally been a single-family dwelling converted to multiple tenancy. Crabgrass and dandelions choked the yard, the two palm trees near the front steps drooped with blight, the windows were curtainless, and there was a fire escape on one side of the house that had obviously been tacked on to satisfy whatever ordinances covered the house's conversion. The block was quiet, the parked cars empty. No Niccoli in sight, only a little girl playing with a broken doll carriage and a woman strolling along the curb with a lethargic poodle. The air was heavy with the rot of unraked grass turning to mulch.

Dearborn let himself into the screened porch and rang the bell, then shaded his eyes to peer through the glass rectangle at the top of the door. He had a quick glimpse of light at the far end of a narrow hall and then it was blocked as someone came out of a room on the left and approached the door.

"Yes?" a light voice called out.

From somewhere farther back in the house another voice called out raucously, "Who's that? Who's there?"

The shadowy figure made no answer.

"How do you do, sir," Dearborn boomed through the closed door.

The door opened and Dearborn found himself confronting an old man in a blue seersucker bathrobe, with bare feet, and scuffs. "Looking for a room?" he asked.

"No. I've come to inquire after one of your former tenants."

Again from out of the back came the rough voice yelling, "Lionel, was that the door?"

"My brother," the old man informed Dearborn.

The voice cried out, "Lionel, answer me!"

"Aren't you going to answer him?" Dearborn asked.

The old man raised his voice to a high treble. "He's looking for a room!"

"As a matter of fact," Dearborn corrected, "I am not looking for a room. I am seeking information regarding one of your former tenants."

"Show him the ground floor rear!" the loud voice instructed.

"It's got hot and cold running water," the old man said obligingly as he motioned Dearborn to follow him down the hall. "Double bed. Twenty-five a week."

Dearborn said a little more emphatically, "I want to ask you about a man named Louis Martin."

"This way." The old man shuffled through a door on his right and Dearborn followed. It occurred to Dearborn that the man might be deaf, so he said loudly, "Martin! I am looking for information on Louis Martin!"

The old man put his fingers to his lips, shut the door behind them, then asked in a high whisper, "How much?"

"How much what?"

"How much for the information?"

"Are you telling me I'm expected to pay for the information?"

"Herb got the last one," was the unperturbed explanation. "It's my turn."

"I am not the first person to make inquiries?"

"The third."

Dearborn was astonished. "Who, may I ask, were the other two?"

"One was a man, medium-tall, dark-haired, about forty-five, tortoise shell glasses. He come yesterday."

Niccoli. So Niccoli had gotten there before Dearborn after all. "What did he ask you?"

"He wanted to know what I could tell him about Louis Martin. And he wanted to see the duffel Martin left."

"Who was the other caller?"

"A woman. This morning. About thirty. Dark hair, big eyes, high cheekbones. Looks like a model. Good figure. Expensive clothes. Herb got her, so I didn't talk to her, but she wanted the same thing."

"Tell me," Dearborn asked, "had you or your brother ever seen her before?"

"Nope. She wouldn't be easy to forget."

Molly Beggs. Dearborn was sure of it. "How much do you want?"

"Fifty."

"Twenty," Dearborn dickered.

"Forty. That's what Herb got and I'm not taking any less."

Dearborn reached into his pocket and removed his wallet. He extracted two twenties and handed them over. "Did Martin have many visitors?"

"None. What socializing he done, he done off the premises. Didn't hang around here, that's certain. Kept to himself mostly. Not the friendly type. Worked down at the radio station. Reported the sports. Slept late most days, and he didn't keep to any schedule. When he left, he skipped. Still owes us a week's rent."

"You more than made up for it yesterday and today," Dearborn reminded him.

"You want to see his stuff?" He led Dearborn across the room to a closet, opened it, and pointed to a scruffy-looking duffel bag lying on the floor. "Didn't take much. Didn't leave much. Didn't have much. Come to think of it, wasn't much."

"Lionel!"

The old man went back to the door and opened it. "Let yourself out," he whispered. "Stick the duffel back in the closet before you go." He slipped into the hall and clicked the door shut behind him.

Dearborn lifted the duffel bag onto the bed, unhooked the top strap, and dumped the contents onto the bare mattress. Two pairs of chinos, two work shirts, a half-dozen pairs of socks, and about the same number of shorts. Dearborn poked around in the heap. There was a pocketknife inside one of the socks, and when he unrolled the chinos he found a shabby cashmere sweater. He pushed his hands into the pants pockets and into the shirt pockets and came up with a toothpick. He was disappointed but not surprised. After all, he was the third person that day to go through the duffel bag.

He began repacking. He tossed a pair of jockey shorts down into the opening, then impatiently reached in to jam it down to the bottom of the sack. He dropped in a shirt and punched it down on top of the shorts. He wrestled with a pair of chinos that caught on the fastening. He balled up the cashmere sweater and wedged it and the chinos as deep as he could into the bag. Then he felt something. He paused with his hand inside the duffel. Something was pinned to the canvas. He ran his fingers over the safety pin, then reached in with the other hand, opened it, and pulled out a slip of paper. Scrawled on the piece of paper in a feminine hand were the words "Tonight at eleven," the signature consisting of one initial, a lacy and elaborately written *M*.

Niccoli had been surprised, to say the least, when he spotted Benjamin loping along the beach at La Playa that morning. At first he had made the obvious connection, believing that where Benjamin was, his father was sure to be. But after calming down sufficiently to appraise the situation he realized that there was at least a chance that bumping into Benjamin had been no more than an odd coincidence. Otto Rothschild had told him that Benjamin was away on vacation, Benjamin had enough money to travel in style, and La Playa was a rich man's resort.

On the other hand, the police file had mentioned Leo Beggs and La Playa, and the old man was hot for making trouble. Still, from what Niccoli could tell, he'd only "borrowed" that police file in order to add the paragraph he'd wanted, a sizzling denunciation of the department, of police investigatory techniques, and of Niccoli himself. And what else would he want? This time there weren't any old friends asking him for help, he hadn't implicated himself in the crime, he had no connection to it at all. No, screwy as it was, Benjamin Pinch's presence at La Playa was probably no more than a coincidence.

Probably. Niccoli couldn't resist that "probably." The old duffer was an oddball. That "probably" made Niccoli nervous. It also made him stealthier, sharper, and more determined than ever to wrap up this case with speed.

As expected, the local police hadn't been happy with what Niccoli had told them, but they had agreed to do what they could to cooperate short of making any outright accusations. If Niccoli came up with a tangible case against Beggs they'd move in. Until then they would walk the delicate tightrope between fulfilling their official responsibilities and kowtowing to the number one man in Silver Beach.

They did what they had to, and thanks to them Niccoli had made the transition from police captain to hotel guard in no more time than it takes to travel from New York to Florida. Of course, it helped that Leo Beggs had taken the bait so easily, but then why wouldn't he, with recommendations that made Niccoli seem like a combination of Columbo, Kojak, and Superman. "Sorry to hear about your bum stomach. Don't know why they'd retire you for something like that. Their loss is our gain. Always glad to get a good man."

Niccoli had started work at La Playa the night before, on

the ten-to-six shift, but before that he'd put in a full day checking on Louis Martin. There hadn't been too much to learn at Martin's boardinghouse except that he'd been a loner, had worked at the local radio station, and had run out without paying his last week's rent. Not even a careful search of the few belongings he'd left behind revealed anything of significance. There was nothing worth confiscating, nothing worth noting in his report as more than "sundry clothing and personal effects."

The police records were more enlightening. They'd received a call on the night of October 5 from Leo Beggs, telling them that he'd apprehended a man in the act of burglarizing his apartment. Upon the police's arrival at La Playa they had found Leo Beggs holding a gun on Louis Martin in the living room of their duplex. Mrs. Beggs, wearing a negligee and in an apparent state of hysterics, was also present. She claimed to have been awake but feigning sleep during the attempted robbery.

According to Beggs, Louis Martin had gained entry to the master bedroom by way of an outside terrace and was in the bedroom when Beggs arrived home from a banquet sponsored by the Florida Sportsmen's Club, of which he was president. Beggs, hearing noises, had gone to the gun cabinet in his library on the ground floor of the duplex apartment, removed from it his Colt .38, and surprised Martin in the act of rifling the jewelry box on Mrs. Beggs's dressing table.

Before the police took Martin away, Beggs lost his composure, expressed regret that he hadn't availed himself of the opportunity to kill Martin, and promised to rectify the error if ever the opportunity arose. His fury, coming as it had after he had successfully thwarted the robber, struck the police as being strange, the fact that a few days later Beggs bailed Martin out of jail leading them to the conclusion that it hadn't been a burglary that Beggs walked in on, and that Beggs had been persuaded, perhaps on threat of scandal, to think twice before making trouble for Martin. Martin skipped town a few days after that and the police decided that it would be politic to let the matter drop without pursuing the fugitive.

The report was of interest on two counts. One was that it supplied a motive for murder and the other was that it mentioned the fact that Beggs owned a .38-caliber Colt revolver, the report itself being purely speculative but the implications being damning. Niccoli was sure he was on to something and the thought was gratifying. He'd stuck his neck out with the higher-ups and he intended to go home a hero. Given a few days' time, he would.

13

"Leo's going to be late," Molly Beggs said. "Fernando called him down to the dining room. Something about Raúl Baki."

"Who's that?"

"Haven't you heard about him? He used to own La Playa Island. He sold it to Leo and now he lives here at the hotel."

"Is he the one who's supposed to be barmy?"

"Now and then he gets to be a problem," she admitted.

"I heard he's looked on as the local character."

"He's a lot more interesting than most of the people down here."

Benjamin gazed appreciatively at Molly Beggs, who was wearing a white gown with spaghetti straps and a cleavage that stopped just short of her navel. "Most maybe, but not all," he informed her with an engaging grin.

"I'll bet you say that to all the characters. Would you like a martini?"

"Thanks."

They were standing in the living room. It looked to Benjamin like a stage set curiously devoid of life. The gray couches were unrumpled, the glass and chrome tables, except for a few sleek art-deco ornaments and a white telephone, were bare, the paintings geometric nonentities. He didn't see a magazine anywhere, or a television set, or an ashtray.

"Like it?" Molly asked, handing him his martini.

"Could use some lint," Benjamin answered frankly. "Maybe a stain or two on the couch or a chipped ashtray."

"Celluloid chic," Molly returned lightly, "which Leo calls class. Well, Leo pays the bills. Want the Cook's tour?"

"Lead on."

He poked his head routinely into the second-floor master bedroom, and the guest room, which was apparently in use but unoccupied at that moment, passed a third bedroom, which, from the sounds of the radio within, was occupied, and followed Molly downstairs to the dining room and kitchen, where she spoke in Spanish to Conchita and Nico, the couple who tended house for them.

"A linguist too," Benjamin noted admiringly.

"Compliments of a Chilean ambassador I once knew."

The general decor remained dismally *moderne* until they reached the library, a room that, according to Molly, had been copied from the library of an English country house and that bore no decorative relationship to the rest of the apartment. It was dark, cluttered, leathery, and Victorian and it was there that Benjamin found what he was searching for, the gun cabinet with its assortment of rifles, pistols, and automatics, all carefully identified with brass plates. Benjamin strolled over to it and ascertained, after a quick glance, that one weapon was a Colt .38. "Your husband collects guns?"

"He likes to shoot. He's an expert marksman. I hate it."

Her words seemed to imply that it was more than guns she hated. Benjamin asked casually, "How long did you say you and your husband have been married?"

"Two years. Two long years."

Dearborn's instructions had been clear. "Employ tact, Benjamin. Gain her confidence. Get her to talk about her marriage. Proof of infidelity. That's what we're after. But tact, Benjamin, tact."

"You and he don't always see eye to eye?"

"You know many couples who do?"

"A few." Benjamin decided to repeat what his father had related to him about the fight the night before but to make it his own. "But from where I was sitting in the dining room last night it didn't look like you and Leo do always see eye to eye."

"You saw us?"

Benjamin nodded. "I guess I shouldn't have brought it up."

"People disagree. What can I tell you?"

"I know this is going to sound crass," Benjamin ventured, "but why'd you marry him? He must be twenty-five, thirty years older than you."

She laughed. "I know this is going to sound crass, but he's stinking rich. Not every model makes a hundred dollars an hour, and not every hundred dollars comes from modeling. Leo wanted a beautiful wife and I wanted a rich husband. From that point of view it was a good bargain. Now I'm stuck with it."

"Why stuck?"

"Because Leo's satisfied with the arrangement."

Benjamin knew he might be pressing too hard, but he chanced it. "You're afraid to walk out on him because he might balk at paying alimony?"

"No," she answered. "That's the least of it."

"What's the most of it?"

"He's got a bad temper."

"And a collection of guns?"

"Look," she said, "could we skip it for now. I didn't really mean to get into that."

Benjamin hadn't made it to the bottom line but he hadn't done badly. Better to stop while he was ahead. It was almost a relief when, a moment later, the doorbell rang.

Benjamin heard the click of heels crossing the dining room and a moment later a man's voice touched with brogue called out, "Evenin', Conchita. Where's my girl?"

"Che's upstairs," the thickly accented voice replied, then added in a brighter tone, "*Como esta*, Señor Reeple?"

The second voice was deeper and held no trace of brogue. "Hungry as usual," came the answer. "What's on the menu?"

"Jool see."

Benjamin looked expectantly toward the circular staircase. The first head to emerge from below belonged to a tall, dark-haired man with a sharply planed face, freckled skin, and slightly buck teeth. Collis McAuley was homely and more Gaelic than his daughter, but the family resemblance was there, in the bone structure, the hair, the dark eyes. "Hello, darlin'."

"Hello, Daddy." Molly met her father halfway across the room and seized him around the waist in a bear hug. "How come you're late?"

"Leo told Alberta she could take the day off. I had to do her bookkeeping for her."

"Damn Leo, anyway."

"No hello for your biggest admirer?" the second man inquired.

"Hello, Stu. Benjamin, I'd like you to meet Stuart Ripple. He's the tennis pro here at La Playa."

Benjamin acknowledged the introduction.

"Nice to have a celebrity on board," Ripple returned heartily. "We don't get to see much basketball down here, but I saw you in a couple of exhibition games you played in Miami a few years back."

Ripple was as handsome in his way as Molly was in hers, but his version was the All-American, blond, blue-eyed, and muscular. Benjamin disliked him at first handshake, a pumping grip that was intended to show off his biceps and threatened to turn into a squeezing match. Ripple's eyes were sharp and appraising and there was nothing warm about his toothy grin.

"Benjamin," Molly said, "this is my father, Collis McAuley. Daddy, this is Benjamin Pinch."

They shook hands and McAuley said, "You play basketball, do you?"

"Not anymore. I retired a while back."

"What's your name again?"

"Benjamin Pinch."

"Well, it's a pleasure to meet you. I don't go for indoor

sports much. Boats and fishing. That's how I like to spend my time."

Benjamin stole a look at Molly. She was unconcernedly pouring two more martinis out of the pitcher.

"Your father's not a basketball fan?" he said in an amused voice.

"Daddy likes boats. Whenever Leo decides to take out the *Seasprite* Daddy signs on as first mate."

So Molly hadn't asked Benjamin to dinner so her father could meet him and she wasn't at all fazed that he'd caught her in the lie. She'd asked him for herself. It made things infinitely more pleasant, answered the question of why she'd been so quick to talk about her unhappy marriage, and answered the question, too, of whether or not she fooled around. She fooled around.

Again the doorbell rang and a moment later they heard Conchita's voice saying, "*Buenas noches*, Señorita Fern."

"Hello, Conchita. Where are they. Upstairs?"

"Sí. Señor Beggs isn't home jet. But the Señora is upstairs."

The latest arrival was a pretty woman, prematurely gray-haired but youthful, dressed in yellow crepe-de-chine dinner pajamas that made the most of her soft curves. "Hi, everybody. I'm not late, am I?" Her eyes lighted on Benjamin with surprise. "Somebody new for a change? Hey, aren't you Benjamin Pinch? Somebody pointed you out to me in the coffee shop this afternoon."

"Yes, he is," Molly answered, "and don't make such a fuss over it. He isn't here to sign autographs. Benjamin, this is Bunny Fern. She's our publicity and public relations director."

"My, my, aren't we lucky?" Bunny Fern crossed the room, held out her hand, and tilted her head to gaze up at him.

Benjamin flashed her his celebrity smile and took her hand.

He dropped it again when there was a sudden explosive cry from the back hall. Everyone turned in that direction as a barefoot apparition dressed in a loincloth over black tights with a dozen braids and a face striped with black and white greasepaint bounded into the living room. "Somebody ask Molly where my fiddle is!"

"In the hall closet," Molly said shortly. "I told Conchita to put it there so she could vacuum your room."

Norbert ran to the stairs and shouted down, "Conchita, I told you nobody's supposed to touch my fiddle!"

"Find someplace to put it where it won't get stepped on," Molly suggested icily.

Norbert addressed himself to Collis McAuley. "Tell her that I keep it in my room. Where else am I supposed to keep it?"

"You'd be better off keeping it at the Monsoon instead of dragging it around behind you everywhere you go," Molly declared.

"What business is it of hers?"

Collis McAuley said sharply, "Molly isn't a 'her.' She's your stepmother."

"Dry up, Collis!"

"Hey, hey," Stuart Ripple joined in robustly, "let's not get carried away, Norbie."

"What's going on?" a new voice demanded roughly. Leo Beggs hove into view followed by a woman who was, Benjamin decided, one of the plainest people he'd ever seen, coarse-featured, with a top-heavy body and a ludicrous tendency to flounce. Behind her was another lady, an old lady with an animated expression and coquettish blue eyes, dressed in a stylish dinner gown of pale ivory lace.

"What's going on?" Beggs repeated. "Norbie, goddamn it, are you startin' trouble again?"

"She stuck my fiddle in the closet," Norbert shouted.

"She shoulda stuck you in the closet with it!"

Norbert sliced the air with a frustrated karate chop and stormed out of the room.

Molly turned to the plain woman and said in a calm voice, as if Norbert had never been there, "Hello, Bertie. I was starting to think you weren't coming."

"I was lending support to Leo." There was a note of smugness to her voice. "I happened to be there when the emergency arose."

"Aren't you always," Molly observed brightly.

"What happened?" Collis McAuley asked.

"Mr. Baki caused a scene in the dining room," Alberta Van Curl said.

"He's off and running again, is he?" Stuart Ripple chimed in.

"I'm afraid so."

"What happened, Leo?" Molly asked.

"You know how Baki likes his special table, away from the window, in the corner facing the door? Fernando alway keeps it free for him. Well, tonight while Fernando was in the kitchen one of the new waiters gave Baki's table away."

"To me," the elegant lady in ivory lace informed them. "I had no idea that the table was permanently reserved. You see, I only just checked in this afternoon."

"When Baki went into the dining room," Beggs explained, "he saw this lady sittin' at his table. Baki went over and asked her to get up."

"He doesn't speak English, you know," the elderly lady said. "I thought he was trying to convey a different message altogether. I invited him to join me."

"Baki got pretty riled up," Beggs went on, "and started to lift this lady out of her chair."

"Oh no," Bunny Fern murmured.

"So when he did that," the elderly lady declared, "I pretended to faint."

"Leo and I got there just then," Miss Van Curl picked up, "and so did Fernando. Leo and Fernando straightened it out."

"It wasn't as bad as it sounds," Beggs reassured them. "Fernando spoke to him in Spanish and calmed him down before too many people noticed what was goin' on."

"And then," the elderly lady added, "Mr. Beggs was kind enough to invite me to be his guest at this private dinner party, which is gallantry above and beyond the call of duty. I am rather disappointed that Mr. Baki turned out to be so unsociable," she went on. "He reminds me of an Arab I once knew. An emir actually. Mr. Baki is a little more excitable but he has the same grand seigneur manner."

"I better introduce you around," Beggs said. "What's your name again?"

"Froebel," the old lady said. "Juanita Froebel."

Benjamin frowned. That name had a familiar ring but he couldn't quite place it.

It didn't remain a mystery very long. When Beggs announced Benjamin's name, the elderly lady said, "Benjamin Pinch? I have an old friend named Pinch. Dearborn V. Pinch. Are you by any chance related to Dearie?"

14

"Juanita Froebel?" Dearborn repeated in a shocked voice. "Are you quite sure about that?"

"Who is she, Dad? I know I've heard you mention her name."

"Juanita Froebel married Orville Froebel in 1919, the year the Prohibition amendment was ratified. I remember it well. The affair was swank but the liquor was execrable."

"Wasn't there something about her china collection?"

"Her porcelains," Dearborn said. "Buzz Beckwith got into difficulties over a game of baccarat and in a moment of desperation made off with her porcelains. I was instrumental in persuading Juanita not to prosecute."

"You think she might recognize you? I mean, it's been a long time."

"I don't think she'd recognize me if I weren't posing as Burgess Roycroft."

"She knew Burgess Roycroft?"

"Juanita ran off to Paris with Buggy in 1921. Didn't last.

_____90

Went back to Orville eventually. Stayed with Orville till he succumbed to a liver ailment in '25."

"You're talking a lot of years, Dad. She might not remember Burgess Roycroft either."

"One never knows, Benjamin. But we shall hope for the best. Now, what were you able to find out about the gun?"

Benjamin took off his dinner jacket and tossed it over a chair. "I not only found out about it, I saw it. It's in Beggs's gun cabinet, a Colt .38."

"How could you tell?"

"It was labeled. A neat little brass plaque." Benjamin crossed to the ice bucket and helped himself to ice cubes. "Have you got any club soda?"

"There's Perrier in the refrigerator under the bar. Where's the gun cabinet, Benjamin?"

"In the library."

"Which is?"

"First floor across from the kitchen."

"More specific?"

"From the garden door you go through the dining room, down the hall, and turn left. From the inside-corridor door you turn right."

"Proceed. Describe the cabinet." Dearborn was sitting in an armchair with his aching feet propped up on a hassock. It was almost two in the morning, and until forty minutes before he had been subjected to Cooky's relentless pursuit. She'd followed him to the dining room, outlasted him in the game room, outwalked him through the grounds, and outsat him at the bar. He'd balked at leaving the hotel to walk on the grounds for fear of running into Niccoli and had finally eluded her by saying he had to go to the men's room.

"It's a wall cabinet," Benjamin explained. "With a glass door about six feet square."

"Did you test the lock?"

"I gave the door a little tug," Benjamin replied, carrying his Perrier to the couch. "It's locked all right. There's a keyhole but no key."

"I suppose the lock wouldn't be too complicated to spring?"

"A lot easier than springing me out of jail."

"We've got to get that gun, Benjamin."

"I've been thinking this over," Benjamin said, "and I'm willing to go along with getting Molly Beggs to talk, including romancing her if I have to—"

"Just one moment," Dearborn interrupted, holding up his hand. "When did romance enter the picture? I don't recall suggesting that you do more than put forth a few discreet feelers."

"Discreet feelers aren't what she's after, Dad. She came on playing the unhappy wife to the hilt. I've seen enough groupies hanging around the locker room door to recognize the breed. I knew it for sure as soon as I met her father. She touted him off as a basketball fan. The guy wouldn't know a basketball from a Ping-Pong ball. As for her marriage, in the fifteen minutes I was alone with her I found out she married Beggs for money, that she plays around, and that she wants to split but something's holding her back."

"Fear," Dearborn said.

"That's right. She's afraid Beggs might turn violent."

"Beggs did turn violent," Dearborn reminded him.

"She doesn't know that yet."

"Not yet," Dearborn reflected. "I counted on the shock value of the news to surprise her into implicating Beggs. But now what you've told me makes me wonder how ardently she reciprocated Louis Martin's affections. How prostrated will she be when she learns of Martin's death?"

"So what if she plays around, Dad. That doesn't mean she has no conscience."

"True, Benjamin, true."

"Or that she won't be shocked when she finds out her husband killed Martin. I'm not worried about that. There's no law against tricking her into talking. But there is a law against breaking into people's apartments."

"I don't expect you to do it," Dearborn advised.

"Dad, promise me you won't try it either."

"I don't make promises."

"Dad, if you don't care about your reputation, have a little consideration for mine."

"Your reputation is another subject entirely."

"No second-story stuff, Dad."

"Trust me."

Dearborn gave a sigh of relief when Benjamin left. With Captain Niccoli already one jump ahead of him, Dearborn had no time to waste. He put on his newly acquired green leisure suit. It might be unorthodox garb for a burglar, but it was certainly more appropriate than a yachting cap and white flannels. He had reconnoitered the terrace again late that afternoon and decided on his equipment. At three, in his stocking feet, he turned out his lights, unlocked his front door, and, armed with a pair of hedge clippers commandeered from the garden shed, an awl from the same source, and a spool of nylon fishing line bought in the shopping annex, he crept out onto his terrace.

The sky was cloudy and there was no moon, but artfully arranged spotlights nestled among the bushes below provided some illumination. Except for the reassuring hum of the air conditioner, there were no sounds coming from the Beggses' bedroom. It was unlikely that, with the air conditioner going and the doors and windows closed, the loud snap of the hedge clippers would be audible. To make certain, Dearborn allowed a full minute to elapse between each cut. The eight-foot hedge was rooted in a planter sunk into the terrace floor, and Dearborn cut the hedge low, about a foot from the soil. The whole procedure took about twelve minutes.

Once Dearborn had removed the cut branches and ascertained that he could squeeze through the resultant foot-wide aperture, he laid the branches down and tied them loosely together at the base with the fishing line. Then he tested his theory that the piece removed would fit back into the empty spot. It fit as perfectly as a jigsaw piece and was held upright by the branches surrounding it. On tiptoe, and holding the branches aloft, Dearborn glided through the opening, turning on the

_____ 93

other side to join the loose branches to the rest of the hedge.

The Beggses' bedroom blinds were closed, but there was still danger that Dearborn would be spotted by the guards. He traversed the length of the terrace almost doubled over, with his head and shoulders just below the terrace wall. The sliding glass door leading into the living room was open and the screen door was unlocked. Dearborn carefully slid it back and stepped into the room. It took only a moment to adjust to the deeper darkness inside and to get his bearings. He had been in the room before and recalled the placement of the couches and the location of the coffee table and bar. He tiptoed with cautious confidence toward the circular staircase.

The staircase was sturdy, but it was made of wrought iron and creaked when Dearborn put his weight on the top step. He went down slowly and waited at the foot to make sure he hadn't been heard. Again he took his bearings. Benjamin had said that if one came in at the garden door, one would walk through the dining room into the hall and find the library on the left. He skirted the banquet-sized table and entered the hall. He peered over a swinging door on his right into a white-tiled kitchen lighted by a luminous clock over the sink and a light that someone had forgotten to shut off over the stove.

To his left was a door, slightly ajar, that proved on investigation to be a storage closet. A few feet farther on he saw a door on the right, probably a spare room, which he didn't bother to investigate. Directly in front of him was the front door leading into the hotel corridor. It was chained and bolted. Next to the door was an umbrella stand, a wall table and mirror and a clothes closet.

Opposite the spare room on Dearborn's left was the open door to the library. He entered. The drapes were drawn and the room was dark. If it weren't for the dim light filtering in from the hall Dearborn would have found it impossible to see.

He took in the jumble of paraphernalia on the desk, the Victorian fireplace, the smoking jacket tossed casually over a chair. He found himself beginning to feel some slight pangs of . . . regret? No, not that. Apprehension. Suppose he were caught? Suppose Captain Niccoli were lurking somewhere? As a matter of fact, if he didn't know better he'd say that someone was lurking somewhere. He stood quite still surveying the room, listening for the telltale signs, the rustles, the swallowing, the breathing that would indicate he wasn't alone, but he heard nothing.

Satisfied that his nervousness was unjustified, Dearborn settled down to the task. He toured the room, banging into chairs and lamps and tables and nearly impaling himself on the antenna of a TV set on the desk, until finally he came across the gun cabinet on the far wall. He bumped his nose on the edge of it as he slunk close to the wall, and the slight blow was sufficient to disengage the latch and send the heavy glass door swinging slowly open. Strange. Hadn't Benjamin told him the cabinet was locked? Dearborn chalked it up to Benjamin's carelessness in checking the lock and congratulated himself on his own good fortune. He had already taxed himself to the limit with the hedge clippers. It was just as well he wouldn't be called on to employ the awl.

He pushed his face up close to the gun display, then pulled his head back and regarded the display from a distance. Neither way could he read the labels. He was too farsighted to see anything close and it was too dark to see anything from afar. He hummed a few dirgelike notes. Why hadn't he brought a flashlight? He had equipped himself with hedge clippers, an awl, and a hundred yards of nylon and he hadn't thought of bringing a flashlight. Like a blind man he reached out and began fingering the plaques. But it was no use. They weren't embossed. He had to find a light.

Stealthily he crossed to the door and made his way back to the kitchen. Rather than trust the swinging door, he stooped and slithered under it. Precious time was lost as he slid open drawers and peeped into cabinets. Finally, as he passed the stove for the fourth time he noticed, on the top, a ceramic container holding a treasure of wooden matchsticks. Hurriedly he grabbed a handful and retraced his steps.

His feeling of apprehension had passed. Things were going well, exceedingly well. The words "all too well" crossed his mind, but he pushed them away. He returned to the cabinet and lit one of the matches on the cabinet's rough underside. The match flared and he held it up. At eye level was the plaque reading "Colt .38" and above it the small lethal weapon Dearborn had come to steal. He lifted it from its moorings, pocketed it along with the kitchen matches, and carefully pushed the glass door shut.

"Easy as pie," he told himself. "Let Niccoli stew over this one."

He returned to the hall and started back through the dining room, pausing near the table to listen. What was that? A door upstairs had opened and footsteps were crossing the living room floor. He judged the distance between him and the garden door. About twenty feet. If the door were chained and bolted like the front door it would take a full thirty or forty seconds to get out. Perhaps whoever it was up there would stay up there. He waited. But his luck had run out. The stairs creaked as the person started down.

Dearborn turned and tiptoed back down the hall toward the front door. Before he reached it he heard footsteps crossing the dining room, and without pausing to judge the wisdom of the move, he grabbed the door knob to the closed room on his right, opened it, and slipped inside.

The scream that greeted him followed so closely on his entrance that it seemed instantaneous and was so hair-raising that Dearborn momentarily lost his powers of locomotion.

"Ah, *Dios!*" the voice screeched.

Dearborn found suddenly that he was having difficulty with his knees.

"Help!" the shrill voice cried and a deeper masculine voice joined in to shout, "Wha? Wha? *Qué pasa, mujer?*"

The male voice triggered Dearborn into action. He catapulted into the hall, dashed to the front door, ignoring the startled figure of Molly Beggs standing a few yards behind him, threw open the door, ran down the corridor, and rushed up the stairs to his own suite.

He jerked the door open, leaped inside, closed it again, and bolted it before throwing himself down on the couch. Then he cocked his head and stared at the door, lifting his hand to pantomime the act of pulling and throwing the bolt.

Something registered. Something he hadn't realized until then. He had flung open the Beggses' front door without unbolting it just as he had flung open his own door. Yet five minutes before he left the Beggses' apartment, when he had looked at the Beggses' front door, the chain and bolt had been in place.

15

The phone wakened Dearborn. As he reached for it with one hand he groped for his watch with the other. Six-thirty. He hadn't gone to bed until three-thirty. He yanked the receiver off the hook. "Is it seven o'clock? It is not." He slammed down the receiver and resolutely turned his back on it.

A moment later the phone rang again. Dearborn bounced into a sitting position and snatched up the receiver. "Stop it! Stop it, I say!"

"Burgess, it's me, Cooky. Listen, don't hang up. I have something to tell you. Guess what happened? Somebody broke into Uncle Leo's apartment last night. One of Uncle Leo's guns was stolen. We were all asleep upstairs. . . ."

Irresistibly Dearborn's bleary eyes were drawn to the top drawer of the bureau.

"He got in the front door," Cooky said excitedly. "He jimmied open the gun cabinet and took one of the guns. Conchita swears the chain and bolt were in place on the front door, but how could they've been? Uncle Leo thinks the guy had a passkey, which means it could've been an inside job."

It certainly was an inside job, Dearborn thought, and by a security guard at that.

"Molly saw him," Cooky went on. "He went into Conchita and Nico's room and Conchita woke up and heard him. She started in to yell and he ran out. Molly had gone down to the kitchen to get an Alka-Seltzer and she saw him come out of their room and run out the front door."

Of course Molly had seen him, Dearborn reflected. The question was, had Molly recognized him.

"But it was dark," Cooky declared. "She said he was just kind of a blur."

That was a relief. But something else was bothering Dearborn. Why hadn't Niccoli taken the gun while he had the chance? It required no more than lifting it off its bracket and yet he had left it there.

"We've been up the whole night," Cooky informed him. "The hotel guards searched the grounds and Uncle Leo called in the police."

Unless, possibly, hearing noises in the hall, Niccoli surmised that someone might be going into the library and he decided not to chance calling attention to the empty space in the gun cabinet.

"Conchita had hysterics. Uncle Leo's furious. He's always so careful about his guns. He has the only key to the gun cabinet and he never lets anybody near it, not even Molly. The police are going to question all the employees and the guests in the Cloister wing. That new hotel guard Uncle Leo hired said it's got to be done."

Blast Niccoli. But of course he still wanted the gun and he must wonder why someone else is interested.

"The police are up there now," Cooky went on, "knocking on doors."

As if to confirm her statement, Dearborn heard voices in the corridor and the sound of knocking two or three doors away. He tossed aside his sheet.

"Burgess, you're still there, aren't you?"

"I am trying to recall where I stashed my bathing suit."

"Why, for heaven's sake?"

"I do not intend to be annoyed with a lot of senseless

questions. I shall quit the premises before those ninnies knock on my door."

"Where'll you go?"

"Didn't you say something yesterday about a cove? Shell Cove, is it? You have access to a motorboat, don't you?"

"Yes, but it's going to rain. The sky's dark, the water's choppy, and I heard thunder a couple of minutes ago."

"I'm not intimidated by a touch of weather."

"It can get pretty rough in a storm, Burgess, especially this time of year."

Dearborn began pulling open the buttons of his pajamas. "Nonsense. Where is your spirit of adventure, Cordelia?"

Cooky was wearing a man's T-shirt and a pink string bikini. Before they married, Jessamine had owned dozens of those little G-string affairs, bits of satin and lace that exposed more than they concealed, but Dearborn had made her get rid of them when she left burlesque.

"Why the big sigh, Burgess?" Cooky asked. "What are you thinking about?"

"Just a passing thought, Cordelia. A reflection on the follies of the past."

Cooky pointed to Dearborn's bathing costume, a loosely tied but capacious terry robe over white boxer trunks, tank top, and rubber bathing slippers. "Talk about the past, that outfit went out with the Charleston. And why the disguise?" Cooky eyed his yachting cap and sunglasses with mistrust. "You had those things on last night and you've still got them on."

Niccoli, Dearborn supposed, had no reason to visit Shell Cove, but there was no point taking chances. He felt in his pocket for the blue silk bandanna that he ordinarily wore with his blazer and that was now serving as a wrapping for the Colt .38.

"I guess," Cooky posited with a speculative glance at Dearborn's jet-black sideburns, "it's because you're afraid your hair will oxidize."

"My scalp and eyes are sensitive to salt water," Dearborn snapped. "Shall we shove off?"

The boat was little more than a skiff with a small fifteen-horsepower motor. It took fifteen minutes for them to circle the tip of the island and motor down to Shell Cove.

"The water is shallow," Cooky said. "I'll have to lift the motor while you pull the boat up onto the sand."

Dearborn slipped off his robe and made a neat bundle of it. He used the terry sash to tie the robe into a compact packet, which he carried over his head when he slipped into the water.

The beach was deserted. The white sand ran back from the ocean for a hundred feet to a clump of scrub pine. Beyond the scrub pine was the area of jungle that Dearborn had seen from the other side of the island when he and Cooky had first driven across the causeway two days before.

Cooky climbed out of the boat and shaded her eyes to look up at the sky. "It's getting close," she said, pointing to the black clouds billowing along the horizon.

"Nonsense. Those clouds are a good forty miles distant."

"I should've made a couple of sandwiches," Cooky lamented. "I didn't have any breakfast."

"Try to put it out of your mind."

"We're going to get stuck here, you know. The tide's starting to go out. It won't be high tide again until six. We will have to stay here at least 'til five."

"You're a wet blanket, Cordelia," Dearborn observed. "If you aren't deploring your condition, you're bewailing your fate."

"I can't help it if things never work out for me."

"They never will with that attitude," Dearborn chastised, trudging off across the sand.

"That's what's worrying me."

Dearborn was looking for a backrest. If he must pass the next few hours on the island he wanted to pass them in relative comfort. He sighted a log up ahead and headed for it. It lay in the sand at the base of a dune.

"Where are we walking?" Cooky asked. "As long as we're here, don't you want to go swimming?"

"I do not," Dearborn replied. He swung in toward the log and halted with a startled grunt as a bush a few yards away began to move.

Cooky saw it too and let out a scream.

Dearborn skipped backward as the bush fell upon him with a savage cry. Raising his fists and prancing sideways, Dearborn shouted to Cooky to run while he delayed the attacker, who was by then spinning a lethal-looking cord with balls attached to either end.

"I won't leave you, Burgess!" Cooky screeched, rushing forward to take up a defiant stance next to him.

"Seize!" a voice exclaimed from within the advancing bush. Dearborn thrust Cooky behind him and prepared to do combat, but the sharp command was followed by an abrupt cessation of activity.

"I think he said 'cease,' " Cooky whispered.

"Roycrap!" the imperious voice called out. "Roycrap, my fran!"

"It's Mr. Baki," Cordelia whispered.

Dearborn was overwrought. He'd been ready to fight to the death and he resented being made a dupe in Baki's war games. "Irresponsible," Dearborn cried. Then, raising his voice, he repeated the word slowly, syllable by syllable: "Ir-re-spon-si-ble!"

"My fran," Mr. Baki returned with equally distinct pronunciation. "Ere-we-spin-ze-bola!" He wound up his cord and balls like a major league pitcher and let fly at a branch of one of the scrub pines. The cord and balls flew through the air and twirled themselves around the branch, snapping it off as efficiently as if it had been hatcheted.

"Ouch," Cooky muttered, "that smarts!"

Dearborn was less impressed by the demonstration than by the fact that he'd been misunderstood. "Damn it, Baki, I didn't ask you to spin the bola, I said you are irre . . . oh, what's the use." A clap of thunder interrupted him.

"There," Cooky said, lifting her head to scan the sky. "I told you it's going to storm. Now what do we do?"

"We shall seek cover," Dearborn said reasonably.

"Where?"

Baki stepped forward and said something to Dearborn in Spanish and turned to point to the foliage behind him.

"If you're suggesting we follow you into that jungle," Dearborn informed him irritably, "we decline."

Baki parted his leaves and shouted "Shailter" at Dearborn, then raised his hands to form an inverted V over his head, and set off at a trot.

"Come on," Cooky yelled. "He knows where we can go."

"The man is a maniac," Dearborn muttered in an outraged voice. "No wonder they booted him out of Cuba."

The rain began falling, large drops that increased rapidly and threatened to turn into a downpour. They hadn't far to go. A hundred feet down the beach Baki cut inland, plunging through the scrub pine into the denser foliage and falling to his hands and knees to crawl under a tangle of impenetrable bush. When Cooky and Dearborn followed they found themselves crawling along a shallow ditch that had been dug under the bushes to emerge at the opposite end into a clearing.

There was a hut at the far end of the clearing. Baki motioned to Cooky and Dearborn to follow and began cautiously circling the clearing so as to approach the hut at an angle. Cooky emulated him, stepping gingerly along the periphery of the circle and following his lead when he grabbed a low-hanging tree branch and swung Tarzan-fashion across an intervening trench.

Dearborn, with a deprecating remark about cowboys and Indians, chose instead to cut directly across open ground with a purposeful stride.

"Roycrap!" Mr. Baki shouted.

Dearborn waved his hand impatiently. "I refuse to indulge your fantasies, Baki. I am not going to swing around in the trees like some—"

The words "half-witted baboon" were cut short as Dearborn's ankle was suddenly snared and he felt his foot pulled out from under him. He landed on his shoulders with most of his back and one of his legs suspended in midair.

"Burgess!" Cooky cried with horror, starting to run toward him.

"Halt!" Mr. Baki cried. He waved Cooky back and zigzagged his way across the clearing to Dearborn's side.

Dearborn had been upended by means of a trigger spring and small wire noose attached to a rope tied in turn to the branch of a tree. It took only a moment to release him but considerably longer to dissuade him from returning to the beach.

Cooky finally prevailed upon him to give Baki another try. "Look, it's dry in there, Burgess. And he didn't mean to do it. He's just bonkers. Norbie told me he raided the main-floor men's room last Monday night. Uncle Leo was still in New York, so it took them three hours to get him out."

Dearborn put out his hand. "What did you say, Cordelia?"

"He raided the —"

"No, no. You said your uncle was in New York?"

"At the International Meeting of Sportsmen's Clubs. He's president of the Florida chapter."

There was another clap of thunder, followed by a jagged streak of lightning.

"Come on, Burgess."

Cooky charged ahead and Dearborn, his energy and good spirits magically restored, lit out after her.

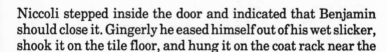

16

Niccoli stepped inside the door and indicated that Benjamin should close it. Gingerly he eased himself out of his wet slicker, shook it on the tile floor, and hung it on the coat rack near the door. Then, uninvited, he walked through the living room and into the bedroom.

Benjamin followed. "What's going on?" He remembered then that he wasn't supposed to know that Niccoli was in Florida. "Captain Niccoli? What are you doing here?"

"Where is he?" Niccoli demanded. "And don't ask who."

Benjamin ran his hand through his hair and tried to sound surprised. "Dad?"

"No. Little Jack Horner."

"How should I know where he is?"

Niccoli stalked back into the living room and crossed to the patio door. He peered out at the deserted rainswept beach. "He couldn't of got far." He turned to confront Benjamin. "Who's Burgess Roycroft?"

"Who? Why ask me? Listen, I just woke up."

"I checked the hotel register. Burgess Roycroft lives at the Grosvenor House on Fifth Avenue. Funny, isn't it. I checked his signature. You could read that handwriting from twenty feet. Just like somebody else I know. I asked the desk clerk what Roycroft looks like. Want to guess? A tall old geezer with black hair, a cane, and a mean temper. Sound familiar?"

"Doesn't sound like little Jack Horner."

"No, it don't, does it."

"Okay, so my father's here at La Playa. So what?"

"What do you know about the robbery?"

Benjamin didn't have to fake bewilderment about that. "What robbery?"

"Leo Beggs's apartment was broken into last night. A gun was stolen. A Colt .38."

Benjamin's jaw went slack. Trust me, his father had said. That's what came of trusting him. He'd added burglary to his list of accomplishments.

"Well?" Niccoli pressed. "What about it?"

"I don't know anything about it," Benjamin lied. Then he added truthfully, "I didn't do it."

"I know you didn't do it. Your old man did it." Niccoli's facial muscles were tight, his face grim. "He's interfering in police business again. I know why he's here and I know what

_____ 104

he's after. The only thing surprises me is that you let him get away with it. I gave you credit for more sense. You know something? I spotted you here yesterday morning."

"You did?"

"I chalked it up to coincidence, crazy coincidence. I must be getting senile. I'm getting as batty as your old man."

Benjamin's brain began to function. Niccoli was laying it out for him. Now all he had to do was play along. "Captain, I came down here to keep an eye on my dad. He didn't ask me to come and, if you want to know, he's sore as hell I'm here. That's the truth. He won't talk to me. He won't give me the time of day. As for his registering under a phony name I didn't know about it until you told me."

Niccoli cocked his head. "You serious?"

"Of course I'm serious," Benjamin returned virtuously. "You know a lot more than I do. What's my father doing here? What's he after? Why the phony name? And what about you? What are you doing here?"

Niccoli wasn't one hundred percent convinced. "I thought you were on vacation?" he returned suspiciously. "Rothschild told me you were away."

"I was away. I got home Sunday. Otto called to tell me he thought my old man was up to something. I checked around and found out he'd come down here, so I got on a plane and came down too. That's all there is to it. Now, what's it all about?"

"The name Louis Martin mean anything to you?"

"One's a comic and the other sings."

Niccoli studied Benjamin's face. "I was surprised you'd let him rope you into anything."

"I've got myself to think about," Benjamin assured him. "Whenever my father gets into trouble, I'm the one who gets the publicity."

"Most celebrities go for publicity."

"Not the kind my father generates."

Niccoli gave ground grudgingly. "Still, you helped him give me the slip last time."

"You mean the Rotten Apple business?"

"Yeah."

"I was only trying to keep my name out of the papers."

"Interfering with the authorities," Niccoli reminded him. "Lucky for you I was sympathetic."

"I appreciated it. I still appreciate it."

Niccoli began patting his breast pocket. After a minute he pulled out a flattened pack of cigarettes and began fumbling inside it. "If I should agree to let him off easy, would you cooperate?"

"In what way?"

"You help me get the gun and I'll give you a chance to get him out of here without the police being any the wiser."

"Sounds okay."

"Then we've got a deal."

"On one condition."

"What's that?"

"I want to know what the hell's going on around here."

"Okay. That's fair enough. It all began when this guy, Louis Martin, was killed. . . ."

It turned into a day-long deluge that churned up the Gulf, shredded the palm leaves, and turned the gardens into a quagmire. Benjamin ordered lunch from room service and hung around until midafternoon waiting for Dearborn to show. According to Niccoli, no one had left the premises. The hotel buses hadn't started running until eight in the morning and by seven the police had already posted men on the road. Knowing his father, Benjamin was sure he'd conned some poor unsuspecting guest, ten to one female, into concealing him somewhere. Benjamin only hoped the con didn't include the kind of snow job that made for complications later.

By one-thirty Benjamin was restless. He had taken up a post in front of the glass doors, through which he squinted at the empty beach and pitted gray water. From what Niccoli had told him, Leo Beggs was certainly a prime candidate for a murder charge. He'd caught Louis Martin in the bedroom with his wife, threatened to kill him, had him arrested, and then, in a sudden about-face, sprung for his bail. Niccoli had two theories about it. Either Beggs had traded the bail for silence or Beggs had wanted Martin freed so he could kill him. Or, just possibly, it had been a combination of both.

Niccoli had found out from his fellow security officers that Molly Beggs had in the past entertained nocturnal visitors, that some of them were local types imported from Silver Beach, and that the guards were generously recompensed for looking the other way when one of Mrs. Beggs's townies came over the wall. At least one of the townies had been someone known to the guards, a man named Louis Martin who hung out in the bars on Cabinet Street when he wasn't hanging around Molly Beggs.

In other words, Niccoli was three-quarters of the way home, and his visit to Benjamin had turned out to be a blessing because it pointed up the foolhardiness of Dearborn's remaining at La Playa. There was no longer any reason for Benjamin to butter up Molly Beggs, they didn't need proof of anything, and Dearborn's theft of the gun had been as unnecessary as it was crazy. All Benjamin had to do now was convince his father of that.

Simple? Not so simple. There were two complicating factors. Pride and money. Of the two, money was the lesser problem. Benjamin might get Otto to loosen the purse strings, but persuading his father to abandon the chase to Niccoli was another story. And Niccoli hadn't offered to sweeten the sacrifice with anything approaching gratitude. On the contrary, if Benjamin didn't get his father onto a plane for New York by nightfall, Niccoli intended to make other, less felicitous arrangements.

By two Benjamin was getting desperate. When the phone rang at two-ten, he vaulted across a hassock to answer it. "Dad?"

"Ben?" It was Molly Beggs. "Hi. I wasn't sure you'd be there."

"Oh, Molly. Hello."

"Are you busy?"

Benjamin was embarrassed. She might not be a paragon of virtue, as Dearborn would say, but he couldn't act the hypocrite now that there was no longer a necessity for it. "I'm getting ready to call the airport," he answered. "I think I may have to fly back to New York today."

There was a silence at the other end.

"Something's come up," he added lamely.

"Something's come up here, too. Someone broke into our apartment last night."

Benjamin tried to sound as if he hadn't already heard. "You're joking. What happened?"

"One of Leo's guns was stolen. The police were here all morning. Now Leo's gone back to Silver Beach with them. Norbie is over at the Monsoon rehearsing. I don't know where Cooky is, and frankly I feel like I need someone to talk to. I thought maybe you'd come over."

"I don't know," Benjamin mumbled, feeling like a fool. "I really ought to . . ."

"Please. Just for a few minutes."

Benjamin wasn't impervious to the voice or to his recollection of how beautiful she'd looked the evening before. Besides, he told himself, he owed her a kind word and maybe a sympathetic ear. "I'll be over in five minutes."

"I haven't played square with you," Molly said, averting her eyes from Benjamin's face.

They were lying in her bed under embroidered sheets, hips and thighs touching. She had just hung up the telephone. "That was Leo. He's still at the police station. He won't be back for a couple of hours."

"Considerate of him to call."

"Yes, but I expected him back sooner."

"You sound disappointed."

"Yes, well, you see, that's why I said I haven't played square with you."

"I don't get it."

"I have a confession. I'm in love with someone. Not Leo. I've never been in love with Leo. Someone else."

Benjamin couldn't think of an appropriate comment. He made some kind of sound to let her know he was listening.

"His name's Louis Martin. I told Leo I wanted a divorce so I could marry Lou."

"Why are you telling me all this?"

"Because, I guess, I'm feeling guilty. Leo threatened to kill Lou. He would, too. So I've been trying to make Leo believe I'm not interested in Lou anymore. That's why I asked you to dinner last night and that's why . . ."

Benjamin propped himself up on one elbow and stared down at her incredulously. "A diversionary tactic?"

"I guess you could call it that."

"You wanted to sic him on me?"

"That's right. I thought I'd try to keep you here until he gets home. I—"

Benjamin slid out from between the sheets and crawled to the edge of the bed. "Where are my shorts?"

"I'm sorry."

"Let me get this straight. You figured that if your husband wants to kill somebody, it's better to kill me than kill Louis Martin?"

"No. That's not it at all!" Molly sat up and locked her hands around her knees. "I was only trying to get Lou off the hook. Leo knows I fool around. He fools around too, for God's sake. It's just that he doesn't want me to leave him. I'm one of his props. Like the chrome coffee tables and the yacht. He doesn't want to let me go. That's all that interests him. My staying. So I thought if I could get him to think I'm not interested in Lou any longer—"

"Where's my shirt?"

"Look, Benjamin, I decided to tell you because I realized it's a dirty trick. I couldn't have gone through with it anyway. I swear I was going to tell you even if Leo didn't call."

"What did you do with my wristwatch?"

She shrugged and reached out to open the drawer of the bed table. Benjamin circled the bed, took his watch out of the drawer, and slipped it on.

"Ben," Molly pleaded, "it was only because I'm afraid for Lou. Please believe me. Give me a chance to explain, all right? Let's go into the living room and talk about it. Listen, you've got no reason to feel so all-fired righteous either."

Benjamin stopped rushing around the room. His panic was subsiding, partly, he realized, because he felt less vulnerable with his clothes on. Only now he was beginning to feel foolish. What right had he to be angry? She hadn't been any more dishonest with him than he'd been with her. And what the hell, they were both being dishonest together.

"Well, what about it?"

"Yeah, sure. Why not. Give me a minute to tie my shoelaces."

17

Benjamin was irritated with himself for getting involved with Molly Beggs. His father was always talking about the traits Benjamin had inherited from his mother. Well, this was one Dearborn had to take credit for. Benjamin was a sucker for a beautiful woman and even more of a sucker for a beautiful woman's tale of woe. The situation had changed. He should stay out of it. No reason now to tell her anything. In fact, plenty of reason why he should not. Leave it to Niccoli. Butt out. And other words to that effect.

But Molly claimed to be terrified of her husband and was still playing dangerous games with him. It could only be because she was really in love with Louis Martin. That probability persuaded Benjamin that she deserved to know the truth. She would learn it soon enough anyway. Why wait to hear about Martin's death from a stranger?

Her hysteria was wild but brief and gave way to an almost eerie composure.

"I'm sorry," Benjamin told her.

"How do you know Lou?" she said shakily. "I've never heard him mention your name."

"I don't know him. I only know about the murder."

"When was it?"

"Last Tuesday."

"How?"

"He was shot," Benjamin told her bluntly.

"It was Leo, wasn't it?"

"The police think so. I'm sorry to be the one to tell you, but I thought it might be easier coming from me than from them."

"How do you know about it?"

"The police in New York are investigating the murder. They sent a guy down here that I happen to know. His name is Anthony Niccoli."

"Niccoli? Isn't that the man Leo hired as a security guard?"

"That's right. He's been working here for a couple of days."

"So he could spy on Leo?"

"That's putting it pretty crudely, but I guess that's what it amounts to."

"Leo did it," Molly said dully.

"It looks that way."

"He was in New York for the Sportsmen's Club convention last week. That's when he did it."

Benjamin hadn't known anything about that, but it would have come out next, just another piece that fit the puzzle.

"When is Niccoli going to arrest Leo?" Molly asked.

"He won't arrest him. He'll turn his information over to the Silver Beach police and they'll arrest him. Then he'll be extradited to New York."

"What information?" Molly asked. "What has Niccoli got?"

"It's not very pretty."

"The sordid details about my affair with Lou?"

"Not just that."

"I see. The wicked lady who drove him to it. In other words, my reputation could get him off."

"It might make it a little easier for him."

She asked defiantly, "Will you testify to my immoral character?"

"That's not funny."

"You mean you weren't collecting evidence in there a few minutes ago?"

"That's even less funny."

"What else does Niccoli have?"

"There's the gun."

"I wondered why someone would want to steal that gun."

"Now you know."

"Isn't that against the law, or something?"

"Are you going to report him?"

She shook her head. Her voice was hard. "I knew it would end like this. I knew it."

"I'm sorry," Benjamin repeated. "I thought I ought to tell you before the shit hits the fan."

"You won't get into trouble with your policeman friend for telling me?"

"I'd appreciate it if you didn't let on you know. It's a hell of a thing to ask. . . ."

"You expect me to go on behaving like nothing happened? How do you think I'm going to face Leo?"

"It's only for a couple of hours. No longer than—"

An explosive cry, an oath, and a wild clatter cut through Benjamin's words. It came from outside and was succeeded by hoarse shouts and a demand to halt. Molly and Benjamin leaped to their feet and ran to the glass doors leading to the balcony. They opened them and went out, hunching their shoulders against the whipping rain.

"It's Nico," Molly exclaimed.

Nico was galloping through the garden. Below them a garden chair lay on its side and the table umbrella, carried by the wind, was rolling across the lawn. Nico raced furiously toward a tall figure that vanished a second later around the corner of the building.

The door beneath suddenly opened and Conchita rushed out screaming, "Nico, Nico!" She tripped over the garden chair and fell.

"Conchita!" Molly shouted down.

"Ay, ay!" Conchita screeched. "Whad iss it? Nico! Ay, Dios!"

Benjamin ran back into the living room and took the stairs two at a time. He burst through the open door and hoisted Conchita to her feet. He was holding her upright when Nico returned, still shouting, but now directing his wrath toward Benjamin.

"Leaf her!" he bellowed. "Chu leaf her!"

"*Es muy bien*," Molly called out from above. "*Le ayudandola.*"

Nico threw himself at Benjamin and Benjamin released Conchita, who promptly collapsed.

"Chu bastard!" Nico cried. "Chu throw her down!"

"Damn it all. Leave me alone."

"Leaf you along? I leaf you along!" Nico wrapped his arms around Benjamin's chest and Benjamin grabbed Nico around the shoulders. Neither of them had a firm footing on the wet patio tiles and they slid around in one another's arms like circus clowns.

The tussle ended when Molly dashed out the front door and dragged Conchita to her feet. "*Bastante! Los ambos ayudenme con ella! Y dejarmos traerla en la casa!* Do you hear me, Nico?"

They brought Conchita indoors and sat her on one of the dining room chairs.

"I thought chu wass him," Nico panted at Benjamin. "The thif."

"What thief?" Molly asked.

Nico answered excitedly, "He wass tall like chu. He had black hair. He ron out the door."

"Our door?" Molly exclaimed. "Just now?"

Nico nodded. "Chus now when I bringin' in the ombrella. I look up and see heem. Then he falls over the chair, peek heeself up, and ron."

Conchita clasped her hands and held them to her forehead. "I see heem in the hall."

"You saw him?" Benjamin said. "Did you recognize him?"

"Chus the back!" Conchita wailed. "I dun know."

_____ *113*

Molly looked at Benjamin in bewilderment. "Who? Oh my God, who?"

"I don't know." He didn't want to drag the name of Dearborn V. Pinch into the picture. It would be a needless complication. It seemed odd that his father would be skulking around the Beggses' apartment again. What did he want this time?

"Chu call the police," Nico told Molly.

"Yes, of course," Molly said. "I'll call them."

Benjamin was depressed. He didn't have enough thumbs to plug up all the holes his father was punching in the dike. He made a face at Molly behind Nico's back and mouthed the words "Not a good idea." Then he said, "Let me do it. I'll use the phone upstairs."

"I yam going!" Conchita suddenly proclaimed in a high-pitched but emphatic yowl. "I yam leafing!"

"You can't do that, Conchita," Molly protested.

"Oh jess I can," she quavered. "I dun stay here no more. Every day sontin' terrible iss happenin'. I dun like. I dun like."

My feelings exactly, Benjamin thought as he climbed the stairs. The sooner we get out of here the better.

The Coast Guard helicopter spotted them at nine that evening and ferried them back, first Mr. Baki, who insisted upon the arrangement, presumably to ensure his safety, and then Dearborn and Cooky.

"Lucky for you," the pilot drawled, "that someone noticed that guy Baki was missing."

"Whoever it was," Dearborn muttered, "took his own sweet time about it." Dearborn's robe sagged from the weight of water it held and he was uncomfortably aware of the soaked bathing trunks plastered to his puckered flesh. He'd turned his yachting cap around to keep the rain from running down the back of his neck, and strands of hair hanging over his forehead dripped water into his eyes.

"It was the maître d'," the pilot explained. "Seems Mr. Baki didn't go in the dining room for lunch, and he never misses his lunch. When he didn't show for supper the maître d' got suspicious."

"Bright boy," Dearborn said, turning to Cooky. "Bright boy, Fernando. You should give him some consideration."

"Tuesday is Fernando's day off," Cooky informed him. "But I'll tell him I'm considering him when I see him. It'll give him a good laugh."

Ironic, thought Dearborn, looking at her. The ordeal had had a beneficial effect on the girl. The rain had washed her face clean, her eyes seemed larger without all that grease, and her hair was lying flat for a change, putting her head into reasonable proportion to the rest of her. Amazing the improvement. She was almost comely.

The helicopter made a noisy descent into the southwest garden, its propeller blades stirring up the palm leaves and scattering the fallen hibiscus blossoms. It was still drizzling, but the worst was over. A handful of people stood under the eaves outside the dining room windows watching the helicopter land. Dearborn picked out Benjamin's six-foot-four frame and next to him Alberta Van Curl. Leo Beggs was there, too, but who was that thickset fellow wearing the raincoat? Not Niccoli, was it? Hurriedly Dearborn turned his yachting cap around and groped in his pocket for his sunglasses.

Benjamin was the first one to reach the helicopter. He wrenched open the door and reached in to help Cooky out.

"Cooky!" Leo Beggs exclaimed, running up to her. "What the hell's the matter with you? What were you doin' in Shell Cove on a day like this?"

"I'm sorry I scared you, Uncle Leo."

"You know about the tides. If we hadn't of sent the Coast Guard over there, you'd of been stuck all night!"

"I know, Uncle Leo. I'm really sorry."

Benjamin helped Dearborn out of the helicopter. "Am I glad to see you! You had me worried there for a while."

"Ssh," Dearborn cautioned, jerking his head toward Cooky and Leo Beggs.

"Listen, Dad—"

"Roycroft. Roycroft, you fool."

"We have to talk."

"Not now. Are you aware of the fact that Niccoli is standing over there?"

"Have you got it?" Benjamin asked, detaining his father with a firm hand. "Where is it?"

Automatically Dearborn stuck his free hand into his pocket and closed his fingers around the gun. "Have you no sense? This is no time to discuss it. I think the man recognizes me."

"It's okay. It doesn't matter."

"Doesn't matter? Of course it matters."

Niccoli broke away from the crowd and walked toward Dearborn. Dearborn squared his shoulders and prepared to brazen it out.

"Hello, Mr. Roycroft," Niccoli said heartily. "Glad to see you made it okay."

Dearborn stared at him in amazement. Had he actually said "Roycroft"?

"We were worried about you. Lousy day for a picnic, Mr. Roycroft."

Dearborn continued to gaze at him in consternation.

"No one knew you and the young lady had gone over to Shell Cove. Lucky someone suggested that Mr. Baki might be there."

Beggs spoke up suddenly. "Yeah, that's right. What's the big idea, Roycroft? I thought I told you to keep your distance from Cooky?"

"Leave him alone, Leo," Alberta Van Curl said, fluttering her hands and looking as if she might swoon. "Can't you see he's exhausted. Look at him." She pulled Leo away, and he held onto Cooky's arm as they walked off, grumbling and still casting nasty looks at Dearborn over his shoulder.

Dearborn was in shock all right. It seemed impossible that Niccoli could stand two feet away from him and not recognize him. In fact it *was* impossible. Niccoli might be calling him Roycroft but he knew it was Dearborn V. Pinch, and if he knew it was Dearborn V. Pinch then someone had told him to expect

Dearborn V. Pinch. Dearborn shifted his gaze to Benjamin.

"Maybe we'd better go inside," Benjamin suggested.

"Why don't we?" Dearborn agreed in a clipped voice. "If you'll excuse me." He started at a fast pace for the door leading into the shopping annex and a moment later found himself flanked by Niccoli and Benjamin. He proceeded on his way, keeping a step ahead of them, and then at the Cloister wing attempted to veer from the convoy formation, breezily calling out, "Good evening, gentlemen," and trotting briskly around the corner. They caught up with him at the foot of the stairs.

"Dad, we've got to talk. Captain Niccoli has something to say."

"Who told him I'm here?"

"Nobody. He found it out himself."

"And why, may I ask, have you allied yourself with him?"

"For a good reason, Dad. Captain Niccoli is willing to forget the whole thing if you cooperate."

"Forget what whole thing?"

"The theft," Niccoli supplied.

"I returned your file folder," Dearborn snapped.

"I'm talking about the gun."

"Why would I steal a gun?" Dearborn asked.

"Dad," Benjamin pleaded, "the picture's changed since this morning. If you'll just cut the crap and give us a chance to explain...."

They had reached Dearborn's door. Dearborn bent down, reached under the carpet, and came up holding his room key.

"That's where you keep your key?" Benjamin asked. "What's the matter with the front desk?"

"It's there and I'm here. That's what." Dearborn opened the door and slipped the key back under the carpet. "I might have known you'd turn traitor as usual, Benjamin," he commented. "You have a bad streak. Not your fault. Genes. Comes down from the maternal side."

18

"What is that man's name, dear?" Juanita asked Cooky. "I thought I heard someone call him Roycroft."

"Burgess Roycroft. That's his name."

"The Roycroft Beverages Roycroft?"

"Yes."

Juanita Froebel had come out onto the lawn to watch the rescue operations. Mr. Baki had been the first arrival, and she'd remained to watch the second landing. That's when she'd spotted the vaguely familiar-looking gentleman with the imposing carriage and the handsome face. She'd been trying very hard to recall where she'd seen him before when someone walked up to him and addressed him as Mr. Roycroft.

"My, my," she noted. "He's as tall as ever. Even taller. I wonder if that's possible?"

"Do you know him?" Cooky asked curiously.

"I knew him," Juanita replied. "I once knew him quite well. And who are—"

"Come on, Cooky," Leo Beggs interrupted, "you've got to change into dry clothes."

He took Cooky's arm and hurried her away before Juanita could find out who Cooky was or fully satisfy her curiosity regarding dear old Buggy Roycroft.

What had Buggy been doing with Mr. Baki, and that young woman? Were they enjoying an innocent outing or was Buggy still up to his old tricks? One would suppose that his tastes had been tempered by the years, but one never knew.

Juanita went back into the hotel and strolled toward the lobby. Buggy had been possessed of an unique imagination and she had found some of his inventions stimulating. In fact they had come in handy later in life when she could no longer rely on youth or beauty to rule the occasion. But Buggy had been a bore, too, and sometimes outrageous. She'd gone along with an assortment of oddities, including the albino garage mechanic and that ghastly duchess with the unhealthy passion for chocolate eclairs. She'd endured and even enjoyed some of the adventures—the interlude in the Tuileries coming readily to mind—but she'd drawn the line at others and abandoned Buggy altogether on the banks of the Seine when he'd arrived in company with those lascivious Siamese twins from Latvia.

Still, that had been a long time ago. Surely Buggy had mellowed somewhat since the old days. She herself had discovered with the passing years that a certain degree of unorthodox activity lent spice to the jaded appetite, but she didn't have quite so many opportunities to indulge herself now and sometimes when the opportunity arose she found she didn't have quite the stamina.

She approached the front desk determinedly.

"Good evening, madam. Can I help you?"

"Young man, I've just learned that I have a friend staying at the hotel, Mr. Burgess Roycroft. Can you tell me which room he occupies?"

"Certainly." The desk clerk checked his files. "Mr. Roycroft is in the Cloister wing. Suite 63. The house phones are over there to your left."

"Thank you. I won't disturb him this evening. I rather think he might have had a tiring day. I shall catch up with dear old Buggy in the morning."

"Look," Niccoli said brusquely, "you're lucky I'm a reasonable guy."

"Open to argument."

"Dad, could you cool it?"

"Withholding evidence, police harrassment, stealing, obstructing justice, you name it," Niccoli declared.

"Why are you here, Captain?"

"What do you mean?"

"You are here because I piqued your curiosity and alerted you to the possibility of Martin's being the victim of a deliberately planned murder."

"Oh, for Christ's sake."

"Dad, cut it out."

Dearborn, in smoking jacket and shorts, was seated at a rolling table supplied by room service. He had bathed, shampooed, and shaved, and was enjoying a light repast consisting of a strawberry omelet, melba toast, watercress salad, and tea. "Under the circumstances, it seems extraordinary that you refuse to acknowledge your debt to me."

"My debt to you?"

"There will be newspaper coverage. The police department does offer commendations to private citizens. And though I won't insist upon an apology, a simple statement of gratitude would, I think, be in order."

"You won't insist on an apology?" Niccoli said wonderingly. "And how would you feel about ninety days in jail?"

"It's almost eleven," Benjamin cut in. "Our plane leaves at midnight."

"There's always another plane, Benjamin."

"Not here there isn't. At least, not on weekdays. The last night flight is midnight. The first morning flight is at seven, and we've got to switch at Atlanta."

"We can always charter a plane if necessary," Dearborn insisted unreasonably.

"We're sitting on the edge of a swamp, Dad. There aren't any private airstrips around here, which means there aren't any private charters. We'd have to phone Miami or Jacksonville or Tampa or one of the bigger cities to send a plane for us. Now look, I've got to pack, you've got to pack, and Captain Niccoli has to arrest a man."

"Where's the gun?" Niccoli demanded.

"All in due time, Captain. First I think we should settle our differences." Dearborn crossed his long bare legs and adjusted the sash of his smoking jacket.

"I'm a cop," Niccoli said irately. "I know what the law is and I follow it. You know what would happen if I pulled the shit you pull? You think my men break into people's apartments in the dead of night and get away with it? Here. Look at this." He pulled a piece of paper out of his pocket and waved it at

Dearborn. "This is a search warrant. If you hadn't gummed up the works I'd of had the gun by now."

"You didn't wait for any search warrant, Captain Niccoli," Dearborn remarked with exaggerated politeness.

"What are you talking about?"

"No need to pretend. Nothing we say here need go beyond these four walls."

"You better talk fast."

"You broke into that apartment yourself last night. You opened the gun cabinet and were about to remove the gun when you heard footsteps, my footsteps, mistook them for the approach of a family member, secreted yourself in the front closet, and a few minutes later amscrayed through the front door. Didn't think I knew that, did you?"

"Are you nuts?"

"Don't deny it. The front door was bolted when I first entered the library. Later, when I was making my own exit, I found the door unbolted."

"Didn't you go in by the front door?" Niccoli asked.

"I did not."

Niccoli turned to Benjamin. "You didn't . . .?"

"After the dinner party I came over here to see my father for a couple of minutes. Then I went back to my own suite and went to bed."

"Come now, Captain," Dearborn said smugly, "your secret is safe with us."

"If there *was* somebody," Niccoli declared stridently, "and I'd be surprised if there was, it wasn't me."

"However," Dearborn continued undaunted, "in return for keeping your little secret—"

"There's no little secret. It wasn't me."

"Wait a minute," Benjamin interrupted. "Hold everything." The peculiar look on his face caused both Dearborn and Niccoli to pause.

"What is it, Benjamin?"

"Dad, what time did you go to Shell Cove?"

"A little before seven."

"In the morning?"

"Of course in the morning."

"Not in the afternoon?"

"There is no seven o'clock in the afternoon. Do you suppose I would jeopardize my life by going out in a small craft in the midst of a violent storm? I went this morning a little before seven. Why? What does Shell Cove have to do with this discussion?"

"Not Shell Cove, Dad," Benjamin returned. "Your whereabouts at two this afternoon."

"Kindly be more explicit."

"During the time I was at Molly Beggs's, this afternoon someone got into the apartment. Nico chased him but he got away."

"Why didn't you tell me about it?" Niccoli demanded.

"I thought it was Dad."

"I? Why should you think it was I?"

"It usually is. Besides, Nico said it was a tall dark-haired man."

"Tall dark-haired individuals are not at a premium, Benjamin."

"The point is that if it wasn't you sneaking around this afternoon, then maybe it wasn't Captain Niccoli sneaking around last night."

"It wasn't me," Niccoli reiterated.

"In other words," Benjamin concluded, "there's a third party involved here."

The men were silent for a moment. Niccoli speculated tentatively, "Another one of her boyfriends?"

"According to Benjamin," Dearborn said, "the lady views her emotional and sexual commitments as separate entities."

"That right?" Niccoli asked Benjamin.

Benjamin grinned sheepishly and flicked some lint off his jacket sleeve. "I'm just guessing," he said, "but I get the feeling that any fooling around she's doing these days she's doing with the hope she'll be caught."

"Explain yourself."

Benjamin repeated what Molly had told him about trying to make Leo Beggs think she was through with Louis Martin.

"You think she'd go so far as to have somebody sneak into the apartment while her husband was there?" Niccoli asked. "I mean, what was she going to do? Parade him past the bedroom door?"

"I don't know about the other night. But I don't think that's what was going on today."

"Why is that, Benjamin?" Dearborn asked accusingly. "Was she otherwise occupied?"

"Leo wasn't at home and she told me she didn't expect him home till late."

"And what," Dearborn challenged, "did you tell her?"

"What was I supposed to tell her?"

"We'll discuss what you were and weren't supposed to tell her later. What *did* you tell her?"

"About what?"

"About Louis Martin."

Benjamin cast around for some way to sidestep that question. He decided on an out-and-out lie and was about to plunge into it when there was a sudden loud report from the direction of the bedroom, followed by an ear-splitting scream.

The three men leaped to their feet. Dearborn shoved the rolling table away from him with such force that it coasted across the floor and hit the front door. Niccoli ran to the bedroom door and opened it. He dived into the room with Dearborn and Benjamin at his heels, then stopped short when he saw that the room was empty.

"It came from Beggses' apartment," Dearborn declared.

"Come on." Benjamin turned and sprinted toward the front door. Niccoli began crowding Dearborn back into the living room.

"No," Dearborn commanded. "Through the terrace." He crossed the bedroom and pulled open the terrace doors.

Niccoli ran past him and halted in front of the hedge. "Now what? I'm not a pole vaulter."

Dearborn grabbed the clump of false hedge and yanked it out. Then before Niccoli could step through, Dearborn straddled the shorn stubble and pushed through the opening.

He was the first to enter the Beggses' bedroom, the first to see Leo Beggs lying across the bed, his hand still on the gun, his head hanging over the edge, and blood gushing copiously from a wound in his temple.

19

Molly Beggs was standing at the bedroom door leaning against the door jamb holding a battery-operated television set. A smiling announcer gazing out of the small screen was promising "quick relief for that tension headache," the ludicrous pitch seeming to Dearborn more macabre than comical.

"Call the Silver Beach police," Niccoli instructed. He bent over the body and placed his ear against Beggs's chest, then straightened up and shook his head. "Tell them what it's about and tell them I'm here."

Benjamin picked up the bedside phone and dialed.

Niccoli had taken a notebook out of his pocket and was jotting something in it.

Benjamin spoke into the phone briefly, hung up, and queasily eyed the body.

"He must of been sitting in bed," Niccoli noted. "If he'd been sitting on the edge his head would of fallen about here." He indicated a point closer to the center of the king-sized bed.

"Odd, that," Dearborn interposed.

"Not really. There's no telling what a suicide's likely to do. I've found them lying on rubber shower curtains surrounded by notes for everyone from their lawyers to their milkmen, and I've found them at the dinner table with their faces in the mashed potatoes."

The sound of the portable television set dropping to the

floor brought them up short. Benjamin managed to catch Molly just as her knees buckled. He carried her back into the living room and was met with a volley of howls that brought Dearborn and Niccoli bounding out of the bedroom behind him.

Nico and Conchita were standing at the top of the stairs. It was Conchita doing the vocalizing.

"Iss che chot?" Nico cried.

"She fainted," Benjamin answered. He carried her to the couch and lowered her gently onto the cushions.

"How did chu get in here?"

"Never mind that now," Niccoli interjected. "Do something about your wife."

Nico put his arm around Conchita's shoulders and began patting her. He said, "We heard a chot."

"Señor Beggs," Conchita choked out between sobs. "*Dónde esta* Señor Beggs?"

"Dead," Niccoli informed her bluntly. "Shot himself."

In the background someone said, "I hear, Steve, it's the thriller to end all thrillers." Niccoli strode back to the bedroom door and picked up the portable television set. He switched it off and deposited it on the nearest table.

Both Conchita and Nico stretched their necks to peer through the bedroom door where Leo Beggs's bare feet and pajama-clad legs were visible lying on the bed.

"Ay, Chico!" Conchita cried.

Niccoli strode across the room and shut the bedroom door.

"I'm all right now," Molly murmured, raising herself to a sitting position.

"Mrs. Beggs," Niccoli told her, "I'm a policeman. I'm with the New York police. I'll explain it all in a few minutes. Right now I want to go downstairs and take a look at the gun cabinet in the library." He started down the stairs.

"Get the woman some brandy, Benjamin," Dearborn instructed.

"Wha chu wan here?" Conchita suddenly exclaimed, noticing Dearborn for the first time. She addressed her husband in a spate of rapid-fire Spanish.

"Che sais he iss the man with the flowers," Nico explained to Molly.

"That is so," Dearborn promptly admitted. "It was meant as a friendly gesture. Unfortunately it was misunderstood."

"Mr. Roycroft and I know one another from New York," Benjamin hastened to explain. "That is, his father and my father are friends."

"Mrs. Beggs," Dearborn asked, waving off Benjamin's explanation as superfluous, "did you see your husband shoot himself?"

"She's not in any shape to talk about it," Benjamin cautioned.

"Yes I am," Molly said weakly. "I had gone downstairs for the TV. I was right at the top of the stairs coming up when I heard the shot."

Dearborn looked around. "Where is Cordelia?"

"Cooky had a sandwich and then went over to the Monsoon. She said she'd come back with Norbie after the club closes."

"So you and your husband were alone?"

"Except for Conchita and Nico."

"Why do you think he did it?" Dearborn asked.

Molly exchanged glances with Benjamin, who suddenly looked extremely uncomfortable.

Suspicion was once more revived in Dearborn's mind. "Benjamin, what do you know about this?"

Just then Niccoli clattered up the steps to announce in a matter-of-fact tone, "It came from the gun cabinet all right." He paused with one hand on the railing. "Something wrong?"

"Did you tell her?" Dearborn demanded of Benjamin.

"Tell her what?" Niccoli asked in a perplexed voice.

"Yes," Benjamin admitted. "Yes I did."

"How did *you* know?" Molly asked Dearborn. "Who told *you*?"

"Captain Niccoli told him," Benjamin answered. "Look, Molly, it was going to come out anyway."

"Benjamin," Dearborn broke in, "it is not enough that you are an idiot. You're an untrustworthy idiot."

"For Christ's sake," Niccoli chimed in, "who told what to who?"

"Benjamin," Dearborn explained, "told Mrs. Beggs that you were going to arrest her husband for murder."

Conchita's lamentations had died down and she and Nico were swinging their heads back and forth as if watching a tennis match. Nico declared incredulously, "Chu wass going to arrest Señor Beggs?"

"*Porqué?*" Conchita cried, "Sutch a good man. A good Catholic. He would not choot heeself. He would not keel no one."

"Maybe you'd better take her downstairs," Benjamin suggested nervously as Conchita's wail picked up volume.

Nico was reluctant to leave, but Molly spoke to him in Spanish, words of reassurance that seemed to have a soothing effect. He supported Conchita to the stairs.

"What did Benjamin tell you?" Dearborn demanded of Molly after Nico and Conchita were gone.

"I'll ask the questions if you don't mind," Niccoli declared.

"He told me that Lou is dead," Molly replied. "He said that Mr. Niccoli is a policeman from New York and that he came down here to arrest Leo."

"What else did he tell you?" Niccoli prodded.

"That it was you who broke in last night and took Leo's gun."

Niccoli started to object, then thought better of it and said instead, "You told your husband I was going to arrest him?"

"I wasn't going to. I promised Ben I wouldn't. But tonight Leo wanted to...wanted to..." She sighed and shook her head. "I told him I wouldn't. We had an argument. I said I was going to sleep in Cooky's room. He got very angry. Very." She stopped and took a deep breath.

"Go on."

"He began calling me names. I answered him back. Then he said something about fixing me good and I said he couldn't make trouble for me anymore, that he wouldn't be around to make trouble. Then I told him he was going to be arrested for Lou's murder."

"How did he take it?"

"He was shocked that you'd found out. He thought he'd covered his tracks. He said he'd never go to jail for it. I thought he meant he'd get out of it somehow. Try and buy his way out. He always thought money would take care of everything. I just laughed at him and left the bedroom."

"Was he in bed when all this took place?"

"Yes. We . . . er . . ." She blushed. "We both were. He didn't try to follow me. I didn't think he would. I thought he'd start calling people. His lawyers. Anyone he could think of that might help him. Maybe Joe Powell, the sheriff."

"The sheriff?"

"Leo thought everybody's for sale."

"You didn't think he'd try to run?"

"No," Molly said simply. "He didn't run away from things. He fixed them. Just like he said."

"Mrs. Beggs," Dearborn said, speaking up in spite of Niccoli's annoyed frown, "you were carrying a television set when we came in. You were sufficiently well composed to watch television?"

"I expected it would only be a few hours before the police came to get Leo. I knew I wouldn't be able to sleep, so I went down to the library for the television set. I stopped to speak to Nico while I was down there and then—"

As she spoke the door chimes sounded downstairs. "That's the police," Niccoli interrupted. "Mr. Roycroft, you want to go back to your place and get that package you're holding for me?"

"Yes, all right. Come with me, Benjamin." Dearborn motioned to Benjamin and together they went through the upstairs door into the second-floor corridor.

"All you have to do," Benjamin said as they walked to Dearborn's door, "is let me turn the gun over to Niccoli and we can wash our hands of the whole mess."

Dearborn fished the door key out from under the carpet. "I shall, of course, turn the gun over to Niccoli. As for getting out of here . . ." He had begun to insert the key into the door lock when unexpectedly the door swung back under the pressure of his hand.

"I guess the waiter didn't shut the door when he brought in your supper," Benjamin remarked.

Dearborn didn't answer. He walked through the living room to the bedroom and from there to the bathroom. Benjamin followed. The bath mat lay on the floor and next to it the rumpled bath towel. An open bottle of shampoo sat on the ledge of the tub and Dearborn's shaving mug and razor were on the sink where he'd left them. His wet robe was draped over the shower curtain rod and a bit of his bathing suit was sticking out of the clothes hamper. Dearborn picked up the wastepaper basket and dumped out the contents. Something heavy fell out along with the wads of Kleenex, empty toothpaste container, bits of cellophane and cotton swabs, something wrapped in a wet blue bandanna. Dearborn scooped it up and carefully unwrapped it. "Give this to the captain with my compliments."

Dearborn went back into the bedroom, opened his bureau drawer, and took out the note he'd found in Louis Martin's duffel bag. "Might as well give him this, too. I found it among Martin's possessions. It's another piece of evidence to add to the file."

"I don't mind telling you, Dad, I'm glad to get this over with. The last hour was no picnic."

"Mrs. Beggs made a grave error in telling her husband that he was going to be arrested, almost as grave as your error in confiding in Mrs. Beggs."

"I kept your name out if it, didn't I?"

"You should have kept everyone's name out of it."

"Don't give me a hard time, Dad. I feel rotten enough about it as it is."

"In that case I won't delve into the circumstances under which you were persuaded to let down your guard."

"I wish you wouldn't."

"For shame, Benjamin."

"Molly didn't expect him to commit suicide. You saw what it did to her."

Dearborn had, indeed, seen what it did to her. The faint

had been a fake. He was sure of that. When she'd sat up there was color in her cheeks, her eyes were bright, and she showed no signs of confusion. And the hesitantly told story about spilling the beans because she was horrified by her husband's sexual advances was preposterous. From what Dearborn knew of her she'd say yes to Jack the Ripper if it suited her purposes. No. Molly Beggs was not the frail creature she pretended to be. He said, "I would have guessed that suicide was uncharacteristic of Leo Beggs. It's an admission of failure. He didn't strike me as the kind of man who would kill himself."

"Dad, it was a spur-of-the-moment decision. You heard Niccoli. There's no way to predict what somebody'll do or how he'll do it."

"Perhaps."

But Dearborn was thinking of the sequence of events as described by Molly Beggs. She and Leo had been in bed. He desired to exercise his connubial privilege. She objected. They argued. She left the room and as a parting shot told him he was about to be arrested. She went to the library, picked up the television set, and carried it back up the stairs. When she reached the second floor she heard a shot and ran to the bedroom door. She discovered on going in that her husband had shot himself. It was not possible. When and how had Leo Beggs gotten the gun out of the gun cabinet?

"Dad, you want me to come back after I give the gun to Niccoli?" Benjamin asked.

"No, Benjamin, I'm tired."

"I'll buzz you in the morning, then."

After Dearborn closed the door behind Benjamin he stood looking into his living room with the same feeling he'd had a few minutes before of something being out of place. Then he realized what it was. When he had risen from the table earlier he had given the table a shove that had sent it rolling across the room to block the front door. But he hadn't had to push it out of the way to enter the door.

Someone else had done that.

20

Dearborn woke early, dressed, and went downstairs. The news of Beggs's death had already gone the rounds. Stanley, the desk clerk, was fending off a group of curious guests who were bombarding him with questions. It would have been impossible to keep the news quiet, what with police and ambulances all over the grounds the night before, to say nothing of Conchita's caterwauling.

Dearborn ran into Raúl Baki in front of the barbershop where he was handing out "FREE CUBA" buttons.

"Hello, my fran Roycrap," Baki called out, affixing a button to Dearborn's lapel.

"Morning, Baki," Dearborn returned. "I see it's business as usual despite the tragedy."

"What travesty?" Baki inquired in a puzzled voice.

"Tragedy," Dearborn repeated loudly. He wondered if it were possible that Baki hadn't heard the news. "Beggs's death," Dearborn boomed.

"Bags?"

"Yes, Beggs. He's dead."

"Dead" was a word that Baki understood. He was astounded and repeated the word in an awed whisper. "Dead?"

"Suicide," Dearborn clarified. "Or so it seems."

"Seaside?"

"Not seaside. Suicide."

"Susayide? What is susayide, my fran Roycrap?"

Dearborn, frustrated, resorted to pantomime. He raised his index finger to his temple and shouted, "Bang!"

Baki recoiled and murmered in a shocked voice, "Bang?"

"I'm talking about Leo Beggs," Dearborn cried in frustration. "Shot! Leo Beggs!"

"Ah!" Baki exclaimed, the light seeming to dawn. He said, "Shot? Leo Bags shot?"

"Himself," Dearborn confirmed. "Blew his brains out."

Baki responded with comprehension and shock. He shoved his "FREE CUBA" buttons into his pocket and proceeded to evacuate the shopping arcade while Dearborn, satisfied that his obligation had been discharged, continued on into the dining room.

Fernando was at the door. "Good morning, Mr. Roycroft."

"Thought you were only on evenings, Fernando."

"I work a full day Mondays and Wednesdays. Tuesdays and Thursdays are my days off."

"You're looking a little wan this morning."

"Mr. Beggs was a friend. He was very kind to me. It was a shock to hear the news."

"My sympathies, Fernando. I know how you must feel."

Fernando led Dearborn to a table near the window. Dearborn was about to sit down when he recognized a familiar voice at a table some distance away. It belonged to Collis McAuley, Molly Beggs's father. He was sitting with a young, good-looking man in tennis whites and a plump, pretty woman in a provocatively cut halter dress.

"I'd rather be over there, Fernando. Not so sunny." Dearborn walked to a table next to the one where Collis McAuley was seated and took a chair back-to-back with his.

Fernando handed Dearborn a menu and walked away. After a speculative glance at his retreating figure, Dearborn concentrated his attention on what was going on behind him.

"I didn't know if I should cancel the lessons today," the man in tennis whites was saying.

"The guests are paying for tennis lessons," McAuley remonstrated. "There's no question of canceling."

The young man must be Stuart Ripple, the tennis pro. Benjamin had mentioned meeting him at Beggs's dinner party.

"The four of us were supposed to go to the jai alai tomorrow night," Stuart went on. "What do we do about that?"

"We go," the young woman said.

"Molly won't go."

"Of course she'll go. The funeral's tomorrow morning. If I know Molly, she won't be in widow's weeds beyond noontime."

"You've got a mean mouth, Bunny," McAuley informed her.

Bunny Fern, Dearborn registered, publicity and public relations.

"Don't be a hypocrite, Collis. You're no sadder about it than she is. I'll bet you're not even going to cancel the Valentine's party Friday."

"That's a hotel function. It's part of the guest program. Like the tennis lessons."

There was a pause and Stuart changed the subject, saying, "I'd never've pegged Leo for a suicide."

"You'd never've pegged him for a murderer," Bunny retorted.

"Keep your mouth shut about that," McAuley snapped.

"Everybody knows about it," Bunny said.

"No they don't. Only a few people know it. And that's all who have to know it. The official story is that Leo was sick and couldn't face up to it."

Dearborn grunted. Captain Niccoli had agreed not to aggravate an already sensitive situation. So far as Niccoli was concerned, the Louis Martin murder case would be marked closed and the report relegated to the files. Whatever explanation Molly Beggs gave out for publication concerning her husband's suicide would go unchallenged.

"I can't believe you can keep something like that quiet," Bunny said skeptically. "I'm not even sure it's right, letting somebody get away with murder."

"He didn't get away with it," McAuley reminded her.

"I suppose not," Bunny reconsidered, "and I guess nobody's mourning Louis Martin either."

"He got what he deserved," Stuart commented. "That con artist was only looking out for number one."

"Not like you, Stu," McAuley jibed.

"What do you mean by that?"

"You think I don't notice what goes on between you and the rich old ladies? It's not all game, set, and match, now is it?"

"Are you ready to order, sir?" a waiter asked Dearborn, sidling up to the table.

Dearborn tried to wave him away but he remained steadfast, smiling expectantly.

"Poached egg on toast," Dearborn said, "and tea."

"Rich old ladies are fair game," Stuart said smoothly.

"Orange juice, sir?"

Dearborn nodded impatiently and the waiter left.

"Maybe they are," McAuley conceded, a steely note creeping into his voice, "but Molly's not fair game, Stu."

"What's the matter?" Stuart returned snidely. "Afraid you might have to share the wealth?"

"You're sitting pretty," Bunny added, taking up the cudgel, "as of this morning."

"I've got nothing to gain by Leo's death," McAuley shot back.

"You were afraid Leo was going to toss you and Molly out, Collis," Bunny declared. "Molly told me that herself."

"Now," Stuart picked up, "you have your little girl all to yourself and your little girl has La Playa all to herself. You don't want anybody queering that, do you?"

"There's one thing you'd both better remember," McAuley declared. "I'm the one does the hiring and firing now." He pushed back his chair and Dearborn heard him walk away.

Dearborn strained to catch the next exchange. Stuart and Bunny had dropped their voices to a whisper.

"It's true," Stuart murmured, "he doesn't have to worry about Leo anymore."

"Nobody has to worry about Leo anymore, darling," Bunny said. "Or Louis Martin either."

"Yeah," Stuart said with satisfaction. "Like the song goes, from now on it's 'just Molly and me.'"

"Uh uh," Bunny disagreed. "It's 'just Molly and me and Bunny makes three.'"

"You really think she'll keep the date tomorrow night?"

"Sure she will, especially when you tell her I've dropped out and it'll only be you and her."

Dearborn restrained himself from turning to stare as they joined in a low conspiratorial laugh and clinked coffee cups.

_____ *134*

On his way out of the dining room Dearborn paused to speak to Fernando. "Fernando, you say you have Thursdays off?"

"Yes, sir."

"Would you be interested in going to the jai alai? I'm going tomorrow night."

"Well, I ..."

"I'd appreciate the company of an expert."

"I'm not sure that I should, Mr. Roycroft. I mean, under the circumstances ..."

"Nothing you can do here. I understand the funeral's going to be in the morning. The sooner life gets back to normal after that, the better."

Fernando nodded half-heartedly. "I do generally go to the jai alai on Thursday evenings...."

"That's settled, then. You live in town?"

"Yes, sir."

"We could meet at the main entrance to the fronton at eight. I'll expect to see you there. Don't change your mind now, Fernando. No ifs, ands, or buts."

Dearborn was admitted to the Beggses' apartment by Nico, who responded readily to Dearborn's sympathetic queries.

"Must have been a shock, Nico. I understand you were talking to Mrs. Beggs a moment before it happened."

"I wass going in the kitchen. Señora Beggs wass chost going op the stairs."

"You didn't run after her, Nico?"

"Concha, che grab my arm. Che dint wan me to go op. Because of the chot, you see. I hear the chot and then I hear Mrs. Beggs ronnin' and then I hear her scream."

"Terrible. Terrible experience, Nico."

"Burgess, is that you?" Cooky met Dearborn at the top of the stairs. Her eyes were swollen and her face, devoid of make-up, was sallow and puffy. In answer to Dearborn's solicitous inquiries she explained that she hadn't been to bed all night but that she'd eaten breakfast and would try to take a nap later.

"Pull yourself together, Cordelia," Dearborn advised. "There's nothing to be gained by making yourself ill."

"I know, but . . ." Her eyes filled with tears.

"Yes, yes, but you mustn't pamper yourself. You're a young girl. You've got a lot of spring. You'll survive this all right."

"I'm trying, Burgess. But Uncle Leo was . . ." Again her eyes filled with tears.

Molly came out of the bedroom. "Cooky," she said, "where's Norbie?"

"He went over to the Monsoon."

Molly shook her head in disgust. "He stinks. He really stinks. I wanted him to get the will out of Leo's wall safe. He's the only one who knows the combination."

"Why do we have to talk about Uncle Leo's will?" Cooky said dispiritedly. "My God, he just died, Molly."

Molly noticed Dearborn and walked over to hold out her hand. "Hello. Thanks for coming."

"May I extend my condolences, madam."

"I appreciate it."

Cooky shook her head. "I can't believe it," she declared. "I just can't believe it. I can't believe Uncle Leo would kill anyone." She appealed to Dearborn. "Did Uncle Leo look like the kind of man who would kill anyone?"

"What does a murderer look like, dear?" Molly interjected. "They don't wear badges, you know."

"That's awful." Cooky turned her back on Molly and walked across the room to stand near the terrace doors.

"Mrs. Beggs," Dearborn said, plunging purposefully ahead, "there is something disturbing me about your husband's death. It's tactless of me to bring it up, but it is something I thought of after I left here last night, and very frankly I have been brooding over it ever since."

"What's that?"

"When did your husband go downstairs and take the gun out of the gun cabinet? You said you left him in the bedroom and went down to the library for the television set and that as you were returning upstairs you heard the shot."

"Captain Niccoli asked me that too, right after you and Benjamin Pinch left."

"He did?" Dearborn tried to hide his disappointment. It wasn't something he'd expected Niccoli to pick up on.

"Leo got the gun yesterday morning," Molly answered. "After the robbery. He put it in the bedside table drawer. He wanted to be ready in case there was more trouble."

"I see," Dearborn mused. "In other words, the gun was not in the cabinet when you went downstairs for the television set."

"Of course not. It was in the bed table drawer. Otherwise how would Leo have gotten hold of it? I went downstairs, I picked up the TV, I spoke with Nico, I came back up."

"Tell me," Dearborn went on, abandoning all semblance of discretion, "did you suspect when you and your husband were in New York last week that he was contemplating violence, that he intended to seek out Louis Martin and kill him?"

"I wasn't in New York with my husband last week."

Dearborn turned to Cooky. "Didn't you say, Cordelia . . .?"

Cooky answered in a faintly puzzled voice, "No. I only said Uncle Leo was in New York."

"He went alone," Molly Beggs stated calmly. "I was here lending my father a hand in the office and keeping an eye on things. I haven't been to New York in ages."

"I misunderstood. I thought you were vacationing with him."

"I wasn't. Talking about vacations," Molly Beggs remarked, "I guess you've had your vacation spoiled by all this, Mr. Roycroft."

"One takes it as it comes."

"Do you intend to stay the rest of the week?"

"I'll stay a little longer."

"I'm really glad," Cooky said pathetically. "I'm glad to have someone to be with."

Dearborn visited with them for a few more minutes and then excused himself. He'd done his duty, and there was nothing more to be learned from Molly Beggs. It was a fortuitous exit, for as he walked down the first-floor corridor he heard a door open and close behind him and turned to see an elderly lady cross the hall and ring the Beggses' bell. Nico, who had just ushered Dearborn out, opened the door and Dearborn heard the lady announce herself as "Mrs. Juanita Froebel to see Mrs. Beggs."

It had been a close call and one that left Dearborn a bit shaken.

21

The funeral took place the following morning. The seaside cemetery with its circling gulls seemed more like a deserted beach than a burial ground and Dearborn, in his gray worsted traveling suit and city shoes, felt out of place among the shells and coral.

Molly Beggs stood at the edge of the grave, her hands clasped before her, her eyes fixed dully on the coffin. She was flanked by Norbert and Cooky, Norbert almost unrecognizable in a seersucker suit, shirt, and tie, and Cooky with a blotched and swollen face, worrying the belt of her dress, alternately twisting and smoothing it with nervous fingers.

Dearborn was relieved to find that Juanita Froebel had declined to attend, but Fernando Alvarez, the maître d', was there and so was Stuart Ripple, both looking appropriately somber. Bunny Fern was surreptitiously primping, tugging at the hem of her skirt and patting her hair, while Alberta Van Curl was clutching a string of prayer beads and mumbling a liturgical accompaniment to the priest's oration. Nico and Conchita, their shoulders touching, bowed their heads in silent prayer. Collis McAuley held himself stiffly and betrayed no sign of emotion, but whenever he looked at Molly his stony countenance softened.

There were others, onlookers who watched the proceedings from a discreet distance. Some were hotel guests, some were friends or acquaintances of Leo Beggs, and some were members of the press. Dearborn had seen press stickers on seven or eight windshields and had overheard one man identify himself as a reporter from the Miami *Herald*. He wondered how many more reporters there would have been had the true story come out.

The ceremonies over, there was jockeying for position as the priest took one of Molly's arms and Stuart Ripple made a dive for the other. Ripple was thwarted by Collis McAuley, who brushed him away and led Molly and the priest toward the head limousine. Ripple insinuated himself between Cooky and Norbert and began escorting them down the path, while Bunny Fern left hurriedly without stopping to speak with anyone, cutting across the cemetery toward the front gates, where she had parked her car. Fernando gathered up Conchita and Nico and herded them toward the road. Only Alberta Van Curl lagged behind, her bosom heaving with suppressed sobs, her prayer beads dangling from one limp hand.

"Are you all right, madam?" Dearborn inquired solicitously.

"I shall never be right."

"Allow me to accompany you to the car."

"I'm not going back with them."

She stressed the word "them" in a way that intrigued Dearborn and made him want to prolong the conversation. "I came by cab," he told her. "You are welcome to ride back with me."

"You're a friend of Cooky's, aren't you?"

"Yes, I am."

"Cooky is a good girl, the only one who never asked anything of Leo. She's just an innocent child. You must look out for her. We all must. She needs our friendship."

"I shall certainly do *my* best."

"Those vultures couldn't wait to bury poor Leo."

"Please, Miss Van Curl, allow me to escort you."

Dearborn wasted no time squiring her to the taxi stand a half block from the cemetery. He chose a cab with a glass partition between front and back, instructed the cab driver to take them to La Playa, then bundled Miss Van Curl into the back seat and curled his own long frame into a corner facing her. As the cab pulled away from the curb the funeral cortege of black limousines rolled past and Dearborn caught sight of Molly's pale face regarding him and Miss Van Curl with speculative eyes.

Once Dearborn and Miss Van Curl were settled, Dearborn attempted to revive the conversation by mentioning Cooky's name again, but Miss Van Curl seemed to have lost interest in Cooky. Instead, quite unexpectedly, she said, "I suppose it would surprise you to know that I was closer to Leo than anyone else at that funeral?"

"Is that so?"

"Leo and I were lovers," she confided.

Dearborn was taken aback. He gazed at her wonderingly.

"I know I'm not a beauty," she said, as if to forestall any suggestion that she were, "but then neither was Leo."

Dearborn thought it impolite to point out that Leo had attributes she lacked, namely power and money, so he merely nodded in what he hoped was a receptive fashion.

"And now he's gone," Miss Van Curl moaned, "out of my life forever."

Dearborn shouldn't have believed her but he did. There was something honest about the woman. She was emotional and affected, but her pale eyes were steady and she spoke with conviction.

"How long," Dearborn ventured delicately, "were you and he . . .er . . .?"

"For over a year."

"No one knew?"

"No. My apartment is just down the hall from Leo's. It was very convenient. Simple enough to come and go undetected."

"A year is a long time, madam."

"We had many things in common, Leo and I. The only

other person Leo felt comfortable with was Cooky, but he saw Cooky only occasionally and of course she's just a child. It isn't the same thing really."

Dearborn nodded sympathetically.

"We complemented one another, Leo and I. We enjoyed one another. We liked the same things. We shared so many pursuits. We worked jigsaw puzzles, read, watched the old movies, planned trips. Leo had never been out of the United States, you see. . . ." She sighed and lapsed into a melancholy reverie.

"I wonder," Dearborn remarked, in an effort to prod her back to the present, "that you and he didn't consider making the arrangement more binding."

"Marriage, you mean?" Miss Van Curl asked, recovering with a start. "We were going to get married."

"What?" Dearborn exclaimed. "You had actually made plans?"

"Leo celebrated his sixtieth birthday a few months ago. It changed him. Suddenly. Overnight. He told me he was going to get a divorce from Molly and marry me. Until then he hadn't considered it. It meant a great deal to him to have all the trappings that go with being rich and influential. That, of course, included a beautiful wife."

"I have heard rumors to the effect that Mrs. Beggs has, upon occasion, how shall I put it . . .?"

"Strayed?"

"Precisely."

"Yes but Leo strayed too. Even before we . . . Not with women like me—that is, not the type one would wish to marry, shall we say. Nevertheless he told me he felt he couldn't cast the first stone. But after Leo's birthday, when he'd made up his mind to get the divorce, then his attitude changed. Someone told Leo that Molly was seeing a man named Martin. Louis Martin. Leo made a great fuss over it. He was really furious. In a way he'd never been before about any of the others. He spied on Molly and one night he walked in on her and this man in their own bedroom."

"Flagrante delicto?"

"Leo had the man arrested for housebreaking. Then he

told him that if he cooperated with the divorce proceedings Leo would bail him out of jail and not press charges. Martin agreed. But when Leo had him released he ran away. Leo was furious. He hired someone to help find him."

"And did he find him?" Dearborn asked, curious to see how much Miss Van Curl actually knew.

"I think not. He didn't tell me he had. But that isn't important. What matters is that we were going to get married anyway. Leo decided to make a settlement on Molly, give her whatever he had to. He knew it would be hard getting her to agree to something reasonable, but he was willing to go as far as he had to. He hadn't ever been in love with Molly. That is why he was able to put up with all those unsavory episodes. But once he decided he wanted the divorce he couldn't bear having her around any longer. They fought. They fought about it just the other day. All day from what I understand."

Dearborn recalled the scene in the garden between Leo and Molly Beggs. He wondered if that had been what it was about.

"But they did settle it," Miss Van Curl continued. "And Tuesday evening Leo came to my apartment to make plans. Leo wanted a real wedding. He was in excellent spirits." She sniffled and took the handkerchief Dearborn held out to her. "Little did I know it was the last I would see of poor Leo." She looked over at Dearborn and said abruptly and vehemently, "She killed him."

Dearborn was startled. "You are speaking figuratively, are you?"

"No. I am not. She shot him. I know what I'm saying. She decided she wanted more than a divorce settlement. Leo's will leaves La Playa to her. That's what she's after."

"Molly Beggs did not shoot her husband," Dearborn said firmly. "Of that I am certain. She had been speaking with Nico downstairs a few seconds before the shot was fired. She hadn't even reached the bedroom door when it happened."

But Miss Van Curl remained adamant. "Leo was happy. He was well. There was no reason whatsoever for him to kill himself."

Molly Beggs might be innocent, but Miss Van Curl had presented a good case for murder, Dearborn thought to himself. On the other hand, she had also presented a good argument in favor of suicide. A man, romantically involved, anticipating marriage and the start of a new life, hears that he is to be arrested for murder. What better reason for pulling the trigger? The question now was which explanation was the correct one.

"What if I were to tell you, Miss Van Curl, that Leo Beggs did have something to be despondent over?"

"I wouldn't believe you."

They were crossing the causeway separating La Playa from the mainland. Dearborn would have to talk fast. "What would you say if I told you not only that Leo Beggs had located Louis Martin but that he had killed Louis Martin?"

Miss Van Curl bounced back aginst the car cushion. "What do you mean? How can you say that?"

"I hope you will keep what I am about to tell you in the strictest confidence. The New York police have been investigating the case. Louis Martin was killed last week and the police suspected Mr. Beggs. They were about to arrest him."

"Leo wouldn't hurt a fly!" Miss Van Curl trumpeted.

"Flies are not at issue."

"How do *you* know about it?"

"By sheer accident I happened to be in company with the police when the tragedy occurred. Molly Beggs knew her husband was going to be arrested. Apparently she told him about it."

"How did she know?"

"It's an involved story, Miss Van Curl, but it appeared to be so upsetting to Mr. Beggs that he took his life rather than face the possibility of prison."

"It's insane! Leo would no more have killed Louis Martin than he would kill himself! He had no reason. He was perfectly willing to have Molly go off with Louis Martin. He only wanted to find Martin in order to name him corespondent!"

It was a good point and, if the rest of Miss Van Curl's story

_____ *143*

held up, a logical one. It was also one that had already occurred to Dearborn, but this wasn't the time to say so.

"I will not believe it," Miss Van Curl declared dramatically. "I will not accept it! A suicide? A murderer? Not my Leo!"

Her puckered, scowling face was defiant, and there shone through the pale unlovely eyes a passion that touched Dearborn and made him more determined than ever to ferret out the truth.

22

"I told you I prefer to travel by train."

"The train's out, Dad," Benjamin informed Dearborn. "Unless there's a cancellation I can't get anything until Monday."

"Monday will be fine."

"That's four days off. I didn't think you'd want to wait that long. I got lucky with the airlines. I got a three o'clock flight today."

"Tourist class?"

"First class."

"Unacceptable."

"Why? You travel first class on ships."

"On shipboard the difference between first class and tourist is more than a free glass of champagne."

"Oh, shit."

Dearborn, in bathing trunks, bathing slippers, and a generous layer of Bain de Soleil, was reclining on a chaise longue near the pool. He was giving a fair impression of indolence despite the fact that the notebook he'd hastily shoved under his derrière was pressing against the tip of his spine. "I shall remain here until Monday and go home by train. I intend to enjoy a few days of relaxation, Benjamin. There's that celebration tomorrow evening—"

"The Valentine's party? Since when have you become a partygoer?"

"I need to rest after all the recent unpleasantness. Which reminds me. Have you seen Mr. Baki? I expected him to show up at the funeral. One would think..." Dearborn suddenly craned his neck to peer over Benjamin's shoulder and then said urgently, "Benjamin, move over a little. Get between me and the red and yellow umbrella over there."

"What for?" Benjamin twisted his head to look behind him.

"Isn't that Juanita Froebel? The one in the diaphanous bloomers?"

Benjamin nodded. "It's okay. She's going the other way."

Dearborn sat up and watched Juanita, svelte and cool-looking in pale blue chiffon beach pajamas and matching head-band, sashay across the pool patio and disappear through the doors leading into the coffee shop.

"She must have been beautiful," Benjamin said. "In fact, she's still beautiful."

"She looks as wacky as ever to me," Dearborn said caustically. "Sent Old Orville into an early grave. Liver trouble. Did I ever tell you about that?"

"Just the other day."

"Bears repeating. There's a lesson in it. There's no end of damage a woman can do to a man if she sets her mind to it."

"You're not going to begin complaining about Mom again, are you?" Benjamin asked. "If so, I'm going."

"Good idea, Benjamin. I'd like to pop into the pool before it gets too chilly."

After Benjamin left, Dearborn returned to consulting his notebook. "System is everything," he murmured. Given a particular set of problems with a corresponding set of theories and proofs, he felt that he must inevitably come up with the correct resolution.

He squinted up at the Beggses' second-floor windows. The garden entrance to the apartment was on the opposite side of the Cloister wing. From here he could see only the rear bedroom windows. The vertical blinds were open and someone inside was rhythmically bending and rising and bending again. Dearborn continued to watch until the calisthenics ceased and the figure approached the window and paused to open the blinds. It was Molly Beggs wearing tan leotards so near her own flesh tone that she appeared almost naked. She reached out of sight for a towel and began rubbing her face and neck with it while she gazed out the window. That she didn't look the part of the bereft widow was not surprising. However, Dearborn thought, Leo Beggs wasn't the only loss she'd sustained during the past week. One would expect that if she weren't mourning Leo she would be mourning Louis Martin.

As Dearborn squinted upward he saw Molly smile and wave. For a moment he thought she was waving at him. Then he noticed Stuart Ripple climbing out of the pool and saluting Molly with a discreetly lifted hand. A second later Bunny Fern's head rose over the edge of the ladder and she climbed out of the water.

Dearborn wasn't close enough to hear Stuart's voice, but he read his lips. "It's Molly," Stuart said, nudging Bunny with his elbow.

Bunny shrugged and Stuart nudged her again. She raised her hand and waved, then pulled off her bathing cap and walked away, hips swaying arrogantly. Bunny's figure, Dearborn noted appreciatively, was ample, a lavish cushioning of firm, well-proportioned flesh. Not one of those stick bodies with no breasts or backside. She reminded Dearborn of the pulchritudinous Emmylou, and he suffered a twinge of remorse at having decided to delay his departure from La Playa. If it weren't for his uncompromising need to tie up loose ends he could soon be with Emmylou in Boise. But no use brooding over it. One couldn't alter one's character no matter how one might long to.

"Bitch," a petulant voice murmured. Dearborn twisted his head to look behind him. He found himself gazing into Norbert's disagreeable countenance. Norbert was wearing suede leggings, a fringed chamois shirt, cambric neckerchief, felt slouch hat, and bass fiddle. He stood out among the naked sun worshipers like an eskimo among Hottentots.

"Norbert?" Dearborn called, drawing Norbert's attention away from Molly.

There was no alteration in Norbert's expression as he shifted his eyes to Dearborn. "You still here?" he asked rudely.

"May I speak with you for a moment, Norbert?"

"The Musk."

"Come again?"

"The Musk. My name is The Musk." Norbert and his bass fiddle rolled themselves over to Dearborn's lounge chair.

"I hope you won't take it amiss," Dearborn said tactfully, "but I am somewhat concerned over your cousin Cordelia."

"How come?"

"She's taking your father's death very hard. I'm sure you are too." Dearborn regarded Norbert's disgruntled expression dubiously. "In your own way, naturally." Dearborn dropped his voice. "However, Cordelia seems particularly disturbed by the thought that your father might have eliminated Louis Martin."

"What do you mean, might have?" Norbert didn't seem to feel compelled to lower his voice to match Dearborn's.

"You think your father shot Louis Martin, then?" Dearborn asked. "I was hoping that I could offer some solace to Cordelia, tell her that there might be some doubt about it."

"Listen," Norbert returned sullenly, "Martin deserved it. He thought he'd conned Molly into taking my father for everything."

"Conned?" Dearborn repeated interestedly. Stuart Ripple had used the same word in relation to Louis Martin.

"Martin hung out at the Keyboard," Norbert went on, "a joint over on Cabinet Street. A friend of mine who works there told me about him. He was a crumb from the word go. My friend told me what he was after. It was a five-letter word beginning with M, but it wasn't Molly."

"You think Mrs. Beggs was victimized by Martin?"

"I said Martin thought he'd conned her. Nobody cons Molly. If I know my stepmother, she was using Martin just as much as he was using her. That's what I told my father."

Dearborn picked up on the inadvertent admission. "You were the one who gave the show away, eh?"

"If you think I feel guilty about it, you're crazy. I got this straight from my friend. Once in a while Molly works in the office. My friend told me Martin figured out this scheme to siphon out money from the hotel by fooling with the books. He had Molly all ready to do it. You think I wasn't going to tell my old man about it?"

"On the contrary, Norbert."

"The Musk."

"I would say that you did exactly what should have been done. And when, may I ask, did all this occur?"

"A few months ago. I gave him the news on his birthday. It was a birthday present."

"I see. Not the kind of gift he might have chosen himself, but appreciated nonetheless."

"I don't want to get into any heavy discussions about it, okay?"

"I understand. But you think that was when your father decided to kill Martin, do you?"

"Sure it was. My old man was a crack shot. Shooting Martin was the first thing he probably thought of. He should of shot Molly, too, while he was about it."

"I hear you are also a crack shot?"

"Yeah, but I shoot at targets, not at people. That's where my father and me parted company."

"I hope you won't take this amiss," Dearborn said, "but I am under the impression that you and your father held differing opinions on many subjects."

"Cooky's been talking to you, right?"

"Yes, she has."

"Well, tell her to mind her own business."

"Is it true?" Dearborn asked bluntly.

"What difference does it make? What's the use of talking about it now? The old man's dead."

Norbert was through being interviewed. He hitched up his bass fiddle and clattered off, leaving Dearborn to puzzle over his look of fury . . . or was it, after all, a look of grief?

Dearborn ran into Cooky coming out of the Beggses' door carrying a manila envelope. She had changed out of her funeral clothes, but in khaki slacks and a gray sweat shirt she looked no less drab. "Were you swimming?" she asked wistfully.

"I was. Why don't you go in for a dip?"

"I couldn't. It wouldn't be right with all the guests watching."

"Nonsense. No reason to walk around with a long face. The obsequies are over, the interment has taken place, the spirit has passed into the ether, so to speak."

"I could go somewhere away from the hotel," she proposed hopefully.

"What have you got in mind?"

"Fernando told me you and he are going to jai alai tonight. I've never seen a jai alai game."

"I'm not sure that's so wise, Cordelia."

"But you said yourself I shouldn't sit around with a long face. Molly told me she's going to visit some friend, Norbie will be over at the Monsoon. I don't want to be by myself."

Dearborn was trapped. There was nothing to do but invite her. "All right, Cordelia, but I don't think you should mention the jai alai to your aunt."

"I'll tell her you're taking me to the movies."

Fine, Dearborn thought. What he would do when they got to the jai alai and found Molly there with Stuart Ripple, he couldn't imagine, but he'd face that predicament when it occurred. "What have you got there?" he asked Cooky, eyeing the manila envelope with interest.

"I have to take it to the front office. Molly wants her father to lock it in the office safe. It's a copy of Uncle Leo's will."

Dearborn's curious expression turned to greed. It was a fat envelope with the name of a law firm imprinted on one corner. It was also, he noted, sealed with a small strip of transparent tape. "Why don't you let me do that for you? I was going to the desk anyway."

"You were not. I just saw you starting up the back stairs."

"I was about to retrace my steps. Forgot my key." Dearborn pulled out his bathrobe pockets and slapped himself here and there to illustrate the point.

Cooky handed him the envelope. "Okay, thanks, Burgess."

"Cordelia," Dearborn ventured, with a pained look at her shapeless sweat shirt, "am I correct in recalling that tomorrow is your birthday?"

"It's my birthday all right. I'm doing my best to forget about it. It's not going to be any fun this year."

"In honor of your birthday I want you to go into the shopping annex to that ladies' apparel shop—what's the name of it?"

"The Feminine Touch."

"Yes. And outfit yourself head to toe. Tell them to charge it to me."

"I couldn't do that."

"And you are to make similar arrangements with the hairdresser."

"Burgess, what would people say? I mean, with Uncle Leo's funeral this morning? How would it look?"

"I'm more concerned with how *you* look," Dearborn began to say, when a clicking sound attracted his attention to the back stairway. He turned. The click wasn't repeated but Dearborn held up his hand and tiptoed toward the foot of the stairs. He heard soft footfalls ascending.

"What's the matter?" Cooky asked.

"Nothing," Dearborn replied, his head still cocked.

But Cooky went to investigate, springing lightly up the steps and rounding the bend. There was heavy thudding on the corridor overhead and then a moment later the sound of someone coming down the main staircase behind Dearborn. He went rapidly back down the corridor, but by the time he reached the foot of the front stairs, Cooky, her hand held up to her heaving breast, was already halfway down. "He . . . he . . . got away."

"Did you see who it was?"

"Yup."

"Well, who was it?"

"Mr. Baki. Carrying his bola. That's what was clicking."

Dearborn was indignant. "Indulging in another one of his little adventures? I wondered where he's been the last day or two. Must be playing at guerrilla warfare again. The man is as mad as a hatter. I tell you he should not be permitted to roam around loose."

"What would've happened to us if we hadn't met him at Shell Cove, Burgess? Without him we wouldn't 've had a dry place to stay or food or water or blankets, or—"

"Booby traps," Dearborn picked up bitterly. "Let us not forget the booby traps. I tell you the man is a menace."

 23

Dearborn examined the will in the privacy of a booth in the men's room. He made no attempt to read it through. It was long, couched in legalese jargon for which he had no patience, and was for the most part concerned with matters that didn't pertain. What did interest him was what portion of his worldly goods Leo Beggs had assigned to the various members of his immediate circle and, more important, whether or not he had bothered within the last three months to alter his will to the detriment of Molly Beggs. So far as Dearborn was concerned, everything rested on that fact.

And apparently Molly was still heir to La Playa. The will was two years old, but there were recently dated notes and business papers stuck into the envelope that dealt with legal matters Beggs had evidently meant to take up with his lawyers at a future meeting. It wasn't surprising that Beggs hadn't yet altered his will. He had been in good health and had no reason to suppose he wouldn't continue to be in good health. But it was probable, Dearborn thought ironically, that he had paid for his procrastination with his life.

The will told all. Upon Beggs's death Molly Beggs inherited the bulk of the estate, including La Playa. Norbert was to receive two million dollars in moneys and stock. Cordelia was to get moneys and stock amounting to a quarter of a million dollars with the additional promise of a wedding settlement in the form of a trust fund amounting to another hundred thousand dollars. Alberta Van Curl was to inherit the complex of apartments called the Silver Beach Cottages, and there was a provision leaving Collis McAuley Beggs's gun collection and his boat, a craft described as a thirty-eight-foot cabin cruiser with twin 330-horsepower engines, named the *Seasprite*. Dearborn didn't know to the penny what such a craft would be worth, but he had seen the boat docked at the marina and estimated that a hundred thousand dollars would not be too steep a price tag.

There were twenty or thirty smaller individual bequests to employees in various of Beggs's enterprises, including La Playa. Most of the names were unknown to Dearborn, but he did see that Nico and Conchita were remembered to the tune of five thousand dollars each and he was amazed to see that Fernando Alvarez, the maître d', was to be the recipient of a twenty-thousand-dollar bequest. Cooky had not exaggerated when she said her uncle had liked Fernando. If anything she had, understated the case.

Assuming that Leo Beggs had been murdered, the will provided evidence that there were numerous people who stood to benefit from his death. Norbert, Molly, Cordelia, Alberta Van Curl, Collis McAuley, Fernando Alvarez, and a veritable army of employees were substantially better off than they had been a few days before.

But most of the people named in the will, Dearborn was certain, had never heard of, much less known, Louis Martin, and there was a connection between the death of Leo Beggs and the death of Louis Martin. The murderer had counted on Louis Martin's murder to make Leo Beggs's suicide appear bona fide. He had to have known that Leo Beggs was about to be arrested. And he could have learned that from only one source, Molly Beggs. The conclusion was that there had been two people responsible for Leo Beggs's murder, and one of them was Molly Beggs. A conspiracy. Collusion of one sort or another.

Molly had set up the murder, created the opportunity, and protected herself with an alibi.

She had made sure that Nico would see her seconds before the shot was fired while she was still too far from the bedroom to have fired it. The murderer must still have been there when Dearborn, Benjamin, and Captain Niccoli burst into the bedroom. No one searched the room. There had been no reason. Had they thought to open the closet doors . . .

Dearborn lifted his head to gaze, trancelike, into space. If they had traversed the terrace to enter the Beggses' bedroom, someone else could have left the same way. After Benjamin had carried Molly Beggs into the living room and Dearborn and Niccoli had followed, Niccoli had closed the bedroom door. That may inadvertently have permitted the murderer to come out of hiding and leave undetected by the terrace. Dearborn recalled the rolling table in his living room. It might have been pushed aside not by someone entering the suite but rather by someone leaving.

With Molly as the pivotal figure, the facts fell easily into place. Dearborn had believed, from the moment his suspicions were aroused, that she was capable of murder. Everything he'd seen and learned during these last few days bore it out. She was cold-blooded, insatiably greedy, an opportunist, selfish, a sneak, as her succession of secret lovers attested, and the one person able to manipulate the circumstances to suit the requirements.

But Molly couldn't commit the murder herself. She would have been too obvious a suspect. The only way she could commit murder and get away with it was by planning it with an accomplice. But who? It had to have been someone who also stood to gain, directly or indirectly, by Beggs's death, someone close enough to Molly Beggs to trust her and to be trusted by her, and someone equally daring and equally heartless.

Dearborn put the manila envelope directly into Collis Mc-Auley's hand with the suggestion that he transfer the contents since the sealing tape didn't appear to adhere as it should.

The ten minutes he'd spent sitting on the cold toilet seat in the men's room had given him a chill. He was eager to get upstairs and into a warm bath. It was probably his physical discomfort that sent him recklessly bounding across the lobby without thought as to who might be wandering around, and when his path was unexpectedly blocked by a twirling parasol thrust against his chest and a soft voice crying, *"Arrêtez!"* he stopped short with an alarmed grunt. The parasol was lowered and he found himself face to face with Juanita Froebel, looking devastating in white silk and pearls. He fell back a step, considering the possibility of bolting around the fountain, but realized it was too late for retreat.

"Buggy!" Juanita exclaimed. "I've been looking all over for you."

Dearborn stalled for time. "Who are you, madam? I don't recall our having been introduced."

"I should hope we've been introduced." She snapped shut her parasol and used the handle to poke Dearborn gently in the ribs. "What does this remind you of, Buggy?" She recited a limerick that Dearborn had never heard before but that relied heavily for its humor on an alliterative rhyme for cumulonimbus.

"It reminds me that I have never been fond of obscene verse with no artistic merit."

"It doesn't remind you of Paris? Of that little *pension* on the Left Bank?"

Dearborn realized that he couldn't go on playing the innocent. If he wanted her to think he was Burgess Roycroft, he would have to offer some sign of recognition. "You aren't..." he declared in an astounded voice, "you aren't..."

"Yes I am, Buggy. Juanita!"

"Well, well, I should have guessed. You are certainly as . . . er . . . stylish as ever."

"And you, Buggy, are as dashing as ever, although I must admit I don't remember you being quite so tall."

"You recognized me, did you?"

"I saw you night before last. Your young friend told me who you are. Cordelia Gillette, I have since discovered."

Dearborn was grateful for the power of suggestion. "How is it I didn't see you?"

"I was outside when the helicopter landed. I thought I knew you. I said to myself, 'I know that man,' and when I learned it was you I said to myself, 'He hasn't changed a whit since I saw him in Paris.' And you haven't."

"You put me at a disadvantage, Juanita. I suppose I should have known you, too. Perhaps I'm not so sharp as I once was."

Juanita waggled an admonitory finger at him. "I don't believe that, Buggy. I don't believe that for a moment. I saw that young woman you were with. It doesn't look to me as if you've lost any of your faculties."

Dearborn felt uncomfortably clammy, not all of the clamminess external. "Cordelia is just a child, Juanita."

Juanita winked. "As sly as ever, Buggy. Where are you going? Would you like to join me for afternoon tea?"

There's nothing I'd like better, Juanita, but there are matters I must attend to. Perhaps we shall run into one another again."

"Run into one another? Why, Buggy, I do believe you're still hurt over my leaving Paris without saying good-bye. I'm really surprised. You were never one to hold a grudge. You knew yourself it would never last. Heavens, if you'd ever for one moment believed I was serious you'd have run away from me."

Dearborn was not one to ignore an opportunity. Here was his chance to offer up a legitimate excuse for avoiding Juanita in future. "You take rather a light view of breaking a gentleman's heart."

"Breaking your heart?" Her delighted peal of laughter

brought smiles to the faces nearby. "You were already carrying on with Violetta Lamarque and her brother."

"Her mother?" Dearborn repeated in a perplexed voice.

"Her mother too? I didn't even know about her mother. I thought Schuyler Possevino was her mother's lover. Well there, you see, you couldn't have been prostrated by my leaving, with a whole family of Lamarques to occupy your time."

"I take exception to your casual view of the matter. I may have forgiven you for decamping but you cannot expect me to resume our friendship after your unconventional behavior."

"You're a fine one to criticize me for being unconventional. What could be more unconventional than Siamese twins?"

"What have Siamese twins got to do with this?"

"Surely you remember Allegra and Cantata?"

Dearborn recognized that he was on shaky ground. He wasn't sure what it was safe to have forgotten and what was not. "Listen here, Juanita, I'd like to go on talking but I haven't the time."

"Then shall we lunch together tomorrow, Buggy?"

"I have a full schedule tomorrow. Can't do it. As a matter of fact, I don't know when I can do it."

"That's too bad. Nothing seems to be going right for me. I no sooner arrived on Monday than there was an awful incident in the dining room. Now poor Mr. Beggs has dispatched himself."

"Unfortunate affair," Dearborn agreed. "Shocking. I understand the man wasn't well."

"Oh, that's hogwash. He killed himself because of his wife."

Dearborn regarded Juanita with surprise. "What makes you say that?"

"He and I had quite a little chat the other evening. I attended a small soiree in his apartment. Mr. Beggs was a diamond in the rough, don't you think? Or didn't you know him? Rather gruff and belligerent, but cast in the hero's mold. At least, that's how I found him. He escorted me back to my suite after the party. He told me his wife is having an affair with someone. Some man from New York, I believe. Name of Lawrence or Lionel or Louis."

"Louis Martin?" Dearborn offered encouragingly.

"How did *you* know, Buggy?"

"Grapevine."

"Cordelia Gillette. Of course. Well, Mr. Beggs told me that his wife had been pretending she'd broken off the affair but that he knew better. He said he had just discovered that very day that the affair was still going on and that he fully intended to do something about it."

"When was this, Juanita?"

"I told you, Buggy. Monday evening. And you see, he did do something about it, although, heaven knows, I think he did a little too much about it. If he was going to kill someone I should think he would have been better off killing Louis Martin than killing himself."

"What prompted him to confide in you? In his cups, was he?"

"Not at all. There was a very handsome young man at the dinner party. Mr. Beggs's wife was flirting outrageously with him. You know I'm not a shrinking violet, Buggy. I took it upon myself to caution Mr. Beggs. I thought he hadn't noticed. But he had. He told me some very unkind stories about his wife. I didn't say so, but I really rather empathized with her in some respects since I once lived through the similar experience of having a husband many years my senior. One does tend to long for greener pastures."

"Orville was a year or two younger than you, I thought, Juanita?"

"Not Orville, Yataro. My fourth husband."

"You've been married four times, Juanita? But why go on calling yourself Froebel?"

"I prefer Froebel to Ujejski, Byngo, or Hiroshige. Can you imagine being called Byngo? I jumped every time anyone addressed me by name. Anyhoo . . . I shouldn't have wanted to hurt Mr. Beggs's feelings or alienate him in any way, so I said nothing at all about that. Mr. Beggs went from a discussion of

Benjamin Pinch—that's the young man Mrs. Beggs was paying so much attention to. Son of Dearie Pinch, as a matter of fact. Do you remember him, Buggy?"

"Vaguely."

"Mr. Beggs went from a discussion of Benjamin Pinch to a discussion of Louis Martin, and that's how it came out."

"Beggs said he had just found out that day that the affair was still going on? How did he discover it?"

"I have no idea. He didn't say. I suppose that someone told him. How else would he have discovered it?"

"I don't know," Dearborn said. "It's something I shall have to think about."

"I would prefer you would think about lunch tomorrow, Buggy. If you refuse, I think I shall have to camp on your doorstep until you change your mind."

She would too, Dearborn thought. She had always been wanting in discretion. If anything, the years seemed to have aggravated the condition. "All right, Juanita. Tomorrow, then. One o'clock in the coffee shop."

"The dining room serves much better food."

"The dining room, then."

"Marvelous. Be prepared to tell me everything about your life, Buggy, from where Allegra and Cantata left off up until the present."

24

Leo Beggs, a week after Louis Martin was killed, believed that Louis Martin was alive. If Juanita Froebel had told Dearborn the truth, and there was no reason to doubt it, then Leo Beggs had not killed Louis Martin.

Dearborn, reclining in his tub, his head cushioned by a folded bath towel, his eyes closed, all but his shoulders and knees submerged beneath the warm water, wrestled with that extraordinary fact.

Leo Beggs had not killed Louis Martin.

And if Leo Beggs had not killed Louis Martin, then who *had* killed Louis Martin?

The answer was chillingly obvious. Louis Martin's death had been preliminary to the main event, part of a plan in which one man was murdered in order to camouflage the second murder. Whoever had killed Leo Beggs had also killed Louis Martin.

Why? Why so convoluted and risky a scheme? It seemed unreasonable and unnecessary. The plot had a Tom Sawyer quality, a kind of "What's the good of a plan if it ain't got no trouble in it" logic that baffled him. No matter how he turned it, tilted it, disassembled and reassembled it, it made no sense.

But, understand it or not, he accepted it and, accepting it, he would be able to turn it to good use. He would not just be looking now for someone with a motive, he would be looking for someone without an alibi.

Dearborn stretched out his arm and plucked his wristwatch from the sink. Six-thirty. He and Cooky were to meet Fernando at the fronton at eight. They would have to leave La Playa at seven-thirty. That gave him an hour to dress and dine. He climbed out of the tub, dried himself, and put on his terry robe. There wouldn't be time to eat in the dining room or even in the coffee shop. He would have to order from room service.

He padded barefoot into the bedroom and made the call, ordering broiled red snapper, wild rice, and pineapple custard, with a bottle of wine from Malescot-St- Exupéry as a stimulant to his frazzled nerves. Dinner taken care of, he examined his wardrobe. Dearborn had never attended a jai alai game and he wasn't sure how informal a note should be struck, but he decided on taupe flannel trousers, cream and beige silk shirt, rust mohair overshirt, and beige and rust cravat, a conservative combination with a touch of distinction. He would dress after he'd eaten.

It was quarter to seven when room service arrived. Dearborn heard the knock and went to admit the waiter. There was a piece of paper lying on the carpet just inside the door, and he leaned down to pick it up. Damned fool. That deranged foreigner was at it again. The handwriting was almost indecipherable, but it was Baki's work all right. Dearborn held it at arm's length.

> BEGGS DID NOT DIED IN VAIN,
> MY FRIEND ROYCRAP.
> VIVA CUBA.
> R.B.

"Good God!" Dearborn exclaimed. "What has taken hold of the man?" He crossed to the coffee table and flung down the piece of paper, then returned to open the door.

Before he reached it he saw the door knob turn. "Just a moment," he called out. "I'm coming."

The sound of a key being inserted into the lock caused Dearborn to halt in his tracks. Surely room service didn't carry keys to the rooms. It dawned on him that it might be Baki, following up his communiqué with an invasion. He fumed at the outrage. "I shall call the management, sir!"

There was a telephone on the coffee table, but Dearborn decided to call from the bedroom, behind locked doors. Who knew what that madman had in mind. He turned, hurried toward the bedroom, and was crossing the threshold when behind him he heard the whoosh of a silencer and saw the bullet smash into the door jamb.

"I don't think we should call in the police," Collis McAuley said. "I think a doctor could handle it."

"The bughouse," Dearborn said tartly. "He has bats in the belfrey. That bullet might have struck me."

"Why did he pick on you?" McAuley asked. "Except for handing out propaganda leaflets and holing up in the public toilets, he hasn't bothered any of the guests. He's certainly never tried to hurt anyone."

"I told Leo a hundred times," Molly declared, "that the man is getting crazier every day."

"But he's never tried to hurt anyone, Molly," her father maintained.

"There's a first time for everything. He shouldn't be allowed to carry a gun."

"I agree with you there, darlin'. I don't know where he got it. But I told the security guards to hold him in his room under lock and key."

McAuley was sitting on Dearborn's couch holding the note from Baki. Molly Beggs sat next to him, and Dearborn, dressed in his taupe flannels, sat opposite eating his newly arrived dinner, but with no great relish. "Baki," he said "believes, perhaps because he was introduced to me by Mr. Beggs, that I am sympathetic to his cause. He has befriended me, his friendship taking the form of my inclusion into his rather bizarre fun and games. Added to that is the fact that I seem to have encouraged him, quite unintentionally of course, in some misapprehension regarding Mr. Beggs's demise."

"Say again?" inquired McAuley.

"I am the one who informed Baki of Mr. Beggs's death. He misinterpreted my explanation to mean that Mr. Beggs had been shot rather than that he had shot himself."

As Dearborn offered this declaration he noted with interest Molly's almost imperceptible start and her warily narrowed eyes.

"It doesn't account for his shooting at you, does it?" McAuley asked.

"He was not trying to kill me," Dearborn said flatly. "You can tell that by his note. I am quite certain of that. He was play-acting. He has fantasized an epic masterpiece with a cast of two, necessitating some doubling in brass. In other words he is playing both villain and hero. As am I."

"The man's loony all right," McAuley conceded, "but I don't want to cause a panic among the guests by spreading it

_____ *161*

around that he's gone berserk. We'll keep him locked up until we can get help."

The telephone rang and Dearborn answered. It was one of the security guards. He handed the phone to McAuley, who listened with a worried look on his face and then said, "All right. Meet me back downstairs in the office in ten minutes." He hung up.

"What did he say?" Molly asked.

"Baki's gone."

"Gone? You mean he's not in his suite? Well, he must be hiding on the grounds."

McAuley picked up the phone and called the front desk. "Stan? McAuley here. Listen, have you seen Baki anywhere around? All right. Thanks." He put down the receiver. "Stan says he hasn't seen Baki for a couple of days. He's been staying in his suite, ordering all his meals from room service."

"He couldn't have gotten far," Molly commented. "You'd better call Joe Powell."

"I'd like to see if we can find him ourselves first, Molly. If we don't get him in the next couple of hours, then I'll call Joe."

"I wouldn't wait too long," Dearborn cautioned, "especially now that Baki seems to have acquired a weapon."

"The guards have weapons too, Mr Roycroft. And seeing hotel guards around won't cause a panic like seeing a load of cops swarming all over the grounds." McAuley searched Dearborn's face. "I'm going to be honest with you, Mr. Roycroft. We've got a situation on our hands here. We're willing to consider anything within reason. It goes without saying that you won't be billed when you leave. Anything else we can do in the way of compensation . . ."

"I do not intend to take action," Dearborn assured him. "I am aware of the fact that you are passing through a time of crisis and I see no reason to add to it by instituting a lawsuit or demanding monetary satisfaction. I am also reluctant to attract undue publicity to myself."

McAuley's relief was evident. "What can I say except thanks. I'll leave a man in the hall until we get him."

"No guard," Dearborn returned. "In the first place, I shall

be out all evening and no doubt you shall have captured Baki by the time I return; and in the second place, the quickest way to arouse comment and curiosity would be to have sentries trotting up and down the corridor. Don't you agree?"

"Where are your new duds?" Dearborn asked in an accusatory tone.

Cooky was dressed in blue overalls, a red-,white-, and green-striped polo shirt, and sneakers. Her hair was teased into an exaggerated Afro, and her makeup was as thick as ever.

"I couldn't, Burgess. I just couldn't. People might misunderstand. About Uncle Leo, I mean. Because, well, you know. Because he left me money. They might think I was ... well, glad about it. I just couldn't."

"What's the difference what people think?" Dearborn demanded. "Why worry about it?"

"I'm sorry, Burgess."

"I think you should wash some of that glaze off your face. There are other ways to attract attention."

"Name one."

"We shall discuss that en route."

"What's that around your neck, Burgess? A camera?"

"Opera glasses," Dearborn informed her. "I bought them in the drugstore this afternoon. Not a very good pair, but they'll do."

Dearborn had rented a chauffeured car. They pulled up in front of the fronton at eight forty-five and Fernando, who had been pacing anxiously back and forth, sprinted over.

"My apologies," Dearborn called through the car window. "No telephone here. Nothing I could do to get in touch with you."

As Fernando opened the car door he looked past Dearborn and saw Cooky. "I'm glad you decided to come, Miss Gillette." His manner was cordial and formal, the perfect extension of his maître d' persona.

"Hi, Fernando. I didn't recognize you in street clothes."

Fernando's appearance was certainly altered. Like many

of the men around him he was wearing the Cuban guayabera and slacks, the casual clothes somehow even more flattering to his dark good looks than the dinner clothes he customarily wore.

Dearborn had picked Cooky up late, passing off his delay as the result of an urgent business call from New York. Now he did the same with Fernando, who accepted the excuse graciously.

Dearborn dismissed the chauffeur and Fernando excused himself to exchange the two tickets he held for three, insisting over Dearborn's objections that the tickets were his contribution to the occasion. He guided Dearborn and Cooky past the ticket taker into the central betting area, a crowded room dominated by betting and cashiers' windows and strategically placed closed-circuit television sets suspended from the ceiling.

The fronton was jammed and already littered with cigarette butts, empty Styrofoam cups, candy wrappers, and discarded tickets. There was a dimly lit bar at one end of the room near the restrooms, a hamburger stand, an ice cream and cold drink counter, and numerous dispensing machines, and according to Fernando there were additional betting areas on either side of the auditorium for the general-admission patrons, those without seats, who could watch the action live from the sidelines.

Fernando purchased three programs and three stubby pencils and herded Cooky and Dearborn to their seats, situated in the first row of the elevated tier back of the orchestra section. Fernando explained that although these were not the most expensive seats in the house—the first two rows of the orchestra were furnished with upholstered armchairs and prices to match—these were the most advantageously placed, affording the best overall view of the court.

Dearborn was not completely recovered from his unnerving encounter with Raúl Baki, but he was determined not to let it interfere with the evening's activities. He was there for a purpose and he meant to carry it out. The seats Fernando had chosen were well suited to his intentions. "Fine," he murmured, patting the leather case slung around his neck. "Splendid. I shall be able to keep an eye on everything going on from here."

25

Game three was just ending and people were rising from their seats to surge toward the betting windows. A handful of women in short tight black skirts, red satin blouses, and headphones began patrolling the aisles. Fernando explained that these were the tele-wager girls and that they took bets from the floor.

Dearborn eyed them appreciatively. The one working their aisle was particularly eye-catching, a redhead who walked with an irresistible bounce. "Looks promising," Dearborn commented affably.

"I think you'll enjoy it," Fernando agreed.

"I should think so."

"It's an exciting game."

"Oh yes," Dearborn responded, tearing his eyes from the redhead. "How's it played, Fernando?"

Fernando explained the game, describing the equipment, the hard ball called the pelota and the curved basketlike racket called the cesta.

"Cooky tells me you were a budding jai alai player yourself, Fernando. Do you still play the game?"

"Whenever I get the chance. They know me here, so I practise with the players whenever I can. Friday afternoons usually."

"Is that so. You'll be on the courts here tomorrow?"

"I hope to."

"You wouldn't like to play with them? Professionally, I mean?"

"I wanted to very much. It didn't work out that way."

"Why not now?" Cooky asked.

"I've lost too much time."

"How old are you, my boy?" Dearborn inquired.

"Twenty-five."

"That's not too old," Cooky declared. "I don't know why you don't try out."

"I have tried out," Fernando said. "They say it would take six months, perhaps a year, to get in shape. I'd have to quit my job. I have family in Miami, three sisters, a younger brother. I couldn't afford it."

"Oh." Cooky looked crestfallen for a moment. Then suddenly her expression turned radiant. She started to speak but was interrupted by a bell and a voice over the loudspeaker announcing the two-minute warning.

Fernando pointed to two large lighted boards at either side of the court. "The players for the next game are listed there and next to them the odds. You can watch the odds change up until the final bell."

"Fernando," Cooky picked up, "you never told me you've got family in the United States."

"My mother came twelve years ago," Fernando explained, "with my brother and sisters. My brother was born here, actually. But my father couldn't come. He was a doctor, so they wouldn't let him leave. I was thirteen, the eldest. Someone had to remain with him. He died four years ago and that's when I decided to get out."

"I know that Mr. Beggs took quite an interest in you, Fernando," Dearborn said. "Why didn't you ask him to lend you some money? I'm sure he would have done so."

"He depended on me. And he gave me my first job when no one else would. I wouldn't have felt right quitting."

"Well, that might all change now," Cooky gushed. "It just so happens that . . ."

Dearborn saw her gloating expression and anticipated

what it was she was about to say. She, like Dearborn, knew what was contained in Leo Beggs's will.

"Cordelia," Dearborn said sharply, "I'd like to see if I've got this betting straight. What is it, Fernando? Win, place, show, quinella, perfecta, trifecta, two, three, five, ten, and multiples thereof?"

Cooky, cut short, seemed to think better of what she had been about to say. She appeared to realize that this might not be the right time to break the news. She shut her mouth determinedly.

Dearborn was satisfied. He wanted to observe Fernando's reaction to the news himself, but he preferred that it be in a more tranquil atmosphere.

The final bell rang and continued to ring with short steady blasts as the lights in the auditorium dimmed and the tele-wager girls left the floor. The court was separated from the audience by a floor-to-ceiling wire-mesh net which, Fernando pointed out, protected the spectators from what might otherwise be a danger from rebounding balls. The bells were replaced by a recording of bullfight music as the jai alai players, sixteen in all, marched in from the sidelines, single file, strode to the center of the court, turned to salute the audience, and withdrew.

Four of the players took their positions on the court. Two were wearing white sashes and two were wearing red. They were the lead-off teams. For the next minute the ball cracked against the three playing walls as it was caught in the cestas, swung, and thrown back at great speed. When one of the white-sashed players failed to scoop up a ball, the white team was retired and replaced by the blue. Dearborn, despite his harrowing experience earlier in the evening, found himself absorbed by the game. When he glanced at Cooky, she was perched on the edge of her seat riveted by the action, and Fernando's handsome face was taut with concentration.

After the game Dearborn handed Cooky a twenty dollar bill and told her that he didn't care to buck the crowd. "You go. I'll do my betting from my seat."

She went with Fernando, and once they were gone Dearborn rose and began sauntering up and down the aisles. His eyes swept the audience. Here and there he recognized a face belonging to a La Playa guest, but it wasn't until he perused the first row of the orchestra section that he spotted Stuart Ripple and Molly Beggs occupying the two center armchairs. Molly was making notes in the margin of her program while Stuart had his arm around the back of her chair and was leaning chummily over her shoulder.

Dearborn was standing in the aisle behind them and a little to the right. He remained there watching as Molly signaled one of the tele-wager girls and handed her a fifty-dollar bill. The girl cradled the headphone between shoulder and ear as she jotted down the bets, then called them in to the betting office.

A cocktail waitress passed and Stuart leaned forward to detain her. He ordered something and turned back to Molly, letting his hand drop from the back of the chair to rest lightly upon her shoulder. She didn't seem to object.

They were sitting, Dearborn was glad to note, a long distance from the spot where he, Fernando, and Cooky were seated, and neither Molly nor Stuart looked as if they intended to do much strolling around. With luck, Dearborn might be able to keep Cooky from seeing them.

When Dearborn returned to his seat he filled in the time before Fernando and Cooky returned by opening negotiations with the redhead. "Ursula, you say? Lovely name. Well, Ursula, you look like the kind of woman might bring a man luck. I'm going to test the theory by wheeling one, three, and five on the singles coming up. Irigoyen, Miro, and Torres."

It turned out that Fernando and Cooky had bet the three, five, six combination and that all three of them won on the five, three ticket. By the time the sixth game was announced, Cooky, forty-seven dollars to the good, had abandoned the numbers for a system of her own. "Bonilla has a sweet face but Gris is too short. I'm going to bet on Sanchez and García. They look as if they're friends. Burgess, what are you looking at through those opera glasses?"

"Nothing at all. What did you say about Gris? He has warts?"

After the seventh game Fernando excused himself to visit a friend in the general-admissions section. A few minutes later, Cooky left to go to the ladies' room and Dearborn took up his surveillance of Molly and Stuart, which ended when Molly got up and left the auditorium. Dearborn shook his head in discouragement. He could only cross his fingers and hope for the best. It was a big place and there were a great many spectators milling about. Perhaps Cooky wouldn't pay much attention to who was in the crowd.

Ursula had stationed herself at the end of Dearborn's row and she singled him out with a provocative little smile. "Not betting, Mr. . . .?"

"Pin—Roycroft," Dearborn supplied, almost tripping himself into an indiscretion. "Burgess Roycroft."

"What would you like, Mr. Roycroft?"

"Now or later?" he returned wickedly.

"You're a bad one," she said with an engaging twitch of the shoulders and a sly wink. "Let's start with game eight."

At the two-minute warning bell, Fernando returned and slid into his seat. He was followed by Cooky, hurrying back with a distraught expression on her face.

"Something wrong?" Dearborn asked, already anticipating what she would say.

"Burgess, could I speak to you alone? Would you excuse us, Fernando?" She motioned to Dearborn to join her in the aisle, but Fernando stood up instead.

"I could use some coffee. Anyone want anything?"

Dearborn shook his head. "No, thank you, Fernando."

"You don't mind, do you, Fernando?" Cooky asked.

"Of course not." He withdrew after flashing a questioning look at Dearborn.

Cooky took his place. "Molly is here with a man," she whispered.

"She is?" Dearborn responded with feigned innocence. "Well, what of it? You're here too, aren't you? With two men."

"Burgess, I saw Molly not five minutes ago standing in a dark corner of the bar talking to some man. She had hold of his arm and she was whispering in his ear."

Dearborn tried to reason with her. "Stuart Ripple is, I'm sure, an old friend."

"Stuart Ripple? Who said anything about Stuart Ripple?"

"I noticed your aunt, Cordelia. I saw her with Ripple earlier. I was going to mention it but I got wrapped up in that last game."

"Well, it wasn't Stuart Ripple she was with just now."

"Of course it was."

"It wasn't."

Dearborn was unconvinced. "It was dark, Cordelia. You probably didn't get a good look at him."

"Oh, please. Stu is a blond and not nearly so tall. If it had been Stu I wouldn't 've been able to see him over all those heads."

Dearborn lifted his glasses to scan the front row of the orchestra. Molly was not there. Stuart Ripple was alone, slouched down in his seat, a drink in one hand, a program in the other.

"Was he wearing blue slacks and a blue-and-white-striped sports shirt?"

"There were people between us. I don't know what color pants he had on, but he didn't have on a sports shirt. He had on a guayabera."

"And he was dark-haired?"

"I told you!"

"A guayabera?" Dearborn swiveled around and trained his glasses on Fernando, who was still in sight, taller than the people surrounding him, dressed in his guayabera, his dark sleek head bent to pass under the archway leading back out to the central betting area.

26

"Could it have been Fernando?" Dearborn asked.

"Why should it've been Fernando?"

"He's tall, and dark, and he was wearing a guayabera. Could it have been Fernando?"

"Wasn't he with you?" Cooky asked. "When I came back to the seat he was with you."

"He had just returned," Dearborn informed her.

Cooky showed her dismay by running tense fingers through her hair, pulling and fluffing it distractedly.

"You told me that Fernando finds your aunt attractive, Cordelia."

"Fernando's not like that. I didn't say he's fooling around with her. He wouldn't do that."

"Why not?"

" 'Cause of my Uncle Leo."

Dearborn suggested diplomatically, "It needn't necessarily have been an assignation."

"Oh no," Cooky murmured, "that's why she was whispering into his ear, grabbing onto his arm. I could see the expression on her face. She wasn't talking about the weather, that's for sure."

"Could it have been Fernando?"

She looked miserable. "It couldn't 've been," she said in a positive tone.

"But it was dark at that end of the bar."

"I told you that before, Burgess. But it wasn't Fernando. It *couldn't* 've been."

She wasn't going to say any more and, indeed, Dearborn didn't think there was any more to be said. It was enough that she had seen Molly exchanging confidences with a tall, dark-haired man who conformed to the description of the man Nico pursued through the garden on Wednesday afternoon.

"I want to go home, Burgess."

Dearborn wasn't ready to leave, but he said indulgently, "All right, Cordelia. I understand perfectly. I shall inform Fernando."

"Isn't he coming back to the seat?"

"He's a discreet young fellow. He may decide to watch the next game from the betting floor. I'll go speak to him and then return for you."

As Dearborn left the auditorium the lights dimmed and the music began. The central betting area wasn't deserted, but the crowds had thinned and Dearborn moved around the floor freely. He assumed that Molly Beggs had already returned to her seat but he didn't see Fernando.

He made a slow careful circuit of the central betting floor. There were a few people at the bar, among them two or three tall, dark-haired men wearing guayaberas, but no one who looked familiar. He moved from the central betting floor to the general-admissions section right of the auditorium, then returned to investigate the general-admissions section on the left.

The crowd was thicker here than anywhere else and it seemed to Dearborn that he had experienced a sudden geographical dislocation. The room seemed to be solidly peopled with dark-haired gentlemen in guayaberas, talking volubly in Spanish, smoking cigars, eating, drinking, and waving their arms. Some were facing the fronton court, some were watching the closed-circuit television sets, and some were wandering around aimlessly, but all were amiable, sociable, and exceedingly noisy.

Apparently the Latin contingent enjoyed a special rapport. Fat, thin, short, tall, young, and old, it was impossible to sort them out. Dearborn was about to abandon the search for a familiar face when he spotted Fernando a few yards away. Dearborn called out to him and thought for a moment that Fernando had seen him until he moved away and was lost behind a pillar.

"Drat!" Dearborn fumed, elbowing his way through the jammed bodies.

By the time he had circled the pillar Fernando was gone.

Dearborn was about to retrace his steps when his attention was once again arrested by the sight of a tall man, just visible above the heads of the crowd. The man showed only a quarter profile, and before Dearborn could shift his position sufficiently to get a clearer look, he moved deeper into the recesses of the room. It might have been Fernando and it might not. The face, the little Dearborn could see of it, had looked like one he'd seen before, but he had been unable to see anything below the neck and the glimpse had been brief.

Dearborn plunged forward, clearing his way with peremptory commands of "Fall back! Step aside! Back off!" When he reached the far end of the room he found himself facing a glass enclosure in which eleven of the sixteen jai alai players sat waiting their turn to enter the court. The twelfth had just entered through a door in the rear. To the left of the players' booth but not leading into it was another door, and as Dearborn fought his way through the packed bodies he saw that door close.

Dearborn reached the door a moment later only to find that it was locked. A small sign next to it read, "For Manager Ring." He pressed the bell and a uniformed guard opened the door a crack and poked out his head.

"I'm afraid I'm late," Dearborn explained fussily and with a note of urgency. "Did the manager tell you where I should leave the envelope?"

"I don't know nothing about it."

"Did he sign the voucher?"

"I told you I got no idea. I just come back from the john."

"I'd better put it on his desk, then."

The guard responded to Dearborn's nonsense by opening the door wider and admitting him to a cement-block corridor lit by bare low-wattage ceiling bulbs.

"Who was the man who came in a moment ago?" Dearborn asked casually.

"I don't know. Irigoyen let him in."

"Where did he go?"

"The locker room, I guess. Or Scrope's office."

Dearborn walked resolutely down the hall, pausing at the

end to scrutinize the small sign with the arrow pointing left. It read "Manager, L. Scrope." A larger sign with an arrow pointing right read "Locker Room." It was a toss-up, but Dearborn turned toward the locker room. As he walked toward the open doorway he heard the sound of footsteps, but when he entered the room it appeared to be empty.

"Anybody here?" Dearborn called out. There was no answer.

There were three aisles of lockers and along the right-hand wall next to the door were a half-dozen open tile shower booths. Dearborn was standing a little to the right of the center aisle. There was no one in any of the shower stalls, and as he moved to the left he could see that the center aisle was empty.

"Hello?" he called again. No one answered. "Fernando?" he called tentatively. All was silent. "I saw you come in," he said calmly to whoever was there. "I have no intention of leaving without talking to you."

He was reluctant to move out of sight of the door, but he would have to do so if he were to flush the man out. He moved to the aisle on the left, glanced along the row of lockers, then quickly moved back to the center aisle. He repeated the maneuver with the right-hand aisle. Without success. The vertical lockers were tall enough to contain a man but not wide enough. The person was hiding, obviously, at the other end of the room, behind the lockers in the center aisle.

Dearborn tiptoed forward. There was a bench in the aisle. It was piled high with an assortment of clothes and sports paraphernalia, folded trousers, underwear, shoes, socks, knee and elbow pads. Dearborn paused as he realized that he was totally vulnerable and in a situation where he might need protection. There was nothing on the bench that would serve as a weapon. He turned back and noticed a fire extinguisher hanging on the wall. He began to take it down, unlatching it quietly and lifting it from its niche.

When he turned back he grunted with shock. Standing at the end of the aisle was a bizarre figure, like a feudal knight, in red tunic and white helmet, the helmet pulled low over his forehead, the wide chinstrap pulled up to cover his mouth. His arm was raised high over his head, a cesta basket was strapped to his arm, and before Dearborn could make a move to defend himself the arm whipped down and the pelota sped toward Dearborn, who barely had time to react. He turned a fraction of an inch to shield himself so that the ball, partially deflected by the fire extinguisher, bounced off and grazed Dearborn's cheek before it slammed into the wall. The force and weight of it sent Dearborn reeling backward, and as he staggered, his attacker raced forward, barreled into Dearborn's chest, and ran to the door.

The second blow knocked the wind out of Dearborn and he slid to the floor dazed and gasping. It was over in thirty seconds, but it took Dearborn another three or four minutes to recover from his shock. He had only just risen to his feet when he heard the jai alai players returning to the locker room.

Dearborn picked up the fire extinguisher and was in the process of replacing it when the players pressed through the doorway. One, carrying a red bathrobe and two white helmets, was complaining loudly in Spanish and making eloquent gestures toward the floor. He stopped, leaned down, and picked up the pelota. He held it aloft and renewed his irritable diatribe. Then he spotted Dearborn and stopped talking.

"Any more extinguishers in here?" Dearborn demanded.

The player stared at him suspiciously.

"I said, any more extinguishers in here?"

The player shook his head.

"When's the last time these were checked?"

The player shrugged.

"If you don't know, I shall have to speak to Mr. Scrope."

Dearborn dusted off his hands and marched out of the locker room, uncomfortably aware of his throbbing cheek and the dull ache in the vicinity of his third rib.

He returned to the auditorium to find Fernando deeply engrossed in a conversation with Cooky. The look he flashed at Dearborn was baleful and he stood up as Dearborn approached, saying coolly, "May I have a word with you, Mr. Roycroft?"

"Oh, Fernando," Cooky wailed, "I didn't mean to start trouble."

"What's this all about?" Dearborn demanded.

"Miss Gillette tells me you've made certain remarks about me and her aunt."

"The best defense is an offense, eh?" Dearborn suggested.

"What is that supposed to mean?"

"Burgess," Cooky pleaded, "I didn't mean to make trouble. Honest."

"There is nothing between Mrs. Beggs and me," Fernando declared.

Some of the people in the surrounding seats showed interest in Fernando's declaration and Ursula, taking bets in the aisle, paused to listen.

"Perhaps," Dearborn said tactfully, "we should continue this conversation outside."

Cooky rose and the three of them made their exit. Once outside, Dearborn, on the theory that he couldn't possibly make things worse, asked Fernando where he had been during the eighth game. "Were you in the locker room?" he asked.

"No. I was in the men's room. Why do you ask?"

"Because I was in the locker room."

"You were in the locker room, Burgess?" Cooky asked. "How come?"

"I was looking for Fernando."

Fernando frowned. "I don't understand."

"Burgess," Cooky interrupted, taking a close look at his face, "what happened to you? You've got a big red swelling on your cheek."

Dearborn put his hand up and winced. "Fellow swung his arm back as I was passing. Terrible blow. Saw stars for a second." He stole a look at Fernando, who was frowning.

"Look, Mr. Roycroft," Fernando said, "I don't understand what's going on here."

"Nothing," Dearborn assured him. "Nothing at all. I'm afraid there's been a misunderstanding all around. My apologies for accusing you unjustly, my boy. I meant nothing by it.

Didn't mean to imply more than a friendship between you and Mrs. Beggs, I promise you."

Fernando looked somewhat mollified. "You'd better put something on that swelling," he said by way of showing that he accepted Dearborn's apology. "And I'd better be getting on home."

Cooky looked a little disappointed, but she said nothing to stop Fernando and a few minutes later they parted company to go their separate ways.

27

Dearborn carried his notebook in his pocket, but he didn't want to consult it in front of Cooky. Instead he leaned back against the car cushions and closed his eyes. He had never considered Alberta Van Curl or Cooky to be suspects, not because of their professed love for Leo Beggs—Dearborn set no store by protestations of love no matter how affecting—nor because he had a personal bias in their favor, but because Molly Beggs was not a woman who would trust or be trusted by other women. She was what Dearborn thought of as the ultimate egoist, the beau ideal of self-gratification, an assessment he was sure his friend Dr. Moltke would second, though no doubt in more scientific and blunter terms.

Now he felt secure crossing Stuart Ripple off his list of suspects. Ripple was average-sized, muscular, and blond, not tall, dark-haired, and slender, and three separate incidents indicated a tall, dark-haired, slender man as Molly's accomplice. It seemed reasonable to eliminate anyone who did not fit that description. As for Bunny, she was inextricably bound to Stuart Ripple. They might be good-for-nothings. In Dearborn's book they were that and more, but they hadn't killed anyone.

Whose names remained? As of now, the name Fernando Alvarez headed the list. There was no question but that Fernando at this stage of the proceedings seemed the most likely suspect. He would not only benefit directly from Beggs's death, he would also benefit indirectly from his liaison with the beautiful widow. He needed the money. Without it he was destined to remain a maître d', not forever perhaps, but long enough to ruin any hopes he harbored of pursuing his chosen profession. The chances were good that, with his background, Fernando was familiar with the use of firearms. He was dark-haired, tall, and slender. He was able to gain entry to the jai alai locker room and he knew how to throw a pelota. It was unfortunate that, excepting a certain Latin reserve, he was such a likable fellow. Still, if it should prove that he was in New York at the time Louis Martin was killed, then Dearborn would have his man. If not, then Dearborn would have to look further.

Collis McAuley was another candidate. McAuley had disapproved of the affair between Molly and Louis Martin, fearful that because of it he might be jarred from his comfortable niche. He stood to benefit both directly and indirectly from Beggs's will and he was tall, dark-haired, and thin. An excellent fit. Except, Dearborn admitted to himself irritably, for one crucial implausibility. Why would Collis McAuley choose to sneak into his daughter's apartment when he merely had to ring the doorbell to get in? Was it to throw suspicion elsewhere? If so, why was such deviousness necessary? That was a point Dearborn couldn't hope to clear up until or unless it was proved that McAuley was Molly's accomplice. Again the practical question was, did McAuley have the opportunity to kill Louis Martin as well as Leo Beggs?

Then there was Norbert. Norbert Beggs was a dutiful but not particularly affectionate son. He stood to inherit two million dollars. He disliked Louis Martin and he gave no hint of possessing even the most rudimentary conscience. But in Norbert's case there were two disturbing factors. Norbert lived in his father's apartment, giving him no more practical reason than McAuley to break in, and he abhorred Molly Beggs ... or appeared to. Unless his attitude toward her proved to be an elaborate hoax, it seemed unlikely that he could collaborate with her in scheming murder. On the other hand, he fit the bill physically. He was dark, he was tall, he was slender, and he had one more point in his favor, or to his detriment, Dearborn thought, according to one's point of view. He was an expert with a gun.

The fourth suspect was more difficult to square with Dearborn's concept of a murderer, but there were too many suspicious factors to ignore. It was Raúl Baki. The fact that he was off his trolley, Dearborn decided, didn't eliminate him as a suspect. Dearborn didn't doubt for a moment that Molly would use her attractions to further befuddle the poor fellow if it seemed to her advantage to do so. A madman might, in many respects, make a perfect accomplice. He could be persuaded to believe anything, perhaps in this case that Louis Martin was an assassin, that Beggs conspired against him, or that Dearborn was another member of a plot to prevent Baki from liberating Cuba. Under delusions such as those, Baki might easily kill someone.

Certainly Baki, whatever his other deficiencies, was not inexpert at handling weapons, and it was even probable that, being a Cuban, he would be conversant with handling the cesta and pelota. He had, after all, shown himself adept at wielding a bola. Baki was a good deal older than Norbert or Fernando and somewhat older than Collis McAuley, but he fitted the bill. He was slender, tall, and dark, in excellent physical condition, and as an accomplice he presented one attraction the others lacked. He didn't require a reward and he was no one to fear. He was non compos and would unquestionably end up in the booby hatch sooner or later. The question here, as with the others, was, could he have been in New York when Louis Martin was killed?

That's what it boiled down to. Opportunity. All of them had access to Leo Beggs. But how many of them could have made the trip to New York the week before?

"What's the matter, Burgess? Don't you feel well?"

Dearborn opened his eyes and sat up. "I feel fine, Cordelia."

"I wish I did. I don't know why I said what I did to Fernando. He'll probably never speak to me again."

"Nonsense."

"Well, you see he isn't having an affair with Molly. I told you he wasn't."

Dearborn felt duty bound to prepare her for the worst. "I wouldn't put too much faith in Fernando, Cordelia. He is an attractive young man and he seems sincere, but one can never be certain."

"Certain of what? Don't you believe him? I do."

It was impossible to say more without saying too much. Dearborn let it go with the simple admonishment to "wait and see."

"I didn't get to tell Fernando about his inheritance, either," Cooky said regretfully. "You know, my uncle left him a lot of money, Burgess."

"Really?"

"They're going to read the will next week. But I was going to tell him beforehand. He's getting twenty thousand dollars."

"That is a large sum. A very large sum. Why do you suppose your uncle left him such a generous bequest?"

Cooky shrugged. "He liked him, I guess. I don't know."

Dearborn consulted his wristwatch. "It's not yet midnight. Would you like to drop in at the Monsoon?"

"Why not," Cooky responded morosely. "I'm going to have insomnia anyway."

"Norbert's band *is* playing tonight, isn't it?"

"Yup. Two sessions. Eight to nine and midnight to one."

Norbert, Dearborn calculated, was supposedly not speaking to Molly. They might not want to risk being discovered in conversation by Nico or Conchita or Cooky. But there had been plenty of time between shows for Norbert to drive to the fronton, meet Molly in secret, say whatever had to be said, and return by midnight.

"The Monsoon it is," Dearborn said agreeably. "We'll have another go at the Mold."

"The Musk," Cooky corrected.

"The muskiest," Dearborn allowed.

When Cooky and Dearborn entered the Monsoon they were shown to a table not far from the bandstand. Dearborn couldn't help thinking that when it came to naming things Leo Beggs had shown an eclectic disregard for consistency. La Playa, Cloister, Tahitian, Tropicala, Monsoon, bore only a tenuous geographic relationship to one another, and the Monsoon was equally divorced from its decor.

Norbert and his group were playing, their instruments another example of unorthodox blending—three stringed instruments: bass viol, violin, and guitar; one brass: a saxophone; one set of percussion instruments: kettledrums, cymbals, and gong; and a piano. Dearborn noted that Norbert, in green fright wig, knee-length tunic over dungarees, and thonged sandals, was less complicatedly got up than usual and would have been able to get into and out of his costume with little or no trouble and no time lost.

The band was playing something deafening, Norbert's bass fiddle and lyric contributions being a monotonous thump, thump, thump and a tediously repetitive phrase that sounded like, but Dearborn was sure could not have been, "Please don't drop the acid."

"I guess they didn't play this kind of music in your day," Cooky commented.

"I was no more partial to 'Yes, We Have No Bananas.' "

"You don't want to dance, I hope," Cooky said flatly.

"I do not."

"That's good, because I can't."

At one o'clock the set ended with a roll of drums and a final thump from Norbert, the group retiring to desultory applause.

"Why don't we invite Norbert to join us?" Dearborn suggested.

"How come you're so friendly to Norbert all of a sudden?"

"I am merely trying to be sociable, Cordelia, jostle you out of the doldrums."

"He won't come out," Cooky predicted. "We could go back-stage, though. Want to?"

"If you'd like."

Cooky led Dearborn behind the bandstand and through a curtain. "Norbie's dressing room is upstairs." She preceded Dearborn up a short flight of stairs, through a door, down a corridor past a number of closed doors, and stopped in front of one that had a shirt cardboard tacked to it on which someone had painted "The Musk" in large red letters.

Cooky rapped. "You decent, Norbie?"

"Nope," came the laconic reply.

Cooky opened the door anyway. Five of the Mildews were lolling on the bare floor while Norbert, as befitted their leader, was sitting on a kitchen chair precariously balanced on two legs and supported by Norbert's feet planted on the dressing table.

"Hey," he said, "I see you brought the old boyfriend. Fellas, you remember Burgess Roycroft. Burgess, remember the boys? Fleece on sax, Spik on guitar, Billy on violin, Skinzo, drums, Riff, piano."

The musicians acknowledged the reintroduction with their own brand of casual cordiality. "Okay, man; way to go, man; hang loose, man; all ri-i-ight," and from Riff, "What's up, man" causing Norbert to respond, "Whatever's not hanging down, man" which good-natured badinage precipitated a round of guffaws.

"Can we stay?" Cooky asked.

"Sure," Norbert replied expansively. "Find a place to park."

Dearborn, encouraged by the welcome, was determined to cultivate it, but he very nearly had the reverse effect when he attempted to move Billy's violin and bow from a stool near the door.

"Hey!" Billy shouted in an anguished voice. "Not the bow, man. Not the bow! Don't you know nothing, man?"

"I beg your pardon?"

"You got any oil on your fingers, you're going to wreck my

bow. Them horsehairs are coated with rosin, man. You want to ruin them?"

"My apologies," Dearborn said with dignity, dusting his fingers and looking unsuccessfully for an alternative perch.

"Either of you guys want to smoke?" Spik asked, taking a deep drag from the fragrant cigarette in his hand and then proffering it.

"I do," Cooky said, accepting the cigarette with a self-conscious peek at Dearborn.

"You?" Spik asked Dearborn.

Dearborn hesitated. Ordinarily he would lecture them on the sins of drug abuse, but he didn't want to appear priggish. Also he felt a sudden nostalgic pang. The smell in the room carried him back over fifty years to the days when he wore his hair slicked back and thought baggy knickers and argyle socks were the last word in spiffy, when marijuana was called bang, when a ladies' man was a cake-eater, when liquor was called hooch, and when it was fashionable to go to hell in a flivver. The differences between then and now, he mused, were purely linguistic. Now one referred to pot and dudes and booze and jetted one's way to Hades, but essentially the vices never changed, only the fashions in vice.

"Don't shock the old guy," Norbert chided, seeing Dearborn's reluctance.

It irritated Dearborn to be so grossly patronized. "Thanks, my boy," he said, plucking the joint from Cooky's hand. "Don't mind if I do."

28

For a while Dearborn sat on an overturned wastepaper basket, then when balance became a problem he lowered himself to the floor and used the wastepaper basket as an elbow prop. His sense of well-being improved as the hours passed, but not his acuity.

It grew later and he grew more lethargic. Sometime around three a conversation took place that seemed relevant to his purpose in being there, but by then he was having difficulty concentrating. It had been initiated by a question he'd directed to Skinzo, relative to the number of nights Mildew and the Musk performed each week.

Skinzo had replied, "We jive every night, man."

"Every night?" Dearborn had asked languidly, inhaling deeply.

"We're grooming for stardom, man," Norbie had explained soberly. "We haven't missed a gig since last August when Spik short-circuited and blew the kliegs."

"Remember that?" Riff had put in wonderingly. "That was a gas. Spik's guitar lit up like *Star Wars*."

"You are saying," Dearborn had pursued ploddingly, "that you six have appeared every night without fail? I find that difficult to believe."

"What's today?" Fleece had asked. "February 13, right? That happened August 24. . . ."

"How do you know it was August 24, Fleece?" Cooky had asked skeptically.

"The day Mount Vesuvius erupted," Fleece had answered improbably. "Seventy-nine A.D. It's on the beer calendar hanging in the can. Billy blew the day Vesuvius blew. So let's see, 31 take away 24 leaves 7, 30 days hath September, plus November, plus 31 three more times and 13 gives 173. We haven't missed one night in 173 days."

"You got a head like a computer," Norbie had murmured.

"What is a paradox?" Dearborn had then asked with equal improbability.

"I came down for the Labor Day weekend on the twenty-ninth," Cooky had contributed lazily.

"Thirty-one take away 2," Fleece had promptly calculated, "plus 30 twice is 60 plus 31 three times is 93 and 13 gives 168."

"A man," Dearborn had quipped, "who walks a mile but only moves two feet." He hadn't thought of that joke in years, fifty-some-odd years as a matter of fact, and had been amazed at how well it withstood the test of time. It had seemed so amusing that he had repeated it not once but twice before the party broke up and it wasn't until the following morning, sitting in bed sipping a steaming cup of black coffee, that Dearborn realized that the real import of the conversation had very nearly been lost to him.

Mildew and the Musk had performed every night since the previous August. Louis Martin had been killed early in the morning, somewhere between six and eight o'clock on Tuesday, February 4, and Edward Roycroft told Dearborn that Martin had been followed the day before he was killed, which meant that Norbert would have had to miss at least one night's performance in order to be in New York on February 3 and 4, which he had not. Dearborn congratulated himself on his capacity to overcome drugs, fatigue, and an almost incomprehensible language barrier to ferret out the facts. It certainly appeared that Norbert was exonerated.

Not so Collis McAuley, Fernando Alvarez, or Raúl Baki, however. The task might be less formidable than it had been, but it was far from resolved.

It was almost ten. Dearborn had gone to bed at four-thirty and wakened, as usual, at seven. Needless to say, he had not awakened refreshed. Quite the contrary. Besides the ugly bruise on his cheek and the painfully sore rib, he was lethargic, swollen-eyed, and a trifle depressed. Still, if this investigation were to be brought to a satisfactory conclusion, he must thrust aside all personal discomforts and push ahead.

Molly sat in front of the dressing table studying her face in the mirror. She had just showered, and drops of water glistened on her naked back. She flipped her hair behind her shoulders and leaned forward to examine the faint shadows under her eyes. She'd be thirty in a few months.

"God," she murmured aloud, "I feel like fifty."

Molly was not pleased with her appearance or with her mood and she blamed both on the old man. There was no question that he suspected her. The question was, how much did he know? She didn't like the questions he asked or his suspicious look when she answered them. He'd been at the jai alai the night before. He hadn't thought she'd seen him, but she had, and so had Stuart.

"Why do you think the old coot's spying on you?" Stuart had asked.

"He's a friend of that New York policeman," Molly had explained. "I think he believes I put Leo up to killing Lou."

"Why would he think that?"

"I suppose he disapproves of me."

"He doesn't even know you."

"He knows I had an affair with Lou. What does he care how unhappy I was. How miserable I was. What does it matter to him how mean Leo was."

"I don't like to hear that," Stuart had remarked. "I don't like to think of Leo making you miserable."

"That's why I took up with Lou, Stuart. I never loved him. I just needed someone. Anyone."

"Why not me?"

"I thought you and Bunny . . ."

"Bunny doesn't mean anything to me. Bunny's just a pal."

"I guess I have a way of getting mixed up with the wrong kind of man," she'd said. "I was glad when Lou finally took off for New York. It was a relief."

"You mean it was over then, Molly? You mean that Leo didn't really have any reason to . . ."

"Of course not. It was a joke. A sick joke. A really sick joke."

"Christ, Molly, I wish you'd let me try and make it all up to you now."

"You're a darling, Stu. If it weren't for that obnoxious old man . . ."

"He's no cop," Stuart had pointed out. "He's got no right to bother you. Why don't you toss him out on his ear?"

"If I show him I care, he'll take it to mean he's on the right track and may really make trouble for me. I think he's a little crazy. He must be."

"Senile, you mean."

"Whatever. Anyway, I'm just waiting for him to give up and go home."

"You know," Stuart had suggested, "it could just be that Roycroft's being here at the jai alai is a coincidence."

"He told me he was taking Cooky to the movies. Instead he brings her here. What do you think?"

"How did he know you were coming, Molly?"

"I'm not sure."

"You didn't tell him, did you?"

"Of course not. But he just doesn't happen to be hiding behind those opera glasses. I'm telling you he's watching us."

"Us?"

"Well, you're with me, aren't you?"

"Come to think of it," Stuart had recalled, "he was sitting at the next table in the dining room yesterday when your father, Bunny, and I were having breakfast."

"You mean you sat down next to him?"

"Just the opposite. The dining room was half empty and he came over and sat down next to us."

"What were you talking about?"

Stuart had reacted uncomfortably to that question. He'd closed off suddenly and withdrawn. "Nothing. I mean I can't remember."

"Did you talk about Leo or me?"

"Bunny was asking your father about the Valentine's party tomorrow night. She didn't know if you'd call it off. Wait a minute. I think I said something about trying to get you to go to the jai alai tonight."

"There's the answer, then. Did you say anything else?" she had pressed. "Anything about Leo killing himself?"

"No. Nothing. Not a thing."

Stuart's vehement denial had made her suspicious. Of course, if her father had been there it must have been all right. Still, she knew better than to trust Stuart. She'd better ask her father about that conversation.

Stuart had asked her then if she wanted him to talk to Burgess Roycroft. She had said, "No, I don't think so. That'll only make things worse. There is one thing, though. . . ."

"What's that?"

"You could tell Benjamin Pinch something for me."

"What the hell's Pinch got to do with this?"

"Nothing really, except that Ben's father went to school with Mr. Roycroft or something like that. That old woman was talking about it at my dinner party the other night. Ben knows Burgess Roycroft and *he* could talk to him."

"About leaving you alone?"

"No, not that. About something else, something I promised to keep quiet, Stu. I can't be the one to let it out, but you could."

"What is it?"

"Raúl Baki's flipped his lid. Altogether, I mean. He tried to kill Mr. Roycroft tonight."

Stuart had been shocked and she'd pulled out all the stops describing the incident. "I think if Ben knew about it, he'd see that Mr. Roycroft left."

"You mean Roycroft doesn't want to leave after something like that happened to him?"

"I told you, he's a little strange."

Stuart had given his word and Molly knew he'd keep it. She picked up her brush and began brushing her hair back off her face. There wasn't anything Stuart wouldn't do for her, or at least, let her think he wouldn't do for her. Him and his dumb girl friend. Did Stuart and Bunny actually believe Molly took them to be platonic friends? Hadn't she caught them looking cow-eyed at one another a million times, groping under tables, snuggling up in dark corners.

Their little plot to move in on her was transparent as air and no heavier. They'd been at it almost a year, with Stuart playing the strong silent type and Bunny buttering her up and pretending to be the kind girl friend. Bull. If Molly didn't find their stupid game useful she would laugh in their faces. Now that Leo was dead she really expected Stuart to pour it on. Okay. At the moment it suited her fine.

She picked up a jar of body lotion and unscrewed the lid. Escape. That's all she thought of now. Finally getting out of this awful place. Not just La Playa or Silver Beach or Florida, but out of the country altogether. Traveling to Europe and to the Orient, settling in Paris or Rome. She dipped her hand into the jar and was spreading lotion over her neck and shoulders when the phone interrupted her train of thought. She got up impatiently and crossed the room to answer it.

"Hello? Alberta? What's the matter? Why are you so excited? What are you saying? He what? When? I don't believe it!"

29

Alberta Van Curl found the note on her desk at nine and called Molly Beggs. Dearborn got it from a bellhop who had gotten it from Stanley, the desk clerk, who had gotten it from Miss Van Curl.

Not trusting third-hand accounts, Dearborn went directly to the source. He found Miss Van Curl slumped at her desk looking doleful. She seemed almost relieved when Dearborn poked his head through the door.

"Oh, Mr. Roycroft. Hello. Is there something . . .?"

"I came as soon as I heard, madam. I thought you might appreciate some friendly support."

"That's very kind. Everyone else rushed off to commiserate with Molly. No one seems to think I should be upset even though I'm the one who found the note. I'm having palpitations. First Leo. Now this."

"I don't wonder," Dearborn said delicately. "Do you, er, have the note?"

"No. Cooky came down and took it."

"Can you by chance recall the wording?"

"It said, 'Baki is making me go with him. Tell Molly he's taking the *Seasprite.*'"

"That's all?"

"Signed 'Collis.'"

"The *Seasprite* is the Beggses' yacht?"

"Yes. A cabin cruiser. Quite large. I suppose Mr. Baki doesn't know how to operate it."

"A hijacking and a kidnapping," Dearborn proclaimed. "The man is certifiable."

Alberta's homely face was paler than usual. She was hunched gracelessly over her desk, her pendulous breasts resting lumpishly on the desktop, her big hands clasped. "Collis made me stay here until six-thirty last night. If Leo were alive..."

"I'm sure," Dearborn acknowledged. "Dreadful thing. Hard on you. Painful."

"I *told* him I don't work overtime. I'm supposed to be finished work at five-thirty."

"Tut tut. Unfair. Reprehensible."

"I've suffered terribly during the last week, Mr. Roycroft."

"Did McAuley leave the office when you did?" Dearborn asked, cutting short the sympathy.

"No. When I left he was putting away the books. He didn't come into the dining room while I was there."

"What time did you leave the dining room?"

"About quarter to eight. Collis usually eats about seven. Mr. Baki came in right after I left."

"How do you know that?"

"Stanley told me. He came through the lobby, walked in back of the counter, and came in here."

"What time was that?"

"A little after seven. If I hadn't left when I did..." She shuddered and closed her eyes.

"Tell me," Dearborn probed gently, "how could Baki have taken McAuley hostage without Stanley's giving the alarm?"

Miss Van Curl opened her eyes and pointed to a door at the other side of the room. "That's an outside door. Stanley thought Mr. Baki was still here in the office when he went off duty at seven-thirty. The night man, Ramon, had no idea anything was wrong."

"In other words, no one even missed McAuley until this morning."

"That's right."

The office door suddenly opened and Benjamin bounded into the office. "Hey, the desk clerk said he saw you come in here. Where were you last night, Da—Mr. Roycroft! I was looking for you!"

"Benjamin? Just the person I want to see. Hop over to the marina and find out if anyone knows anything about Mr. McAuley's abduction."

"Mr. McAuley was abducted?"

"Oh, Mr. Roycroft," Miss Van Curl wailed, "we're trying to keep it quiet."

"Mr. McAuley was abducted," Dearborn confirmed, "by Raúl Baki last night. About seven o'clock. Looks like they went off on the Beggses' yacht. Go see what you can find out, Benjamin."

"Didn't anybody call the police?"

"We've called everyone," Miss Van Curl declared, "the police, the Coast Guard, everyone. They'll be here any minute."

"What do you think the police are going to say if they catch me playing detective?" Benjamin objected.

"If you refuse," Dearborn threatened, "then you will remain here to comfort Miss Van Curl and I shall go."

Benjamin regarded Miss Van Curl unenthusiastically. She turned woebegone eyes on him.

"Take your choice, Benjamin. The marina or Miss Van Curl."

"I'll call you from there."

Miss Van Curl pointed to the outside door. "That's the quickest way. It brings you out on the east side of the hotel."

Dearborn noted and commented on the fact that Benjamin had to unlock the door to let himself out.

"The door has an automatic lock," Miss Van Curl explained. "You can only open it from the inside and it locks again when it closes."

"I see. So of course no one became suspicious. It wasn't until you came in this morning and found the note that anyone realized McAuley was gone."

"Mr. Roycroft," Miss Van Curl said broodingly, "do you believe in divine justice?"

"I do not believe in divine anything, madam."

"Collis has an absolute obsession about those books. The accountants come in at the end of February to start work on the tax returns and Collis is a man possessed for weeks beforehand. Look. Look at his desk."

McAuley's desk was piled with ledgers and stacks of paper.

"For the last two weeks," Miss Van Curl went on self-righteously, "he's done everything but sleep in here! He expects everyone else to do the same. Mr. Baki knew just where to find him. If that isn't divine justice, I don't know what is!"

Dearborn squinted at the grim-faced Miss Van Curl. "The last two weeks, you say?"

"Day and night," Miss Van Curl confirmed.

"Surely he took some time off. A long weekend, perhaps? Perhaps the weekend when Mr. Beggs was away? You know, 'When the cat's away'?" Dearborn forced a small chuckle. "Perhaps he took that Monday off? Or Tuesday perhaps? Went fishing? Took a little boat cruise?"

"Collis loved it when Leo went away," Miss Van Curl sniffed. "It was the one time he felt as if he were truly in charge. He couldn't wait for Leo to go so he could make my life miserable. 'Do this, do that, fetch this, carry that. You're late, Alberta, you took too long for lunch, Alberta, you'll have to stay late again tonight, Alberta.'"

Dearborn clucked absent-mindedly. He wondered what

Miss Van Curl would say if she knew she had just provided the despised Collis McAuley with an alibi.

"And that Raúl Baki," she continued peevishly. "Nobody could every handle him but Leo and Fernando Alvarez. When Collis is in charge, Mr. Baki gets away with the most outrageous things. Do you know he raided the men's room in the hall outside the dining room two Mondays ago? He locked the attendant in one of the booths and wouldn't let him out or come out himself until five in the morning."

How could he have forgotten that, Dearborn wondered. Cooky had told him about the men's room incident. Two alibis for the price of one. That explained the whereabouts of both McAuley and Baki during the hours that Louis Martin was stalked and killed.

"Fernando called in sick that day," Alberta Van Curl was saying, "so he wasn't around. . . ."

"Fernando did not work the Monday before last?" Dearborn picked up.

"No. He called in sick."

"And Tuesday is his day off?"

"That's right."

Dearborn fell silent. He heard nothing further of what Miss Van Curl had to say. He was concentrating on what he must do next, so much so that he didn't hear the phone ring.

"Benjamin Pinch," Miss Van Curl announced, thrusting the phone at him.

"What is it, Benjamin?"

"The night watchman at the marina doesn't go on duty until eight when the marina closes. No one was around when it happened except for one of the small-boat attendants, a kid named Juan who was tying up the last of the bicycle pontoons when Baki and McAuley went by. He said McAuley looked a little funny, but he didn't think too much about it. He didn't see a gun, but he said Baki looked like he was carrying a couple of duck pin balls attached to a rope. They got on the yacht, and after a couple of minutes they weighed anchor and shoved off."

"Is that all you found out, Benjamin?"

"One more thing. Something Baki said. The kid didn't

think anything about it then. Baki was always talking about it."

"What's that?"

"The kid heard Baki say something about going to Cuba."

"You're late, Buggy."

Juanita was, as usual, modishly dressed and coiffed, her diminutive figure flattered by the simple lines of a pale yellow linen shirtwaist dress, her white hair fashionably high-lighted with a blue rinse and pulled into a classic chignon.

"Sorry, Juanita. Was talking to the assistant manager out there. Quite a hullabaloo over McAuley."

"Exciting, isn't it?" Juanita agreed. "I never expected Mr. Baki to turn out a criminal. But one would guess that if he were going to take someone hostage he would choose a more affluent guest. Then again, I suppose he was thinking of Mr. McAuley's daughter. Mrs. Beggs can certainly afford to pay a substantial ransom."

"You've got it wrong, Juanita. Baki isn't holding McAuley for ransom. He took McAuley because McAuley knows how to run the boat. It was the boat he was after."

"The boat? Why would he want a boat? Where is he going?"

"I suspect that V.C. Day is close at hand."

"V.C.? You mean he is going to invade Cuba? How thrilling!"

"You were always a sucker for romance," Dearborn commented snappishly. "That's probably why you married so often. Tell the truth, did any one of your husbands turn out to be as romantic as you expected?"

"Why, Buggy," Juanita asserted, "*all* my husbands were romantic. But nothing lasts forever, darling. You know that."

Dearborn didn't want to discuss Burgess Roycroft, so he interrupted the conversation to order lunch. They decided on the escabeche de gallina, which was a cold pickled chicken, and Dearborn ordered, as an accompaniment, a chilled vintage Sancerre. The distraction was temporarily effective, the meal reminding Juanita of a trip she'd taken to the Andes in 1939 with a gentleman named Ignacio Frutos. "You know, the Andes are five thousand miles long," she reminisced. "They stretch from Tierra del Fuego to the Caribbean. I don't remember the Andes too well, but I'll never forget Ignacio."

Dearborn hoped to confine Juanita to her South American reminiscences by ordering the Brasileiaras, Brazilian coconut cookies, for dessert. The ploy backfired when Juanita said, "Speaking of Brazil, Buggy, do you know who I met a few years back? Emerson Fittipaldi."

Dearborn regarded her blankly.

"The racing driver!"

"Oh yes," Dearborn returned in a mumble. "Yes, of course. Fittipaldi. I don't follow the sport much anymore. Getting a bit ripe for that sort of thing."

"Racing used to be the most important thing in your life," Juanita reminded him. "Or," she revised coyly, "the second most important thing. Which reminds me. How is Sophie? Is she still alive and well?"

"She ... er ... as well as can be expected," Dearborn replied, having no idea who Sophie was.

"And Winthrop?"

"The same, the same."

"And do you keep track of Amelia? I know you and she haven't spoken to one another in over forty years. And what about dear Edward? I sent Amelia a silver spoon when he was born. Just for old times' sake, you know. I've never met Edward, but every once in a while I see him when I'm in New York and go to the symphony."

"Edward?" Dearborn returned. "Edward? My nephew Edward, you mean?"

"Of course, Buggy. That adorable boy. How is Edward?"

Dearborn hadn't anticipated that Edward's name would come up, but he was relieved to find that there was at least one person he could talk about knowledgeably. "He couldn't be better," Dearborn replied. "Saw him just before I came down here. Visited him in his apartment. Lives alone. Hasn't married."

"Of course not," Juanita said. "I never expected he would, even with that cherub face and those curls. Plays his violin beautifully, though, doesn't he?"

"He certainly does," Dearborn confirmed. "He's a fine musician, solid citizen all around."

"I have a friend. Fanny Tyler. Do you know Fanny Tyler, the actress?"

Dearborn did, indeed, know Fanny Tyler. He'd seen her not too long before in connection with the Rotten Apple affair, but he wasn't so sure that Burgess Roycroft had known her. He waggled his head in a way that he hoped could be interpreted as either yes or no.

"She told me that Amelia still refuses to speak your name or hear it spoken. She asked me if I ever hear from you. Now I shall be able to say I saw you. Anyway, Fanny watched little Edward grow up. She talks about him from time to time. She told me that he's talented but that he lacks that quality, that *je ne sais quoi* that one needs to be a concert soloist. He takes after Amelia's side of the family, the Nordic looks, the lackluster personality. He reminds me of Olin. Do you remember Olin?"

"Can't say I do."

"Amelia's husband! Your brother-in-law! How could you forget Olin!"

Dearborn decided the time had arrived for a drastic shift in subject. "Juanita, there's something I wish to discuss. . . ."

"What is it, Buggy?"

"What is it," Dearborn murmured, casting around for inspiration.

"Did it have to do with the Valentine's party this evening? I have absolutely no one to go with. I was going with Drew Pinckney Le Maire—do you know him, Buggy?"

"No," Dearborn answered, hoping that Drew Pinckney Le Maire wasn't another relative.

"But we had a little set-to this morning over the Gaza Strip, so I told him I wouldn't go with him."

"Well, no, Juanita, that wasn't what I was going to talk

about. As a matter of fact, I am already committed to taking Miss Gillette to the party."

"She's going? With her uncle just buried?"

"I persuaded her to do so. Better than sitting around brooding."

"And it's Cordelia you wanted to talk about," Juanita burst out with sudden understanding. "You want me to take her in hand."

"Yes," Dearborn conceded gratefully, grasping at straws.

"I'll be glad to do it, but I'm afraid she's going to need more than talking to. She needs new clothes and three or four hours with a beautician. . . ."

"Carte blanche, Juanita. Anything goes. Just put it on my bill."

Juanita was thrilled. She picked up her napkin, dabbed her lips with it, and pushed back her chair. "Marvelous! I love it! I absolutely love it! I shall call her right now. I do hope she's free this afternoon. Oh, is it all right, Buggy? You don't mind if I excuse myself?"

"Not at all," Dearborn said generously. "Go right ahead. I'll find some other way to amuse myself."

30

Dearborn arrived at the fronton by taxi at a quarter to three. The advance-ticket sale window was open and the woman behind the counter directed him to the players' entrance on the south side of the building. When he tried to enter by that door his way was blocked by a guard who demanded identification.

"Dearborn V. Pinch," Dearborn announced, then recognizing his error, added quickly, "who is an old friend of mine, wanted me to look up Fernando Alvarez. I understand that Mr. Alvarez is using the court today."

"Just give me your name, buddy."

"Burgess Roycroft."

"Wait here."

Fernando appeared wearing a white uniform and helmet and unstrapping a cesta from his arm. For a moment Dearborn felt a twinge of recollected apprehension, then rejected it as unworthy of him.

"Mr. Roycroft? Nothing's happened at the hotel, has it?"

"As a matter of fact," Dearborn replied, "something has. I thought you might want to know about it. Can we go somewhere and talk?"

Fernando led Dearborn through a maze of hallways and doors to the empty auditorium.

"You're not still put out with me, Fernando?" Dearborn prompted, as they settled into the last row of the orchestra.

"I didn't want Miss Gillette to have the wrong impression of me," Fernando replied.

"I'm sure."

"Is that why you're here? To talk about that?"

"No," Dearborn said. "I wanted to tell you about Collis McAuley and Raúl Baki."

Two of the jai alai players were on the court lobbing a ball with powerful strokes against the wall, the rhythmic crack of pelota against concrete providing a hypnotic accompaniment to the story of McAuley's abduction.

Fernando's first question was how Molly Beggs had received the news.

"Not too well, I expect," Dearborn responded. "I haven't seen her."

"Mr. McAuley was supposed to preside at the Valentine's party tonight," Fernando said. "I'd better call Mrs. Beggs and see if I can help. I'll tell her I'm coming in."

Fernando started to rise and Dearborn put a restraining hand on his arm. "Just a minute. Before you go, there's something else I'd like to tell you."

Fernando sat down again.

"How much do you know about Leo Beggs's will?"

"Nothing."

"He never spoke to you about it?"

"No. Why should he?"

"Because you are in it, my boy."

Fernando looked mildly interested but not overly surprised. "How do you know that?"

"Collis McAuley told me," Dearborn answered, choosing to assign the responsibility to the person least likely to give him away prematurely.

"It was generous of him to remember me," Fernando said politely, looking as if he didn't understand what Dearborn was getting at.

"It is not an inconsiderable sum," Dearborn went on.

"Oh? I don't suppose Mr. McAuley told you how much?"

"How much would you think?"

"A million would be nice," Fernando replied with a wry smile, "but I wouldn't turn down a hundred."

"Twenty thousand," Dearborn informed him.

There was a moment's silence. Then Fernando whispered, "Dollars?"

"That is correct."

Fernando slid back into the seat and whistled. "Dollars?" he repeated. "I don't believe it."

It was part of a well-rehearsed script, no doubt intended originally to impress the lawyers and assembled heirs but pressed into service for Dearborn's benefit. Dearborn watched him interestedly. Fernando was either a naturally gifted actor or he had been practicing in front of a mirror.

"Why?" Fernando asked finally.

"To be perfectly honest, Fernando, that was a question I intended to ask you. Not that it's any of my business, of course, but I do admit to a certain curiosity." Dearborn anticipated that the answer would have to do with Beggs's wanting to reward Fernando for loyalty, efficiency, and good works in general.

"It was a bribe, Mr. Roycroft, a twenty-thousand-dollar bribe." Fernando shook his head unbelievingly.

"What kind of bribe, Fernando? A bribe to do what?" Dearborn prepared himself for the obvious answer. *He wanted me to stay at La Playa, continue to lend my support . . .*

"Will you keep this confidential, sir?"

"You may rely on me."

"He wanted me to marry Miss Gillette."

Dearborn was jarred out of his complacency. "Cordelia?"

"Mr. Beggs promised me a promotion if I persuaded her to marry me. He said Mr. McAuley would be retired and I would be made manager. He thought I was crazy to refuse, but the way I looked at it, even if she did reciprocate my feelings, I couldn't agree. Not under those conditions."

"Even if she did reciprocate your feelings?" Dearborn murmured.

"The fact that I wanted to marry her had nothing to do with it. That's what I told Mr. Beggs."

"You wanted to marry her?"

"You promised to keep that quiet," Fernando reminded him.

"Cordelia?"

"I know it's hopeless. 'The desire of the moth for the star, of the night for the morrow, the devotion to something afar from the sphere of our sorrow' . . ."

"What are you reciting there, Fernando? Keats?"

"Shelley."

"Good Lord."

"I refused Mr. Beggs outright. I would not permit myself to stoop so low."

"Where does the twenty thousand come in?" Dearborn pressed, taking a firm hold on himself.

"I asked Mr. Beggs to lend me twenty thousand so I could go out on my own. He said no. He didn't want me to leave La Playa. But he said he'd give me twenty thousand as a kind of bonus if I'd change my mind about Miss Gillette."

"Good Lord."

"I couldn't tell you about that last night. It was a private matter between Mr. Beggs and me. I didn't want to say anything about a loan in front of . . . er . . . her. When I kept refusing he said he'd write the twenty thousand in his will so nobody could call it a bribe. I thought he was joking."

"And when did all this take place, Fernando?"

"About a year ago."

"You didn't make any attempt to engage Cordelia's affections?"

"I wouldn't do that. Not so long as I worked for her uncle."

Dearborn believed the story of the twenty thousand dollars. Leo Beggs's concern for Cooky had been real enough and he had been a man who thought everything was for sale. He'd bought himself a wife. Why not a husband for Cooky? What Dearborn didn't believe, and was hard put to understand, was Fernando's claim to be enamored of Cooky. The only explanation Dearborn could think of offhand was that he intended to forestall speculation regarding an attachment between him and Molly Beggs. He felt he should pursue it, but he didn't want to be sidetracked from the main issue. Counting on a surprise tactic to throw Fernando off guard, Dearborn said, "Didn't you tell me you always work a full day on Monday?"

"That's right."

"But on Monday, February 3, you didn't work. Is that right?"

Fernando looked perplexed. "Monday, February 3? When was that?"

"The Monday before last."

Fernando nibbled his thumbnail contemplatively and said after a hestitation, "That's right. I didn't work that Monday."

Dearborn had expected a glib alibi and was stalled by Fernando's circumspection. He found himself having to justify his reason for asking. He cast about for a suitable explanation and decided that an oblique rendering of the truth would suffice. "Miss Van Curl was telling me that Mr. Baki created something of a scene that Monday night. She said Mr. Beggs was in New York and Mr. McAuley was unable to cope. She said it was a pity you weren't there. She said you can usually handle Baki."

"How did the subject come up?"

"We were saying that Mr. Baki seems to have a fine instinct for choosing his time well. I presume you were home ill that day?"

"No," Fernando responded uninformatively.

"Playing hooky, eh?"

Fernando did look somewhat abashed, but he avoided answering by saying, "Look, Mr. Roycroft, I'd like to call the hotel now if you don't mind."

Dearborn was disappointed, but he had no intention of giving up. "Mind if I tag along?" he proposed. "If you're going back I'd like to accompany you."

"Sure. I'll drive you. My car's in the parking lot."

Dearborn waited on a bench in the locker room while Fernando changed and went to the public phone in the hall to call Molly Beggs. Dearborn sat with his hands folded over the knob of his cane, his chin on his hands. He blamed himself for not having been clever enough to trick Fernando into an admission, or at least an alibi.

"Ready to go?" Fernando called from the locker room door.

Dearborn got up from the bench and followed him down the hall to the door.

The parking lot was nearly empty. Only a few cars dotted the immense expanse of tarmac. Fernando led the way across the lot. He was twenty feet ahead of Dearborn when one of the parked cars started up and headed for the exit. Dearborn paid no attention to it. He was looking down, his mind occupied by the dilemma he faced, how to prove that Fernando had been in New York on the days in question. Without that proof there would be no case against him. It was evidence needed to compel the police to reopen the case.

The loud screech of rubber tires brought Dearborn's head up with a jerk. The strange car had made a wide U-turn and was racing back across the parking lot. Dearborn saw it swerve toward him and pick up speed. Fernando had stopped and was watching. Dearborn felt a surge of anger at having allowed himself to be so easily duped. She must have followed him there. The tables had been turned. He'd been tricked by the two of them, Molly and Fernando.

The car was only a few yards away. Instinctively, Dearborn bent forward and threw his hands up over his head. A second later he was hit, the impact throwing him to one side and causing him to roll over two or three times before he came to rest on his back. He heard the car tires skid into another turn and he kept his eyes shut. When he opened them seconds later he found himself staring up into Fernando's frightened eyes.

"It's okay," Fernando said grimly, rolling his weight off Dearborn. "It's gone. Are you all right? I didn't hurt you, did I?"

It took Dearborn a moment to catch his breath. Then he muttered weakly, "Fernando, tell me something. No evasions. No side-stepping. No monosyllabic answers. Where were you on Monday, February 3, and Tuesday, February 4?"

Fernando studied Dearborn's face with a look that seemed to assume the fall had inflicted some irreparable damage, then said, "My friend José Miro has a cousin who runs a jai alai school in Miami. He's looking for an instructor. José and I drove to Miami to see him."

"Could you prove it?"

"What?"

"Could you prove it if you had to?"

"If I had to," Fernando answered in a bewildered voice.

Dearborn groaned and sat up. His cane lay beside him and he examined it closely before feeling himself for broken bones. Then he allowed Fernando to help him to his feet. He dusted himself off and said, "I should have realized it."

"What's that, Mr. Roycroft?"

"That anyone who recites Shelley on the one hand is not apt to be contemplating mayhem on the other."

31

"Dad, what's this?" Benjamin was sitting on the couch holding the note Baki had sent Dearborn. " 'Beggs did not died in vain, my friend Roycrap. Viva Cuba.' "

"What are you doing with that? How did you get in here? Don't tell me the maid let you in again?"

"You always leave the key under the carpet, remember?"

"It isn't left there for your convenience."

Benjamin got up, dumped the piece of paper on the coffee table, and strode to the bedroom door. He pointed to the splintered door jamb and to the circular bit of metal buried in it. "What's this?"

"Whom do you think you're talking to? May I remind you that you are addressing your father?"

"I don't need any reminding, thanks."

"I've had a long day, Benjamin." Dearborn sighed and dropped into the nearest chair. He was almost too weary to argue. In less than twenty-four hours he'd been shot at, attacked with a pelota, and nearly run over by an automobile. He was bruised, aching, and despondent, and there was a two-inch gash in his ebony cane.

"I'll tell you what it is, Dad. It's a bullet. Raúl Baki shot at you."

"Who told you that?"

"Stuart Ripple."

"Who," Dearborn said drily, "no doubt got it from the fair widow."

Benjamin slapped the door jamb with the open palm of his hand. "The guy tried to kill you. How come nobody called the police?"

"No need to cause a panic in the hotel."

"It's better to let him go around picking people off? Now he's kidnapped Collis McAuley. How do you feel about that?

Don't you realize that if you'd called the police they could have stopped him before he caused any more trouble?"

"It is true, Benjamin, that Mr. Baki is deranged. And he has, no question about it, abducted Collis McAuley. But he did not shoot at me."

Benjamin rubbed his hand over his face and tried again. "Dad, you know who I spoke to this afternoon? I spoke to Niccoli."

"You did? You called him?"

"No. He called me."

"What for?"

"I don't know exactly, but something fishy's going on. He wanted me to ask you a couple of things."

"What things?"

"About the Colt .38 for one. According to the Silver Beach police, it isn't the Colt .38 that's registered in Leo Beggs's name."

"It is the one that killed Louis Martin, isn't it?"

"Yes, but Niccoli doesn't believe you took it out of Beggs's gun cabinet."

"What does he think I took it out of, Benjamin?"

"He says he can understand Beggs killing Martin with an unregistered gun, but he can't understand why Beggs would put the gun in his gun cabinet afterward."

"It did not, of course, occur to him that Leo Beggs did not put the murder weapon into his gun cabinet."

"What do you mean?"

"You are as lacking in imagination, Benjamin, as Captain Niccoli. The gun which is in the possession of the New York police is the murder weapon, but it did not belong to Leo Beggs. Beggs's gun, the registered Colt .38, was removed from his gun cabinet and replaced by the murder weapon all right. But not by him."

"What are you saying? That it was planted?"

"Precisely," Dearborn assured him with conviction. "Planted by the person who killed Louis Martin and conspired with Molly Beggs to kill her husband. Molly is a beautiful

———205

woman and totally unscrupulous. I never doubted that she was capable of murder, even though it was clear that she could not have committed the murders herself. And when I saw the will. . . ."

"You saw the will?"

"With my own eyes. The will leaves La Playa to Mrs. Beggs. We are talking here of a multi-million-dollar enterprise. We are talking about a broken marriage, an impending divorce, a monetary settlement that would have been only a fraction of what is contained in the will, and a woman whose seductiveness is unrivaled."

As Dearborn said these words he studied Benjamin closely. "You wouldn't disagree with that, would you? No, I thought not."

"Murder?" Benjamin exclaimed. " Again murder? You're back on that murder kick again?"

"Two murders, Benjamin."

"Niccoli warned me," Benjamin groaned.

"Killing Louis Martin was step one," Dearborn went on calmly. "Making it appear that Beggs killed Martin and then committed suicide was step two. On the night of the murder Mrs. Beggs went downstairs, ostensibly to get the portable television set, but actually to establish an alibi, while the murderer, hidden upstairs, shot Leo Beggs. The only point that disturbs me," Dearborn mused, forgetting Benjamin for a moment, "is that Beggs was shot with his own gun. If his gun were in the bedside table as Molly Beggs claimed, one would think it would have been more readily accessible to him than to the murderer, that there would have been an outcry, a struggle for the weapon. . . ."

Benjamin began to fidget. He had been in Beggs's bedroom a few hours before Beggs was murdered. As a matter of fact, he had been in Beggs's bed.

"What's the matter, Benjamin? Is something itching you?"

"There wasn't any gun in the bedside table," Benjamin was forced to reveal. "So where's your theory now?"

Dearborn studied Benjamin before saying, "You are quite certain?"

Benjamin nodded, looking embarrassed.

"Obviously, then, the murderer already had the gun in his possession."

"Oh no," Benjamin muttered. "You're not going to give up, are you."

"Molly Beggs must have given it to him earlier in the day. Either that or the murderer took the gun himself . . . the man Nico chased from the apartment while you were upstairs rummaging around in the . . . er . . . bedside table."

"Why not let Molly take it?"

"She might not have known which weapon to choose."

"Hold it," Benjamin walked to the bar. "I want a drink."

"Pour me one, too. I've had a trying afternoon. Whiskey and soda. That's it, of course. Molly's accomplice, knowing that Beggs was out, slipped into the apartment, chose the weapon he intended to use on Leo Beggs, and stole it out of the gun cabinet."

"And was caught by Conchita."

"Exactly. I found out," Dearborn went on, "quite inadvertently, from no more disinterested party than Juanita Froebel—"

"I thought you were hiding out from Juanita Froebel?"

"Don't distract me in the middle of a thought. I found out that, the day before he was killed, Leo Beggs still believed that Louis Martin was alive, was in fact making plans to deal with Martin in some unspecific but malicious manner. What more convincing proof is there that Beggs had not murdered Martin?"

"Oh, sure," Benjamin interjected. "Very convincing. I can see this eighty-year-old lady up on the witness stand."

Dearborn threw him a scornful look. "I had already constructed a sound case, starting with the basic framework, which was my conviction that Louis Martin had been murdered with malice aforethought—"

"Sound? You didn't have any sound reason for thinking that."

"Martin didn't *look* like someone who had been mugged."

"And Leo Beggs didn't look like he committed suicide, I suppose?"

"Exactly."

"Well, he sure as hell looked it to me."

"No doubt. Anyway, I hammered away at it. Reason and logic formed the basis for seeking a mercenary motive. Once the motive was established, the chief suspects stood out like so many sore thumbs."

"A result of all that hammering, I guess."

"If you'd rather I didn't continue . . ."

"Don't stop, Dad. This is better than 'The Movie of the Week.' "

"It boiled down to five suspects, all men, all fitting the physical description of the man Nico chased, all of whom had possible motives. I have been investigating those five suspects—"

"While I've been breaking my balls to get those damned train reservations—"

"Eliminating them one by one."

"And?"

"I have eliminated them all."

Benjamin stood with the two whiskey and sodas poised in midair. "All?"

"All."

"Congratulations. The perfect crime."

Dearborn signaled to Benjamin to hand him the glass. "I am not going to mouth the obvious."

"No such thing as a —"

"Precisely."

"Yeah? Well, how's this for obvious? Didn't it occur to you that if there are no murderers there might not have been a murder?"

"And didn't it occur to you that if a bullet was fired at me, then someone fired it?"

"That nut Baki fired it."

"Benjamin, what else did Captain Niccoli want from me?"

"He wants to know more about Edward Roycroft. He wants me to get a detailed account of your meeting with Edward Roycroft."

"Why?"

"I don't know why. He didn't tell me why."

"Why didn't he call me directly?"

"Because he didn't think you'd talk to him."

"He's absolutely right. And I'm not going to talk to you either. It's almost five and I'd like to rest before the festivities tonight."

"You're not still going to that Valentine's party, are you?"

"I am. And so are you. I have gotten you a date for the evening."

"I've already got a date for the evening," Benjamin declared vehemently. "At least, I had one. Now I'm not so sure I should keep it. I'm not sure what this Baki character's apt to do next."

"A date with whom, Benjamin?"

"The travel agent from the hotel. Who else have I had a chance to meet?"

"You were taking her to the Valentine's party?"

"I was taking her to this little French restaurant she told me about in Silver Beach."

"Good. So there's no chance of running into her here."

"Dad, I told her I'm picking her up at her place at eight."

"Forget it. Forget it. You'll have to tell her you can't make it. You are escorting Juanita Froebel to the party."

"Juanita Froebel? I'm giving up Lucia Cerrito for Juanita Froebel?"

"We are going as a foursome, Benjamin."

"Who's the lucky fourth? Don't tell me. Let me guess. You're taking Lucia Cerrito."

"I am escorting Cordelia Gillette."

"Sounds like a fun evening."

"We shall meet in the Starfish Lounge at seven-thirty and proceed from there to the Monsoon."

Benjamin had been ready to put his foot down until he

heard that it was to be a foursome. Niccoli had told him to stick close to his father. It had been part solicitude and part threat, and Benjamin had no intention of ignoring it.

"I assume from your silence that you intend to cooperate, Benjamin?"

"I'll go," Benjamin agreed grudgingly. "What the hell."

"Are you certain," Dearborn inquired as Benjamin walked to the door, "that Captain Niccoli didn't tell you why he is suddenly so interested in my arrangements with Edward Roycroft?"

"I didn't ask him and he didn't tell me."

Dearborn shook his head in discouragement. "The acorn doesn't fall far from the maternal oak."

32

Dearborn blamed the knocking about he'd suffered for the fact that he hadn't immediately recognized the significance of Niccoli's phone call to Benjamin. But he didn't intend to brood over it. As soon as Benjamin left he picked up the telephone himself and called New York. He allowed the phone to ring a full ten times before deciding that Edward Roycroft wasn't at home and might be at rehearsal. The switchboard operator got the number of the Metropolitan Symphony Orchestra and put through the call.

"Let me speak with Edward Roycroft," Dearborn demanded of the man who answered.

"Who?"

"He is one of the violinists," Dearborn explained impatiently.

"Nobody's here."

"Of course somebody's there," Dearborn insisted. "I can hear the orchestra in the background."

"I'm just an electrician. Call back later."

"Put someone else on the phone," Dearborn commanded. "It's imperative. Heads will roll, I promise you."

"Sure, sure," the man answered in a bored voice. "Just a minute."

Dearborn tapped his fingers on his knees and hummed tunelessly while he waited. Finally another voice got on the wire, this time a soothing female voice. "I'm sorry, sir, we can't interrupt the rehearsal. Mr. Uberdini is very strict about that. Perhaps I could take your name and have the party call you?"

"This is a matter of life and death, madam."

"Who is it you wish to speak to?" the soft voice inquired with maddening imperturbability.

"Edward Roycroft. Edward Roycroft."

"Hold on, please."

Dearborn got up and paced the room as far as the length of telephone cord would allow. Almost two minutes passed before another voice came over the wire, again a woman's voice but this time older and reedier. "Excuse me," she asked, "you're trying to reach Edward Roycroft?"

"I am," Dearborn exclaimed, "and I do not wish to hear that Luigi Uberdini will not excuse him."

"I'm sorry. Mr. Roycroft isn't here this week. There was a death, in the family, I believe. Someone very close to him, at any rate. Have you tried the apartment?"

"I have."

"You might try again. I'm sure you'll get him eventually. Do you wish to leave your name just in case?"

"Not necessary," Dearborn informed her. "Thank you and good-bye."

His hum picked up volume. He pressed his finger to the disconnect button, then released it. "Give me Miss Juanita Froebel's suite, please."

He listened to the staccato buzz, then heard Juanita's light voice answer. "Hello?"

"Juanita? Burgess Roycroft here."

"Oh, Buggy, I was about to call you."

"You were? What for?"

"I wanted to tell you that I spent the entire afternoon with Cordelia. I even sat in the hairdresser's with her for three and a half hours."

Dearborn had forgotten about Juanita's project to turn Cordelia from duck to swan. "Splendid," he responded absent-mindedly. "But that's not the reason I called. I wanted to know if you've made arrangements with anyone to attend the do this evening."

"No, I haven't. I did think of calling a gentleman I met by the pool this morning, Horsley Stytch. You remember him, don't you? He ran on the American Action ticket in 1940? A Stytch in time? But he has a gimpy leg and I do so like to dance."

"Rest easy, Juanita. I have found you an escort."

"How lovely. Who is it?"

"I believe you know him. Benjamin Pinch."

"Dearie Pinch's son? How nice."

"He told me he wasn't taking anyone and I suggested you. He said he'd be delighted. I thought perhaps we could make it a foursome. Four might be livelier than two."

"Oh, Burgess," Juanita bubbled, "you rogue. A pas de quatre."

"What are you talking about?"

"You're such a voluptuary."

"I fail to see . . ."

"It is certainly more acceptable than Siamese twins."

What was the woman babbling about? "Benjamin will pick you up and we'll meet in the Starfish Lounge at seven-thirty. Is that all right?"

"It's perfect, Burgess. Just perfect."

Dearborn was to pick up Cooky at seven-fifteen, but he made sure to leave his suite at ten to seven. He met Norbert at the foot of the stairs. Norbert was wearing beaded mascara and a shade of pink greasepaint that made him look feverish. He was dressed in a sleeveless black lace tunic, skintight white satin trousers decorated with black polka dots, an eye-riveting codpiece in scarlet, and hip-high scarlet boots. As always, his bass fiddle was appended to him like a giant tumor. He presented a startling contrast to Dearborn in white dinner jacket, pleated evening shirt, and black tie.

"Well, if it isn't old Burgess," Norbert greeted Dearborn cheerfully. "Going to pick up Cooky? You've got a wait. She's been sitting in the tub for the last hour and a half."

"You look like you've been sitting in something yourself," Dearborn returned starchily as Norbert and his fiddle brushed past.

Conchita opened the door. In answer to Dearborn's query about Cooky she replied, "Che's not ready. Chu can wait in there." She gestured toward the library.

"Is Mrs. Beggs anywhere about?" Dearborn asked.

"Che's upstairs."

"Will you kindly ask her if I may speak with her, please."

Conchita led him to the library door, ushered him in, and closed the door with a look so untrusting that Dearborn half expected to hear the lock click into place.

Dearborn checked his watch. Four minutes before seven.

The last time he'd been in the library it had been dark. He wondered at the fact that he'd been able to avoid stumbling over anything. The room had more booby traps than Raúl Baki's hideaway in Shell Cove. Besides the desk and gun cabinet, there were a couch, two armchairs, hassocks, a drum table, file cabinets, a curio cabinet, two military chests, mirrors, paintings, oriental scatter rugs, and dozens of knick-knacks, framed photographs, ashtrays, bowls, figurines, the kind of geegaws Dearborn abhorred.

It occurred to Dearborn that of all the rooms in the apartment, this was the most likely one in which to hide something. He had no doubt that Leo Beggs's safe, for instance, was in the room, and to satisfy his curiosity he wandered around peeking behind mirrors and pictures, looking for it. He found it behind a painting of a fat Napoleonic soldier astride a chestnut bay, a round steel plate with a combination lock. Dearborn had overheard Molly admit that only Leo and Norbert knew the combination, and since it was inaccessible to her, it was uninteresting to him. He began idly opening the desk drawers, then rummaged through one of the military chests, and when he stopped to look at his watch again he saw that it was twelve minutes after seven.

He was poking around in the curio cabinet when Molly Beggs opened the door and walked into the room. She was wearing an ivory satin peignoir and her waist-long hair was arranged into one thick plait over her shoulder. Her guarded expression gave way to surprise and hostility when she saw what Dearborn was doing. "What are you looking for?" she asked sharply.

Dearborn put down the porcelain Buddha he was holding. He didn't answer until he had crossed the room to stand directly in front of her. "I was looking for the other gun," he answered nonchalantly.

"What other gun?"

"Your husband's Colt .38. The one he kept in the gun cabinet."

"The police have it," Molly asserted. "You gave it to Captain Niccoli yourself. Remember?" She spoke calmly but in a clipped tone that showed she was exercising self-restraint.

Dearborn said gravely, "There is no point, madam, in each of us continuing to pretend that we do not know what the other is thinking."

Molly studied his tranquil face without betraying any emotion herself. After a moment she walked to the drum table, opened its single drawer, removed a gun, and handed it to Dearborn. "I don't know what you want with it," she said. "It's meaningless. It proves nothing. I found it there yesterday and just left it."

"You put it there," Dearborn suggested.

"So far as I'm concerned," Molly said coolly, "Leo put it there. I don't think the police will argue with that."

"Do you think they'll argue with what I intend to tell them about you, Mrs. Beggs?"

"What to you intend to tell them?"

"That you were responsible for your husband's death."

"That's idiotic. I didn't shoot Leo."

"You had an accomplice," Dearborn pointed out. "It was he who pulled the trigger."

"That's ridiculous. I have too much on my mind right now to be bothered with your wild ideas. My father is out there in the ocean somewhere with that maniac. How dare you come in here and upset me with those crazy accusations!"

"I wonder how worried you really are, Mrs. Beggs. You and your accomplice haven't allowed your father's abduction to interfere with any of your evil machinations."

"I'm not staying here to listen to any more of this." She turned toward the door.

"Mrs. Beggs," Dearborn said quickly, "you said a moment ago that it was I who had removed the murder weapon from the gun cabinet. How did you know that?"

She paused with her hand on the doorknob and then slowly turned back. "Benjamin said so."

"He did not. He led you to believe that Captain Niccoli broke into the apartment and made off with the gun."

"You're too trusting," she parried. "Your son is the one who told me that my husband was about to be arrested. He's also the one who told me that it was really you who broke into the apartment and took the gun. He may deny it, but it'll be his word against mine."

"Did Benjamin also apprise you of his filial attachment to me?"

Molly remained unflustered. "He's not very good at keeping secrets, is he?"

Dearborn looked at his wristwatch. Seven-fourteen. Cooky might walk into the room at any moment. "And did Benjamin tell you that I was hired to come down here and gather evidence against your husband?"

"Yes, he did."

"And perhaps that I was not satisfied with what I found?"

"What did you find?"

"I found out who your accomplice is."

"Oh? Care to enlighten me?"

"It's Edward Roycroft."

Molly began to laugh. "Edward Roycroft? I never saw the man in my life."

"You planned this adventure from the first. You suggested that Martin go to New York to stay with Edward Roycroft. You planned to have Roycroft kill Martin and then kill your husband. You conceived of the notion of using me as a dupe."

"The entire story is ridiculous. Edward Roycroft was a friend of Lou. I never heard of him until after Leo killed himself."

"He's here somewhere now," Dearborn insisted. "I called New York. Edward Roycroft hasn't been seen since the murder."

"How would I have known that you'd discover Lou's body? How *could* I have planned such a thing beforehand? Don't you see how impossible it is?"

"You could not have planned to involve me beforehand, but you could take advantage of my involvement once it occurred. If it hadn't been me Roycroft hired, it would have been a professional detective. I simply saved him consulting the Yellow Pages."

"No one would ever believe that."

"Then why are you so afraid of me that you have made three separate attempts on my life?"

"Oh, I think you're crazy. Call the police, then. See if they'll believe you."

Dearborn took a deep breath. "I have an admission to make, Mrs. Beggs." He smiled slyly and with what he hoped was a degree of obsequiousness. "It has to do with the reason I accepted Edward Roycroft's proposal."

Molly gazed at him with hard eyes.

"It was money." Here Dearborn hemmed and hawed. "To put it bluntly, I am destitute."

"You?" she ridiculed. "I'm supposed to swallow that?"

"Mr. Roycroft is convinced that I intend to donate the money to charity. Don't you find that equally naïve?"

She frowned. "What happened to your money?"

"Bad investments, dwindling capital, an unfortunate run of gambling luck. For the last five years I have been totally dependent upon Benjamin for support. I am not, of course, in danger of starving, but many of my activities have been severely curtailed. Even the trip here was financed with money given me by Benjamin who, incidentally, knew nothing about my purpose in coming here. He insisted on accompanying me to make sure I didn't become reckless, gamble my vacation away, as it were. For a man unaccustomed to answering to anyone, it has been an ordeal."

There was enough truth in Dearborn's recital to give it the ring of authenticity. It was hard to tell, however, from Molly's face whether or not she accepted it.

"I took a great risk tonight," Dearborn went on. He licked his lips nervously. "You were holding a gun in your hand a moment ago." Dearborn had been relatively certain the gun wasn't loaded. "It would have been wiser to go straight to the police...."

"They wouldn't believe you."

"But I thought perhaps you would be interested in some sort..." He repeated the two words with a reptilian hiss. "... some sort of an arrangement." He glanced again at his watch. It was seven-twenty. Cooky was five minutes late.

"What do you want?"

"A man in his twilight years," Dearborn murmured mawkishly, "doesn't need much, the freedom to travel, to enjoy the little luxuries...."

"You're wrong, you know. But if paying you will get you out of here... how much do you want?"

Dearborn heard footsteps in the hall. "Perhaps," he said slowly. "Let us say..." He dragged the words out.

"Wait a minute," Molly declared. She turned to face the door. "Cooky's coming."

Dearborn gave a sigh of relief. Then he said quickly, "Later, then? Perhaps later? Tonight, I mean?"

"Where?"

"I'll leave that to you."

"The marina," Molly suggested. "After the party. Let's say at three."

"Fine," Dearborn agreed as the library door opened. "That suits me fine."

33

The willowy creature standing at the library door was wearing a clinging gown in gossamer shades of mauve, apricot, and dove gray. Her close-cropped cap of ringlets was coppery brown, her complexion smooth, with a tawny blush, her lips touched faintly with cinnamon rose. Garnets glittered in her earlobes and around her neck on a chain so delicate it was barely visible.

"Cordelia?" Dearborn hazarded.

"Four hundred and eighty-nine dollars and sixty-four cents' worth, counting the manicure," she acknowledged.

"Spending Leo's money already?" Molly commented astringently. "You have some nerve criticizing me for the way I behave."

From the manner in which Cooky chose to ignore Molly, Dearborn assumed that they had quarreled. This was confirmed by Cooky a few minutes later on their way to the Starfish Lounge. "We had a fight all right. She got home the same time Norbie and I did this morning. I called her a tramp."

"What did she say?"

"The same thing she said a minute ago. But, Burgess, it's not the same at all." Cooky turned to him with a distressed look. "Is it?"

"Not in the least," Dearborn concurred.

"I do feel bad about Collis. Not that I like him very much. He's never been friendly to me. But I think it's terrible what happened. I suppose Mr. Baki will let him go as soon as Collis takes him wherever he's headed."

"Let us hope so."

"Mr. Baki wouldn't actually hurt anyone."

"Not deliberately, perhaps," Dearborn agreed.

"I don't even think she's particularly worried. She doesn't worry about anyone except herself. She certainly never worried about Uncle Leo. Screwing around with every—"

"No need to be coarse, Cordelia. It doesn't suit the new image."

"Even if she hated Uncle Leo," Cooky persisted. "Even if he did kill Louis Martin."

"That's something we're going to have to talk about, Cordelia."

"What do you mean?"

Dearborn was going to have to break the news to Cooky before the evening was over. It would be too great a shock to call in the police without giving her any forewarning, but when he broke the news he wanted Juanita and Benjamin there. Maudlin sympathy and female hysterics were not emotions he found it easy to deal with.

Dearborn realized, too, that it was going to be difficult to persuade the Silver Beach police to accept his assertions regarding Molly Beggs. They would never arrest Molly and Edward Roycroft on Dearborn's say-so alone. A bald recital of the facts was going to be met with suspicion and, even more likely, incredulity. He would have to offer more. Much more. He would have to flush out Edward Roycroft and then present witnesses to back up his accusations.

That's where Cooky and Juanita would come in. Cooky's role would be supportive. Her status as a family member would add weight to Dearborn's accusations, and Juanita, as a disinterested party, would back up Dearborn's identification of Edward Roycroft.

Dearborn didn't anticipate any difficulty getting Edward Roycroft to come out into the open. His presence had been assured when Dearborn arranged the meeting at the marina. Molly wasn't, after all, really meeting Dearborn to talk about blackmail. She was coming to kill him, and for that she needed Roycroft.

It was because of that, that Benjamin would also be required to be there. Much as Dearborn would prefer to keep him out of it, he couldn't. It would be up to Benjamin to step in at the critical moment, prevent any harm to Dearborn's person, confiscate the weapon or weapons, and detain the culprits while Dearborn phoned for the police.

Dearborn had thought it all out carefully. It only remained to apprise Benjamin, Juanita, and Cooky of the parts they would be called upon to play. This would take skill and tact, to say nothing of self-restraint, since Benjamin's reaction would be predictably negative. However, Dearborn was, as always, confident of his ability to carry it off.

"Let's not discuss your uncle now, Cordelia. I have asked Benjamin Pinch and Juanita Froebel to join us. I think I see them over there at the bar." Dearborn refrained from adding "again in my blue dinner jacket," but reminded himself to have a few words with Benjamin during a more placid moment about his sneak attacks on Dearborn's wardrobe.

Benjamin did a double-take when Dearborn strolled up with Cooky on his arm, and Cooky compounded the shock by once again translating her appearance into dollars and cents.

"What do you think of her?" Juanita demanded of Dearborn. "She's an eyeful, isn't she?"

"No more than you, Juanita," Dearborn offered cordially, taking in her écru gown, the silver paillettes on bodice and sleeves, her delicate shawl of cocoa lace.

"We ladies," Juanita returned coquettishly, "are fortunate to have two such handsome escorts. If I didn't know better, I'd say you two were brothers. You certainly resemble one another. Same height, same physique, same . . ."

Dearborn and Benjamin exchanged quick glances and Dearborn rushed in to suggest that they repair to the site of the evening's fete, offering Cooky his arm.

The Valentine's party was to be held on the beach in front of the Monsoon. Traditionally, the management footed the bill for this lavish last fling of the winter season. Two bands would alternate and the featured entertainers from the Tropicala nightclub would perform twice, once at nine and again at midnight, with Norbert and the Mildews raising their own brand of Ned from a bandstand placed a discreet distance from the center of activities.

Pits had been dug in the sand for bonfires, and buffet tables were set up along one edge of the pavilion, with half a dozen hearts-and-flowers ice sculptures as centerpieces. On the menu were salads, cheeses, pâtés, relishes, an assortment of hot and cold entrées including squab and roast beef and lobster, and mountains of fresh fruit and pastries. The bar was open, with three bartenders in attendance, and a dozen bus-boys were ranged around the pavilion ready to whisk away the dirty dishes.

It was a warm night and the setting was beautiful. The rain that had inundated the coast earlier in the week was gone, and the only reminder of it was the white fog that hung over the hotel, curling in around the Japanese lanterns and blanketing the tops of the palm trees.

People were already trickling onto the pavilion floor, many with drinks in their hands, a few already holding plates and greedily inspecting the buffet tables. One of the bands, a far more staid-looking group than Mildew and the Musk, were playing, the melodic sound inspiring Dearborn to wave his free hand in gentle accompaniment.

"It's foggy out there," Benjamin observed.

"I feel like we're walking in clouds," Cooky agreed.

"Romantic," Juanita added, nudging Dearborn with her shoulder.

One of the Mildews, Billy the violinist, passed by carrying his violin case. It reminded Dearborn of Edward Roycroft. "Perhaps we should find ourselves a spot to park," he suggested.

Dozens of tables had been set up around the edges of the pavilion, and Dearborn led the way to one.

"Benjamin," Dearborn instructed, "you and Cordelia go for the drinks. Juanita, what would you like?"

"A stinger, I think."

"Make it two, Benjamin."

After Cooky and Benjamin walked away, Dearborn said, "Juanita, I have something to say."

"What is that, Buggy?"

"Your presence at La Playa is a lucky coincidence."

"Thank you, Buggy. I feel the same way."

"Yes. Well, I'm glad you do. However, what I meant to say is that it is lucky in the sense that it provides me an opportunity to ask for your assistance."

"Not another girl, Buggy."

"No, no. It's about Cordelia. I have to break some news to the girl. Very unpleasant news. I thought it would be well to have a sympathetic female around."

"To pick up the pieces? Buggy, you heart-breaker, you."

Dearborn shook his head impatiently. "You have the wrong idea. It's about Cordelia's uncle."

"Leo Beggs? Goodness. Don't tell me he was also given to hedonistic excesses."

"Who said anything about excesses, Juanita?"

"After all, Buggy, Siamese twins . . ."

"I'm not talking about Siamese twins. I'm talking about Leo Beggs's death."

"His suicide?"

"To be perfectly blunt about it, Juanita, his murder."

It was difficult to tell whether Juanita was shocked or thrilled. "Murder?"

"Keep your voice down. No need to broadcast it."

"Murdered by whom?" Juanita whispered.

"Well now, that's the next thing."

"His wife," Juanita declared. "It was his wife."

"Perhaps," Dearborn conceded. "As a matter of fact, probably, if not without a doubt. However, it was not Molly Beggs who pulled the trigger."

"Of course not. That kind of woman is too clever to deliver the coup de grâce. She prevailed upon one of her lovers."

"Correct."

"Which one, Buggy?"

"Juanita, let me ask you this. How much do you know about Edward Roycroft?"

"Your nephew? What has Edward got to do with this?"

"There is a connection. Now, didn't you tell me that Fanny Tyler has talked to you about Edward upon occasion?"

"Yes, she has."

"What did she tell you?"

"She told me that he has talent but that he lacks the charisma to—"

"Yes yes, I know about his lack of charisma. You told me that before. What else did she tell you. Money, for instance. Does he have any? Is he independently wealthy? Did his father leave him anything?"

Juanita said with faint irritation, "He's *your* nephew, Buggy. Why are you asking me all these questions? I know that you're not on speaking terms with Amelia, but you told me yourself you see Edward from time to time."

"He's not much of a talker," Dearborn improvised.

"I don't know anything about his financial status, Buggy. He must earn a decent amount from what he does. And his father had money. He left Amelia well off. Edward couldn't be poor."

"What about his past? What has Fanny told you about that? Has he ever been in any sort of jam?"

"Jam? Why are you asking me these silly questions? Buggy, I swear, if I didn't know that Edward is a homosexual I would think you are implying that *he* is Molly Beggs's lover."

Dearborn hopped backward in his chair and worked his mouth without uttering a sound.

"What is it? Are you choking? Did you swallow the wrong way?"

"Edward is homosexual?" Dearborn asked in a shocked voice.

"What's wrong with that? Why are you suddenly behaving so peculiarly? I didn't expect you of all people to behave like a prig about it. One is what one is. And certainly homosexuality is more acceptable than Siamese—"

"Again the Siamese twins, Juanita?"

"I distinctly remember that Greek waiter you befriended in 1932, Buggy. It wasn't even all the rage then like it is now. Surely you must have known about Edward and the Maestro?"

"The Maestro?"

"Edward has been Luigi Uberdini's *amoroso* for years. Why, when Edward had his operation—"

"What operation?"

"Surely you remember that he had a spinal fusion two years ago. He couldn't move for six months. He had to lie flat on his back."

"A spinal fusion," Dearborn repeated in a stricken voice, remembering Roycroft's slight limp. "You mean he can't run or climb?"

"Or twist or turn or bend or reach. Except in moderation, of course. He's only been playing again since last spring. I said to Fanny at the time, it's lucky he's a violinist and not a ditch digger. Even so, he has to have a special chair and I understand he can't manage harmonics without fading away altogether."

A kaleidoscope of images passed through Dearborn's mind. A man running from Nico, a man with his arm raised over his head to throw a pelota, swiftly dashing past Dearborn through the door, climbing over a planter on Dearborn's terrace.

"What's the matter, Buggy? You look very strange."

"I suppose I do."

"Here come Benjamin and Cordelia," she added in a disappointed voice, "and you haven't yet told me what I was waiting to hear."

"Let me assure you, Juanita, that you haven't told me what I was waiting to hear, either."

34

Dearborn was thankful it would be seven hours before his meeting with Molly Beggs. He wasn't shaken in his convictions regarding her, but to say that he was disconcerted by the unexpected turn of events was an understatement.

He had felt a few hours before as if he had pulled the iron out of the fire by zeroing in on Edward Roycroft as the unlikely but totally logical killer. Now he was facing something that ran counter to the rules of reason. Two and two did not add up to four. The irrefutable, the incontrovertible facts had turned out to be specious and misleading. Was it possible that the confrontation later that night would also contradict the laws of plausibility? It was unnerving to think about, but think about it he must.

Which brought up the question of Benjamin. Dearborn was unsure about confiding in Benjamin. Molly Beggs had not admitted her guilt or conceded the existence of an accomplice. Benjamin had scoffed earlier at Dearborn's inability to fix on an accomplice. What was Dearborn to tell him now? That he had, through an act of brilliant deduction, arrived at the one man who had motive, opportunity, and no alibi and then proceeded to eliminate him as unequivocally as he had the others?

For once Dearborn couldn't blame Benjamin for being skeptical. Not only would Benjamin refuse to cooperate, he would probably find some underhanded way to prevent Dearborn from keeping his appointment. For, of course, Dearborn intended to keep the appointment. Although now he would keep it alone. Juanita's presence under the circumstances would be useless, and if Benjamin were not going to be there Dearborn had no intention of placing Cooky in jeopardy.

These thoughts were running through Dearborn's mind as he and Cooky decorously circled the dance floor. Cooky was distracted, too, but for a different reason. She was concentrating on mastering the fox-trot, fervidly whispering "one two step, one two step" into Dearborn's ear while clinging to him with damp hands.

When the music stopped, Dearborn began escorting Cooky back to the table. They bumped into Fernando in front of the bandstand. He was wearing dinner clothes and carrying a sheaf of papers. "Hello, Miss Gillette. Mr. Roycroft."

"Fernando."

"How do you feel this evening, Mr. Roycroft?"

"Bearing up, Fernando."

"What's the matter?" Cooky inquired. "Weren't you feeling good, Burgess?"

"Had a near-miss with some teen-ager playing games with his father's car," Dearborn explained.

"I wish I'd gotten the license number," Fernando declared for the dozenth time.

"Forget it. Nobody got hurt. That's all that matters. What are you carrying there, my boy?"

"Notes for the welcoming speech. I don't mind telling you I'm nervous. I've never had to speak in public."

"You'll be fine," Cooky told him.

"Mr. Roycroft," Fernando said. "I've got news. Do you remember what I told you this afternoon about my trip to Miami?"

"To visit your friend's cousin?"

"Yes, that's right. Well, he called me this evening. He wants to hire me."

"Hire you?" Cooky interrupted. "To do what?"

"Teach jai alai," Fernando said.

Dearborn held out his hand. "Congratulations. When do you start?"

"The first of March. I explained that I have to give notice."

"You're leaving?" Cooky broke in again.

"It's something I've wanted to do for a long time," Fernando said to her.

"Yes, I know. It's wonderful but ..." She paused and then continued, "But you're leaving."

"I thought I couldn't do it because of my family. Even when

I went to Miami for the interview I wasn't sure I'd be able to accept the job. As it turns out, the salary wouldn't be enough, not without the money Mr. Beggs left me . . ."

"What do you know about that?" Cooky exclaimed, again incredulous. "Are you talking about Uncle Leo's will? Burgess, did you tell Fernando about the will?"

The music had begun and it was difficult to talk over it. Dearborn stalled for time. "Let's get away from this bunch," he said. "We can talk better over there." He led them away from the pavilion onto the beach. Only a few yards from the dance floor the fog closed in thickly around them, muffling the sounds of the orchestra and isolating them from the rest of the guests.

"Burgess, did you?" Cooky reiterated. "Did you tell him?"

Dearborn could think of no way to explain himself and so he diverted the attack. He tapped Cooky on the arm. "Do you have any idea of the pain you have caused this young man?"

"What are you talking about, Burgess?"

"You have broken his heart."

"What?" Fernando exclaimed. "Now wait a minute!"

"Stay out of this, Fernando," Dearborn commanded. "I am addressing Cordelia."

"I don't know what you're talking about," Cooky repeated. "How could I break Fernando's heart?"

"You couldn't," Fernando interposed vigorously. "It must be some kind of misunderstanding."

"It certainly is," remarked Dearborn. "The two of you have been misunderstanding one another for quite some time. Cordelia, I have been telling you since we first met that you should not be wasting your time on me when there are so many eligible young men at the hotel. I believe I pointed to Fernando as a prime example."

"Burgess!" she cried in a scandalized voice. "If you're trying to fix up something between Fernando and me—"

"It's a waste of time," Fernando hastened to say.

"You see," Cooky remonstrated with Dearborn. "You heard him. I'm sorry, Fernando. It wasn't my idea."

"I'm sure it wasn't," Fernando assured her. "I know you have no interest in me."

"Of course not," Cooky agreed in a voice that quavered slightly.

"Cordelia," Dearborn said, "Fernando has told me that he is in love with you."

"If you don't mind, Mr. Roycroft," Fernando burst out, "I'd rather you didn't keep saying that!"

"This is the first time I've said it," Dearborn pointed out.

"You're acting very silly, Burgess," Cooky remarked primly.

"Romance does have its silly aspects. That is not to say that it doesn't have its place. The fact remains that Fernando, for reason or reasons unknown, has eyes for you, Cordelia." Dearborn quickly held up his hand to quash any further objection. "What's more, Fernando, Cordelia is gaga over you as well."

Fernando said apologetically, "Please don't be embarrassed, Miss Gillette. I know it's not true."

Cooky said unexpectedly, "I haven't denied it, have I?"

"And she's not going to," Dearborn prophesied.

"You aren't?" Fernando asked.

"Why should I?"

Fernando's pained expression was suddenly replaced by a delighted smile.

"Look at him," Dearborn said to Cooky. "Fernando would have declared himself long ago if you weren't always such a wet blanket."

Both of them seemed to be at a sudden loss for words, and Dearborn, sensing that he had successfully distracted them from the subject of his indiscretion, said, "I'm not fond of cloying scenes. If you two will excuse me . . ."

Cooky showed up again briefly to sit with the group while Fernando made his welcoming speech. Then she and Fernando disappeared for good. Juanita, on the other hand, showed no signs of running out. On the contrary, as the evening progressed she became increasingly lively and began inviting other guests to join them at their table. By midnight their ranks had swelled to nine, including Drew Pinckney Le Maire, with whom Juanita had made it up, and Horsley Stytch, who proved, gimpy leg or not, to be an indefatigable dancer.

Once or twice earlier in the evening Juanita had attempted to coax Dearborn into telling her more about what by then she assumed was merely a supposition concerning Leo Beggs's death. Dearborn had parried her questions until she wearied and dropped the subject. When it got to be one o'clock Dearborn, yawning and stretching, excused himself. Benjamin rose with him.

"Where are you going, Dad?"

"I think I'll turn in."

"I'll walk back to your room with you."

"I don't need an escort, Benjamin."

"I wouldn't mind stretching my legs."

Dearborn had no choice but to accept Benjamin's companionship back to his suite and to endure the indignity of having to bathe, undress, and climb into bed before Benjamin could be persuaded to leave.

"You never know what that crazy Baki might do, Dad."

"That crazy Baki," Dearborn informed Benjamin sarcastically, "is no doubt at this very moment attempting to storm Morro Castle."

Dearborn didn't leap out of bed the minute Benjamin left. Benjamin was enough of a sneak to pop back in just to make sure Dearborn was asleep. He occupied the next half hour going over all the facts in the case as he knew them. They added up the same way each time. He had gone wrong somewhere and he didn't know where.

One thing he did know, and that was that he was deliberately placing himself in danger by going to the marina alone. He was too realistic to believe that arming himself would lessen the peril, but there was, he believed, one thing he could do to protect himself and that was to convince Molly Beggs that he had anticipated the possibility of foul play and had left a letter telling all. There was the chance, of course, that she wouldn't believe him, but he was relatively optimistic that she would.

It was a little after two when he left his suite, crept past the Beggses' door, and went downstairs. He left by the back exit, circled the dark swimming pool, and walked through the gardens behind the Bay wing of La Playa. The fog was thicker now than it had been an hour before, and Dearborn had no difficulty in remaining inconspicuous. The marina was deserted except for the night watchman, who was comfortably ensconced in the cockpit of a small aluminum runabout, apparently asleep. Dearborn walked past him to the far end of the U-shaped marina. He had forgotten about the watchman and it made him more secure to know that, asleep or awake, there was someone there besides himself.

There were benches facing the water at the end of the dock and Dearborn sat down on one of them. When he glanced back he saw that fog shrouded the hotel and road. He could barely make out the shapes of the boats moored in the slips behind him. He had forty-five minutes to wait, and he fell into a reverie that centered, not upon Molly Beggs or Leo Beggs or murder, but upon the fair Emmylou marking time in Boise while he faced the music here.

Then, in the midst of his daydream, he actually did hear music, the low thrum of a guitar. For a moment he thought it came from the beach on the other side of the hotel, but he realized that the party should have ended by then and that what he was hearing came from in front of him, not in back of him.

It was guitar music and he listened to a pensive voice singing softly in Spanish, "*Cuba, tierra querida, Cuba, de mis amores...*"

Dearborn squinted and leaned forward. There wasn't any light out there, but what was that dark shape looming up out of the night? The singing stopped, but the boat continued to approach, a ghost ship quietly floating out of the gloom. It was a large yacht, Dearborn noted, but it wasn't until it was a few yards away that he was able to read the name on the bow. The *Seasprite*.

Dearborn stood up, and as he did so he heard a voice whisper hoarsely, "Roycrap. Roycrap my fran." A moment later a loop of heavy rope sailed past Dearborn's nose and settled around a piling.

35

"Son of a bitch," Benjamin muttered. He slipped the key back under the piece of carpet, closed the door to the suite, and went downstairs. He checked the most obvious places first. Dearborn wasn't in the lobby or in the shopping annex. The coffee shop was closed, and so was the Starfish Lounge, and when Benjamin went out back to see if Dearborn might have returned to the Monsoon, he found only the cleanup crew working out there to clear up the aftermath of the party.

Benjamin went back to check the desk. "Did Mr. Roycroft order a taxi anytime in the last hour?"

"Nobody's ordered a taxi," the desk clerk assured him laconically.

Benjamin hadn't seen him cosying up to any of the ladies at the hotel. There wasn't anyone playing cards in the card room. Then where was he? Maybe he'd strolled down to the marina. There had been a Coast Guard boat down there during the afternoon and some Coast Guard helicopters circling around looking for Baki. Maybe his father had gone down there to see what was happening. Benjamin went out the front door, circled the hotel, and loped down the road to the marina.

It looked quiet. There didn't seem to be anyone around. No. Wait a minute. There was someone. Benjamin stepped behind a bush to observe without being observed. Was that Dearborn? No. It was the night watchman climbing up out of a runabout moored to the near end of the dock. Damn. Benjamin started to walk away, then stopped again. A tall figure had materialized out of the fog and was approaching the watchman. Again Benjamin thought it might be Dearborn, and he stepped off the sidewalk to lose himself in the shadows. The figure, who had by then engaged the watchman in conversation, was standing with his back to Benjamin, stooping forward with his head bent toward the shorter man.

When Benjamin saw the tall figure reach into his back pocket, withdraw a gun, and point it at the watchman, Benjamin reacted with shocked disbelief, his shock compounded by his confusion over whether or not the gun wielder was his father. If it were, then Benjamin didn't want to rush back to the hotel shouting for the guards. On the other hand, father or no father, he couldn't stand by and let him wave that pistol around.

The two figures were standing in the dark, mist swirling around their ankles, a few yards from the closest of the yellow dock lanterns that cast puddles of light along the length of the wooden dock. Benjamin bent down, untied his shoelaces, and slipped off his shoes. He began to creep forward, praying that the watchman would have the presence of mind to keep a poker face when he spotted Benjamin moving toward them.

But Benjamin hadn't taken more than two steps when the tall figure grabbed the watchman by the shoulder, pivoted him around roughly, brought the butt end of the gun down on the back of his neck, and began grappling with the prostrate form, tugging it toward the edge of the bulkhead that flanked either side of the U-shaped dock. The viciousness of the attack brought Benjamin up short. It certainly wasn't Dearborn over there, but there wasn't time now to do the rational thing and go for help.

Benjamin started forward again, running on the balls of his feet, hoping he wouldn't be heard, controlling his breathing so he would have breath enough left to bring the man down. He wasn't that close when a voice to his left called out quietly, "Ben?"—stopping him in his tracks and causing the man with the gun to whirl, release the watchman, and point his gun at

Benjamin. Benjamin raised his hands above his head and stood very still.

Molly Beggs was crossing the road. "Put your hands down. Nobody's going to shoot you."

Benjamin looked dubiously at the man with the gun and slowly lowered his arms.

"Finish what you're doing," Molly instructed, and Benjamin watched as the man pushed the watchman's body over the edge of the bulkhead back into the runabout, then climbed down, stepped over the inert body, and began tinkering with the motor.

"What's he doing?" Benjamin asked.

Molly didn't answer. After two or three minutes the man gave the motor a push. It fell neatly into the water and sank.

"Now when Gus wakes up," Molly noted with satisfaction, "he'll have a good story to tell about being robbed."

Benjamin, like Dearborn, had an instinct for circumspection. He realized the wisdom of not asking questions when Molly said next, "Where's your father? Why didn't he come with you?"

"He'll be here," Benjamin hastened to assure her. "I got here first, that's all."

She knew Dearborn was his father. Benjamin wondered if Dearborn had told her that or if she'd found out some other way.

The man with the gun joined them. He was young and dark, and Benjamin noticed, as he approached, something he hadn't noticed before. The man walked with a slight limp.

"We'll wait out on the dock," Molly said.

"I think I'd better go back and get my shoes," Benjamin suggested.

For the first time the man spoke. "Forget the shoes," he said.

It sounded ominous and Molly's smile wasn't particularly reassuring, either.

"Whatever you say."

The three of them walked out onto the dock. The far end was lost in fog, and with each step Benjamin took he felt more committed to a disagreeable fate. So his father had been right after all. When it came to trouble, no one was better at looking for it, finding it, or dragging Benjamin into it. "Fuck," Benjamin muttered.

"It's your own fault," Molly said coolly. "If you and your father had gone home two days ago you would have saved yourselves a lot of trouble."

"If you and your pal had stuck to adultery, *you'd* have saved us a lot of trouble," Benjamin returned morosely.

"You know," the man with the gun observed pleasantly, "I never thought I'd be socializing with the Super Runt."

"You call this socializing?"

"It's as close as you and I are going to get."

"What did I ever do to you?" Benjamin inquired politely, with some dim view to arousing the man's sense of fair play.

"Ball my girl?"

Uh oh, Benjamin thought. Wrong approach.

"Forget it," Molly cut in. "I told you I don't want to talk about that again. Sit down, Ben." She pointed to the bench at the end of the dock.

Benjamin did as he was told. Sandwiched between Molly and the man with the gun he felt suddenly very helpless. He tried to decide what to do. Arguing wouldn't help. He was sure of that. Pleading didn't seem to hold out any more hope.

"What time is it?" the man asked.

"Three," Molly answered.

He could, Benjamin contemplated, lean over to tie his shoe and then pitch himself into the drink, that is, if he were wearing shoes. . . .

"He should be here by now," the man said.

"We'll give him ten minutes' leeway," Molly suggested.

He could grab the gun and hope the bullet didn't hit anything vital, but even as an alternative plan it somehow lacked appeal.

"Tell me," Molly asked conversationally, "did your father really intend to blackmail me or was that just part of the plot to get us here?"

"My father's apt to do anything," Benjamin said glumly.

"He might do it," the man remarked, "but I don't figure you as the type to throw a game."

"Would it influence you any if I named my price?" Benjamin asked hopefully.

"We're not in the market."

"I come pretty cheap," Benjamin added with an attempt at levity.

"You're going even cheaper," the man informed him matter-of-factly.

Benjamin was losing his taste for conversation. He sat staring at the fog two yards ahead of him and tried to imagine the rest of eternity as a wall of fog. So long, world. The only thing left, he decided, was to warn his father off. When he heard footsteps on the dock he'd shout. He'd be able to get in one good yell before that bastard pulled the trigger, and with the fog this thick his father might just stand a chance to get away.

The minutes dragged on. Finally Molly said, "He's not coming."

The man poked Benjamin with the gun and said menacingly, "Your father's not bringing the police, is he?"

"Don't be a fool," Molly said. "I've been on the phone all day talking to Joe Powell about Daddy. Nobody's been filling his ears with stories, and he wouldn't believe them if they were. He's too good a friend."

"You've got a lot of good friends," Benjamin observed lightly.

"Enough."

Benjamin eyed the man next to him and then said, "I thought I was one of them. That was a nice story you laid on me."

"I thought so. Poor abused wife desperate to keep husband from killing sweetheart, not knowing it was already too late, sacrificing her reputation for the sake of love. I thought I played it pretty well."

"There were a couple of minutes there," Benjamin agreed, "where you had me fooled."

The man with the gun prodded Benjamin, none too gently.

"Let's get him in the boat," Molly said suddenly, standing up and pointing to a dory bobbing from a mooring at the edge of the dock. "We'll dump him and come back for his father."

"I still don't feel right about the old man. He's a sneaky little bastard."

"He's a lot easier to handle than this one."

"What's the matter with me?" Benjamin murmured. "I think I've been pretty cooperative so far."

"I don't relish going back to the hotel, that's all," the man said. "How are we supposed to get Pinch out of his room and back down here without attracting attention? Besides, someone may recognize me."

"There aren't that many people around. We'll go out the back way."

"With him kicking and yelling?"

"He won't kick and yell. Don't worry about it."

"What do you think people will say if they find my bullet-riddled body floating in the Gulf?" Benjamin asked, hoping a graphic image might jar them to their senses.

"We're not going to shoot you," the man promised him. "We're going to arrange for you to get drunk and then have a boating accident."

Benjamin remembered seeing a movie once where the bad guys had forced liquor down the throat of the good guy. It had been messy and brutal, and it wasn't something he felt he could face with equanimity. In fact, he knew he couldn't. A bullet in the back was no pleasanter, but it was considerably more dignified.

"Come on, Ben," Molly said. "Get up on your feet. It's time to go."

It occurred to Benjamin then that the only reason Molly's pal hadn't knocked him out already was because he would be in no condition to swallow if he were unconscious. That was a point for him. It gave him a chance to try to save himself. He decided to make a dive for it as soon as his feet hit the deck of the dory. He was a good underwater swimmer, and if he made it into the water he could count on the fog for protection. A couple of good strokes would carry him out of sight.

He got up and followed Molly to the edge of the dock, then stood back as directed while she grabbed the mooring line, pulled the dory toward her, and stepped down into it.

"Your turn," the man with the gun said to Benjamin.

Molly had turned to lean against the stern of the dory in order to hold the boat close to the dock. Benjamin put one foot down into the boat and then felt, rather than saw, the abrupt movement behind him. Something had gone wrong with his calculations. He was about to get clobbered after all.

He jerked his head to one side as the gun came down hard on his ear and shoulder, sending him sprawling. He tried to get up, but the man had leaped into the boat behind him and was raising the gun again. Benjamin put his arm up in front of him to try to ward off the blow.

It was this defensive movement that blocked Benjamin's view of the bola streaking through space, but if his vision was impaired, his hearing was not. He distinctly heard, as the man slumped down on top of him, a composed and familiar voice say, "I find it diverting that you should characterize *me* as a sneak, Mr. Martin."

36

"He is Louis Martin, is he not?" Dearborn challenged.

"Sure he's Louis Martin," Joe Powell confirmed. "I'm not arguing that. I'm just trying to understand what you're telling me here."

"I'm telling you that he killed Leo Beggs and that a week ago he killed a man named Edward Roycroft." In an aside to Benjamin, Dearborn added, "It will come as a shock to Juanita to discover that Edward Roycroft is dead."

"Not so much of a shock as discovering that Burgess Roy-croft is dead," Benjamin reminded him.

"I don't like it," Powell complained. "I don't like the idea I had to lock up Molly Beggs. I wish to God New York would get back to me."

"I'm not defending Martin," Collis McAuley interjected, "but Molly's innocent. He must of roped her into it."

"I'm afraid that's not true," Dearborn pointed out. "It was a collaborative effort, as I'm sure Mr. Martin, who is not the type given to gallant gestures, will soon bear out."

The Silver Beach police station was a storefront office squeezed between a dry-goods store on one side and a doughnut shop on the other. The small front room, ordinarily deserted until nine, was at eight-thirty crowded with tired people, some of whom were drinking coffee and eating doughnuts, others of whom were simply gazing with glazed eyes at the faded linoleum. Four were policemen. Dearborn and Benjamin shared places at either side of a scarred wooden rolltop desk. Norbert was asleep, sprawled on a bench against the wall. McAuley, with a stubbly chin and rumpled clothes, sat alone on a wooden bench next to the water cooler, and Fernando, his arm around Cooky, leaned against the back wall.

Joe Powell, the sheriff, was seated between Dearborn and Benjamin, leaning back in his chair, one knee propped up against the edge of the desk, hands folded over his stomach. "Okay, give it to me one more time."

"I started to say that while Mr. Baki, Mr. McAuley, and I were offshore waiting for the fog to lift—"

"Wait a minute. You say Baki took you hostage along with Mr. McAuley?"

"Not exactly. So far as I can understand, I was being rescued from assassins and conscripted for an invasion of Cuba—"

"Jesus Christ. . . ."

"Apparently Mr. Baki had been secreted in a secluded spot in Shell Cove all day and was returning to La Playa for some reason. . . ."

"Supplies," McAuley muttered. "There wasn't any food on board."

"He discovered me sitting on the dock, assumed that I was there to rendezvous with him, and encouraged me to board the yacht."

"Forced you, Dad," Benjamin qualified.

"It was while I was sitting on the deck contemplating my situation that I remembered something Juanita said to me at lunch today. It was a remarkable perception, almost like mental telepathy. Not that I believe in that sort of thing, but it did have the quality of an explosion, a flash of insight—"

"Yeah," Powell cut in flatly. "What was it?"

"Juanita referred to Edward Roycroft as having a cherub face and curls. She also mentioned his Nordic features. The man I knew as Edward Roycroft did not have a cherub face, curls, or Nordic features. It became suddenly clear to me that I had been right about the man who had hired me being the murderer but that I had gone wrong in believing the murderer was Edward Roycroft.

"Everything fell into place immediately. I recalled that the body I discovered in front of the funeral home had a round face, blue eyes, and blond curls. There was something else about the body. There was a bruise under the chin, a discoloration that might have come from constant rubbing, like the rubbing from an instrument held under the chin day after day, year after year. Then I thought of Billy—"

"Who's Billy?"

"A member of Norbert's band. Billy's attitude toward his violin is protective in the extreme. No one may touch the violin or the bow, especially the bow. He explained how delicate they are, how easily ruined, and yet Edward Roycroft had seemed indifferent to my handling *his* violin and bow. Didn't even seem to notice it.

"Edward Roycroft never returned to work after the murder. Now I know it was because he was dead. The man who hired me limped. I thought the limp resulted from the bad back which Roycroft suffered. It was more probably the result of a leg wound inflicted on Louis Martin during the war in Vietnam. At first I couldn't account for the attack on me in the locker room at the jai alai, but Louis Martin is a former athlete and he worked as a sportscaster for the radio station in Silver Beach. He gained entry to the locker room with his press pass. Juanita Froebel told me that something happened last Monday to refuel Leo Beggs's animosity toward Louis Martin. I suspect it was that Leo Beggs caught a glimpse of Martin skulking around La Playa and concluded that he was there to meet Molly."

"Where do you come in?" Powell demanded. "That's the part I'm still having trouble with. I don't get why they were trying to kill you."

"I feel confident, Sheriff, that the facts when they're sorted out, will bear out my reconstruction. Martin, in his guise as Roycroft, told me that he was supposed to stay with Roycroft for a few weeks but that he had stayed for four months. He claimed that Roycroft was pleased to have Martin stay, but I suspect otherwise. Edward Roycroft's intimates, as well as himself, would have been inconvenienced by a guest who overstayed his welcome to that extent. Perhaps Martin and Roycroft quarreled about that. Or perhaps they quarreled over something else. It could be that Roycroft found out about Martin's status as a fugitive or that he objected to some new skullduggery Martin was into. I don't pretend to know the exact reason, but I am sure that one morning there was a quarrel and that during the course of that quarrel Martin killed Edward Roycroft.

"After he killed Roycroft it must have occurred to him that if the body were identified as his it would give him a chance to get away. He waited until evening, dumped Roycroft's body in front of the funeral home, and, in order to make the killing look like a mugging, dropped his own wallet into a nearby mailbox. When the police called the next day Martin, pretending to be Roycroft, went downtown to identify the body. He probably intended to leave town after that but somewhere along the line he changed his mind. It would be my guess that Molly Beggs had something to do with it.

"I fear that I also had something to do with it. There was considerable publicity at the time of the Rotten Apple affair. Roycroft must have mentioned the fact that his uncle and I had been at Harvard together. It was Martin's recollection of that which probably started the wheels turning. Beggs was in New York at the time, Beggs had threatened Martin, Molly was about to be sent packing and written out of the will. The opportunity to turn the circumstances to his and Molly's advantage must have been too tempting to pass up. It would have been dangerous to involve the police but a private investigator, handed the evidence and persuaded to notify the police, would provide the perfect explanation for Beggs's suicide. The one development which Molly and Louis Martin didn't anticipate, and which surprised me as much as it must have surprised them, was that the police should have delved into Martin's background and that they then became suspicious of Beggs themselves."

"As usual, Dad," Benjamin observed, "you misjudged Niccoli."

"Not misjudged, Benjamin. Underestimated. There is a fine distinction."

"So you were set up," Powell prodded.

"Some of the evidence was there for the finding. The rest was arranged. Molly followed Captain Niccoli to Martin's boarding house, not, as I first supposed, to get something, but to leave something, the note which she pinned inside the duffel bag. The same was true of Martin's visit to the Beggs's apartment the night I was there. I couldn't understand why the gun cabinet was open and the gun still in place. It was because Martin had just removed the registered Colt .38 and replaced it with the murder weapon, which I was intended to find."

"Burgess," Cooky spoke up, "why didn't you believe Uncle Leo committed suicide?"

"Your uncle wasn't the type to commit suicide. I had a long talk with Alberta Van Curl, who apparently knew your uncle intimately. . . ."

No one had noticed that Norbert had wakened until he chimed in with "He was screwing around with her."

"No one," Dearborn said disapprovingly, "asked for that tidbit of information."

"It's true."

"It may be true," Dearborn reproved, "but it is not relevant. What does pertain is the fact that your father was about to divorce Molly in order to marry Miss Van Curl, unlikely as it seems."

"Molly never mentioned that to me," Benjamin interrupted.

"Molly Beggs knew you are my son. She told you only what she wanted you to repeat to me. In other words, you were quite thoroughly cozened, Benjamin."

The phone on Powell's desk rang and he picked it up. His end of the conversation consisted mostly of grunts and expletives, and when he hung up his expression was somber.

"Was that Captain Niccoli?" Dearborn asked.

"Lieutenant Galton. Niccoli's already on his way down here."

"Well?" Dearborn demanded impatiently.

"Somebody named Umberni or Umbertino—"

"Uberdini?"

"Yeah, that's the name. Seems he's been making a big stink. He was in Paris or something for a week and when he got back last Monday he wanted to get in touch with Edward Roycroft and he couldn't find him. So he's been calling the police and filling out missing persons reports and making a pain of himself generally. Then yesterday Niccoli got there with Martin's mug shots and prints and they found out they didn't match up to the stiff in the icebox. Niccoli put two and two together, and late yesterday afternoon he called in this Umberni to make the identification."

"And?"

"It's Roycroft, all right."

"Of course it is," Dearborn said complacently. "It could be no one else."

"What do you mean you're not going home?" Benjamin bawled. "I've reserved two connecting bedrooms leaving at five. You know how I got those bedrooms? I stood around the train station for four and a half hours waiting for a cancellation. It cost me seventy-five bucks in bribes. Now you're telling me you're not going?"

"I have matters to clear up. For one thing, I feel I owe it to Mr. Baki to find him more comfortable accommodations."

"Jail's not good enough for him?"

"He's not in jail. He has been transferred to the Silver Beach Infirmary."

"What's that? The local bughouse?"

"It's a sanitarium for the chronically depressed. Not the sort of place for a man like Baki. After all, he saved both our lives, Benjamin. He deserves better than the Silver Beach Infirmary."

"All right. We'll have Otto make some calls, see what he can do. You don't need to be here for that."

"Then there's the matter of the five thousand dollars."

"I told you, Dad, I talked to Otto. He says he'll sign the check, no more argument."

"And lastly there's Ursula Spangenberg."

"Who?"

"Forced by circumstance, namely a good-for-nothing loafer of a husband who was last seen boarding a plane for Phoenix in 1967, to stand on her feet all evening, every evening, except for Sundays, taking bets for a paltry salary and whatever tips she can pick up. . . ."

"Oh no," Benjamin groaned.

"Whose one ambition is to buy a luncheonette where she can act as cashier and earn her living sitting down. . . ."

"I think I'd better sit down."

"And who has asked me for advice and moral support. . . ."

Benjamin shut his eyes and lowered his head into his hands.

"Which I cannot, in all good conscience, deny."

ABOUT THE AUTHOR

EDITH PIÑERO GREEN is the author of *Rotten Apples*, *The Mark of Lucifer*, *The Death Trap*, and *A Woman's Honor*. She lives in New York City and on Fire Island with her husband and two sons.